"AN INCENDIARY MIX OF SEX AND MONEY . . . SET IN *BONFIRE OF THE VANITIES* TERRITORY AND REPORTED WITH THE SAME COOL, RELIABLE VOICE AS *PRESUMED INNOCENT*"
Publishers Weekly

She was alone, asleep, clothed. She lay on her side of the bed, her eyes closed, her hair spread dark against a sea of white lace pillows. She wore a dusky pink and silken nightgown, which rose to her neck and then fell away. Unseemly, I thought. In the time I had known her, only once had she come to bed dressed.

Perhaps she'd heard my breathing. Or her antennae, still keen, had sensed some subtle change in the surrounding atmosphere.

She didn't stir, but I realized abruptly that her eyes were open, black pellets in their misty pale nests.

She saw that I was holding a gun.

"Go on, Tommy," she said quietly, staring up at me with steady contempt. "Do it. Show me you have the guts."

~THE~ STARK TRUTH

PETER FREEBORN

AVON BOOKS ◆ NEW YORK

AVON BOOKS
A division of
The Hearst Corporation
105 Madison Avenue
New York, New York 10016

First Avon Books Printing: November 1990
First Avon Books Special Printing: May 1990

Printed in the U.S.A.

RA   10   9   8   7   6   5   4   3   2   1

For the woman I love,
also known as J

PROLOGUE

I parked at the edge of our property under an overhang of branches. The night air blew cold in my face. I walked in through the trees, keeping to their shadows, trampling their fallen leaves, so as to skirt the wide lawn. Already I could see the white columns lit by hidden floods, the ground floor with lights on here and there—part, I knew, of the random security system. A pinpoint of red by the front door confirmed that the system was on.

No matter. I already knew she was home.

I went in through the garage, using my key. The old Aries stood there, next to her new and little-used Mercedes. I paused behind the cars, glanced into the tool bin, then entered the house through the back hall. Silently I passed the servants' quarters, the kitchen, the pantry, crossed the dining room and came out onto the marble floor of the center hall, where, just four months before, I had watched her flee up the stairs in tears, tripping over her dress.

Partway up the stairs I held my breath, stopped. The

hall lights behind me had just gone out. I turned, saw a
new and dimmer light coming from the living room.

The system at work.

It was near midnight. Silence.

I waited outside our door in the carpeted upstairs hall,
hand outstretched, listening.

Nothing.

Then I turned the knob.

She was alone, asleep, clothed. The beaded Victorian
floor lamp with the large lime green shade was still lit
in the far corner of the room, casting a faint light over
her. She lay on her side of the bed, her eyes closed, her
hair spread dark against a sea of white lace pillows. The
covers, silk figured sheets under a lacy down comforter,
were pulled up to her breasts. She wore a dusky pink and
silken nightgown, which rose to her neck and then fell
away. Unseemly, I thought. In the time I had known her,
only once had she come to bed dressed.

I beheld her. I stood over her. I listened to our breathing: hers, my own. I said my last silent good-bye, feeling,
even as I gave inner voice to the words, a faint rekindling
of desire. I suppressed it.

Even so, what would it have taken? What sign, what
beckoning? Even at that last twelfth hour?

I had my answer momentarily.

Perhaps she'd heard my breathing. Or her antennae,
still keen, had sensed some subtle change in the surrounding atmosphere.

She didn't stir, but I realized abruptly that her eyes
were open, black pellets in their misty pale nests.

She saw that I was holding a gun.

"Go on, Tommy," she said quietly, staring up at me
with steady contempt. "Do it. Show me you have the
guts."

PART ONE

1

We first met at a party. It was the firm's annual bash at Tavern on the Green. There'd been an early snowfall that year, and the world outside the restaurant's frosted windows gleamed in the white Christmas lights that hung from the trees. A five-piece band played Cole Porter—Night and day, da-dum da-dum, you are the one—but later in the evening, after the clients went off and the partners left with their wives and girlfriends, the band would switch into rock for the associates and the paralegals, the secretaries and the messengers who got to rub elbows annually with those of us from the twenty-first floor.

Attendance at the party, at least for the Cole Porter period, was compulsory for yours truly, as it would be at the Partners' Dinner some two weeks later. That would be private, at the Century Club, black tie, no spouses. But at both functions the booze flowed as though there'd be no New Year.

"I bet I can guess what you're thinking." Her voice

next to me broke my reverie. "You're thinking, What a waste of money, and some of it's mine."

For the record, she had it wrong. In point of fact I remember what I was thinking: whether the percentage of the women at the party who would end up in bed with men they'd never spoken to before would vary from the previous year. I myself doubted it would. The only difference would be the condoms. Condoms had made a comeback.

"Well?" she persisted at my side. "Am I close?"

"Close enough," I answered, jostled by the crowd as I turned to look at her. "How'd you guess?"

I had on my clients' smile, just in case.

"I was watching you from across the food," she said, gazing up at me. First impression: appraising eyes, wide apart, almost as dark as the wavy black hair. Broad cheekbones; full scarlet lips. "You were scowling. As though you disapproved."

"Of the food? Or the cost?"

"Both," she said.

Very smartly turned out, I noticed, in black silk, padded shoulders. On the short side, full-busted. I was standing too close to her to see her legs.

Manicured hands with red nails.

I liked the way she stood up to being examined.

"Who are you?" I said.

"Just a single woman at a party," she answered directly. "Possibly a client."

"A client of whose?"

"Yours, maybe."

"Mine? But you look too young to be a widow," I said, out of habit.

"Nobody's too young to be a widow these days."

"I'm sorry," I said, again from habit. "Deeply sorry."

For some reason this seemed to annoy her.

"Not to worry," she said sharply. "There's no reason at all to be sorry."

I thought I recognized the type. Most widows I've known want at least the appearance of mourning, bereavement, want condolence or the formality of condolence, leaving room, then or later, for more intimate tears, the still more intimate confessions of helplessness, fear, loneliness, with appropriate commiseration from yours truly. But every so often you run into one, refreshingly enough, who can't wait to get past the formalities and down to the brass tacks, such as how much is the estate worth and how soon can she get her hands on the money.

"I'll tell you what else I know about you," she said. "You've been married and divorced. But if I'm right, it didn't happen recently."

"How do you know I'm not just single?"

"You're too good-looking," she said. "No man as handsome as you could have escaped marriage unless he's gay, and you're not gay."

"And why divorced?"

"Something in your expression."

"You mean when I'm not scowling?"

I meant it lightly, but she didn't take it that way.

"I'm not sure how to describe it," she went on. "Not sadness, exactly, or bitterness. Maybe a little of each. It's more of a wary look, as though you'd been in somebody's bed and didn't like what you saw. A little cynicism. Cruelty, too, I think. Makes you look older than you actually are."

"Sad, bitter, wary, cynical," I enumerated, smiling as if in apology. "Cruel to boot. Gee, that's not a very promising description."

No comment from her.

"Well, how old do you thing I actually am?"

"Around forty, give or take. Not quite, I'd say."

In fact, I'd just recently turned forty-one. And almost four years had gone by since Susan and I had signed off on our divorce and gone our separate ways, she with the children, I with the bills, which—or so I liked to think— was what had kept me locked into Trusts and Estates, and holding hands with widows bereaved and unbereaved, and standing tall at Christmas parties playing Psychoanalysis by Facial Expression with prospective clients.

"What about the divorce stuff, though?" I asked her. "What makes you so sure I wasn't divorced yesterday?"

She laughed at that, her dark and sparkling eyes animating her expression.

"Well, you're bored, for one thing. You've had enough time to find out being single isn't as much fun as you thought it would be. Besides, any man who's just been divorced is in a panic about food. He doesn't know how to cook, hates eating alone. If you'd just been divorced, you'd have been stuffing yourself here, even though the food's mediocre. As is, you've hardly eaten a thing."

True enough. It also made me curious as to just how long she'd been watching me.

The band had stopped playing. Break time, union rules. Break time, too, for the party—a signal to those on the make to extricate themselves if they'd made a mistake, change partners, check out the remaining action or leave if there wasn't any. In the commotion I spotted Mac Coombs, the venerable *capo da capo* in the firm since my father's retirement. That's Dwight MacGregor Coombs, Senior Partner and former Undersecretary of State, shaking hands and exchanging quips as he headed for the exit and the livery service that would take him home to New Canaan. And I knew that my fellow lemmings, the senior members of our illustrious firm, would take his departure as a sign that they could, and even should, go home. But as the others began to leave, my unsolicited partner simply stood her ground, gazing up at me, dark-eyed and full-lipped, her cheeks flushed.

I knew she wasn't my type, not at all, a recognition which irritated and intrigued me at the same time. Quite clearly she was offering herself.

"Anyway," she said, her eyes fixing mine, "I'm glad you haven't eaten."

"Why is that?"

"Because it means you're going to take me out to dinner."

2

We went to La Banquette, a French bistro way west in the Fifties. Out of some sense of decorum, perhaps, I'd stopped going there for a time after the divorce, but the food was too good to stay away from forever. The narrow, mirrored main room of the restaurant was bordered by tables for couples sitting side by side on leather-covered benches, leaving the center alley free for the waiters and their trolleys. For groups larger than two, or those preferring intimacy, there were a few alcoves in the rear, almost like private dining rooms. My usual table was in the main room, but as Georges, the maître d', explained apologetically, this night, so close to Christmas, the situation was hopeless. " After all," he said, scolding me, "Monsieur didn't call for a reservation." But then he led us back to one of the alcoves and, with a Gallic flourish, said that for Monsieur and his beautiful guest, and given the holiday season, the wine would be on the house.

Also knowing, I assume, that the gesture, given the

10

holiday season, would be recognized in my annual gift.

En route in the taxi, we had gotten around to introducing ourselves. Katherine Goldmark Sprague, meet Stark Thompson III. Kitty, meet Tommy. Or, as I think she was the first to point out, Kitten, meet Tom.

"People call me Kitty," she told me. "Someday I'll get around to dropping the Sprague. People know me professionally as Kitty Goldmark, anyway."

"But you *are* widowed, didn't you say?"

"Yes."

"I still say you seem awfully young for that."

"I know. I was; he wasn't. But if you don't mind, I'd rather not go into that."

"Done," I said. "But it so happens I know a Goldmark. Ted Goldmark. Dumb question: You're not related, by any chance, are you?"

"By some chance, we are," she answered. "In fact, not by any chance at all. Teddy's my brother."

I remember that she shifted her body so as to face me in the taxi, the silk of her dress slithering on the seat—an unconscious movement that, I was to learn, invariably accompanied some confession.

"The truth?" she asked, then answered herself: "The truth. I was at your party just now because of Teddy. I had some business at his office this afternoon, and he more or less dragged me along. What he actually said was: 'If you've got nothing better to do, come along and I'll introduce you to some boring lawyers.'"

"That sounds like him," I said. "But it surprises me that you had nothing better to do."

"Don't be surprised at anything," she countered. "Anyway, when I saw you there, I asked him who you were. I said, 'Why don't you introduce me to that boring

lawyer over there? The handsome one.' Do you know
what he did? He *refused*! He said you were the smartest
one in the bunch but that you ran too fast a track for me.
Can you imagine? My own brother? I made a bet with
him on the spot.''

''What kind of bet?''

''That I could pick you up before the party was over.''

''And how much did you bet?''

''A hundred dollars.''

''Not bad,'' I said, amused. ''Looks like you won.
Tell me, though, what else did he say about me?''

I realized that I enjoyed making her talk, not so much
for her voice, which had that loud, New York sort of
brassiness, but because of the body language that accompanied her conversation. The bristling indignation, for
instance, over her brother.

''Actually,'' she admitted, ''I'm not as clairvoyant as
all that. It was Teddy who told me you were divorced,
though he didn't know for how long. I guessed that part.
He also said you had a reputation as a skirt-chaser, *Social
Register* level. Is that true?''

''Overstated, I'd say. And what else?'' Then, seeing
that she hesitated: ''Come on. It's always salutary to hear
what other people make of you.''

''Well, he said the major mistake of your life had been
to stay at a law firm that had your father's name on the
door. A still living and famous father, in addition. He
said you were smart enough—and well connected
enough—to have chosen your ticket almost anywhere—
in politics or business as well as the law.''

She hesitated again. I imagined that she was translat-
ing, maybe censoring, what Goldmark had really said,
but our arrival at the restaurant stopped the conversation.

I also, as I soon discovered, liked watching her eat.

We sat across from each other in the alcove, Kitty with her fur still around her shoulders while Georges hovered over us. She ordered steamed lobster with lemon butter only, over Georges's objections, but after she'd debated the subject of sauces with him, half in English, half in French, the maître d' reluctantly conceded. Then, when we were served, she set to work, bibless, with cracker and pick, dismembering the red crustacean. With accomplished gestures, she picked it clean, sipping white wine. And questioned me the while, pushing, probing.

I gave her my life story, the once-over-lightly version, something I'd learned to do with wit, brevity, and—true enough—a certain cynicism. Usually this sufficed, but not with Kitty. It was as though she wanted to strip me clean, too. I managed to hold her off, but just barely, and stranger still, the sparring aroused me.

She had crème caramel for dessert, I a double espresso and a double cognac.

"You don't seem very satisfied with it," she said, licking caramel sauce from her spoon.

"With what? My life? Or talking about it?"

"Both."

"Well, I wouldn't say that, exactly." Then, a familiar line of self-judgment: "Maybe being buried alive has its points."

She didn't react.

"Probably it's the money," she said.

"What money?"

"You don't make enough," she said, eyeing me levelly across her spoon. Why she should have thought that, I've no idea, even though it happened to be true. She did know—in fact I'd alluded to it myself—that I came from wealth, the "Funds," as it was known, product of the nineteenth-century merger of the Starks and the Thompsons, which by clan honor and tradition no one touched except in extremis. And even then . . .

But that, I saw, wasn't her point.

"Do you really believe money's the only way people can measure themselves?" I asked her.

"If there's another way," she said, "please tell me what it is."

"But just money? The accumulation of money?"

"No, I didn't say that."

"Then what? Material goods? Power? Self-esteem?" Maybe the subject irritated me because it made me think of the firm, and the firm of my father. "Well, I wasn't brought up that way."

"To tell you the truth," she said, running her tongue across her upper lip, "I wasn't either."

"Then . . . ?"

I'd been watching her mouth during dinner, the movements of her lips, her tongue. The scarlet was now gone from her lips, but they remained full, glistening, the color of dusky rose. I watched them curl now, then open into a smile, and her tongue licked across her upper teeth.

"Because it's sexy," she said.

"Money's sexy?"

"Yes," she said, her lips spreading into laughter. Then she reached across, touching my hand, holding it a moment, her red nails arced onto my wrist. "It's just a joke, Tommy. Come on, this has been a lovely meal, but let's get the check."

Amen, I thought. Perhaps I even said it.

Georges brought the check in a paisley folder on a white china plate, and I simply scrawled my signature across the back and handed it to him, explaining to Kitty that one of the civilized practices of La Banquette was the itemized monthly bill, to which they added a fifteen percent service charge.

"And what do I go down as?" she asked with a smile. "Business or pleasure?"

"It'll have to be pleasure," I answered with mock rue. "I forgot altogether that you said you were a potential client. We haven't even talked about that."

"Let's not. I'd rather call you and make an appointment."

"Good."

We walked—her suggestion—she in the heavy red fox which hung almost to the tops of her high heels, I in the old alpaca-lined greatcoat I'd bought in Italy some five, six years before, pre-divorce. She linked her arm easily through mine, and from time to time our hands touched, held, pigskin to suede, and our breath came out in little puffs in those dark and empty streets of the West Fifties.

We talked, but I'd be hard pressed to say what about. She ran her own business, some kind of party-catering outfit, maybe it was that. Or Sprague, her married name. I'd known Spragues in school, but apparently her Sprague hadn't been one of mine. I remember her saying something about the Osborne, that ornate hulk of faded Victorian splendor at Fifty-seventh and Seventh, diagonally across from Carnegie Hall, but whether it was that she'd always wanted to live there or had never understood how people did I couldn't tell you. And that, of course, was because I was traveling my own single track, sure in the knowledge of where we were going to end up, and relishing it.

We reached her building, one of the newer towers on Central Park South, where, from high up, the snowy park stretched straight, broadly, between the verticals of east and west. I imagined making love to her on that snowy blanket. We faced each other under her canopy. Her cheeks were flushed, the tips of her ears pink, her eyes aglitter. I held her arms firmly, fingers deep into her fur, while her hands touched my lapels, and the smell of her, the heavy musk of her perfume, rose strongly, mingling with the fumes of my cognac.

I kissed her, bending her back lightly, tasting her.

"I think I should come up with you now, Kitty," I said, inhaling her.

I saw her eyes go dull, the way women's often do at the moment of acquiescence. But then abruptly alert, small, a fleeting angry glance. She looked down, away, and her hands pushed at me.

"No," I heard her say. She was shaking her bowed head, her hair in my face. I heard something indistinct, like "I don't want this," or "I don't want it this way."

"I don't get it," I said, still holding her. "What's wrong?"

"Nothing," she said. Her voice was muffled. "I'm sorry. I don't want—"

"For Christ's sake, Kitty, you've been asking me all night! Who picked who up?"

"I'm sorry, I—"

With that she tore loose from me, yanked her arms free. Her black hair swirled. Her eyes, I saw, were wet with tears.

"I said I'm sorry," she repeated, glaring at me. Then, stiffly: "Thank you for the evening. I hope you'll call me again."

I felt something approximating rage—an unaccustomed feeling—erupt inside me.

"What am I supposed to do?" I blurted out. "Make an appointment with you?"

She took that like a slap, mouth agape, which was how I'd meant it. Then she suddenly swiveled on her high heels, pivoting on hard cement, and I saw a uniformed doorman push open the glass door for her. She turned back to me from the doorway.

"Call me," she said aloud. That was all, and she disappeared into the lobby in a blur of russet fur.

3

I came back to the office around three, one Friday afternoon a few weeks later, to find Kitty Goldmark sitting in the armchair next to my desk, a leather portfolio at her feet and her fox coat flung over the couch behind her.

No appointment, needless to say. In theory my staff was free to make appointments for me without my knowing about it, but only with established clients, and I'd had a clean slate for that afternoon except for a meeting of the Recruitment Committee.

"Well," I said, closing my door behind me. "Happy New Year, Kitty. If you don't mind my asking, how did you get here?"

"On foot."

"I mean, without an appointment?"

"What difference does that make? You're available, aren't you?"

She glanced at my desk, at the corner next to the computer console where I kept my calendar. It turned out she'd arrived a bit after two and, claiming she was a new client and had already talked to me, had simply browbeaten her way past my secretary. While waiting for me, she'd had enough time to inspect the premises pretty thoroughly and form her opinions, which, I learned later, were largely negative. Sterile space, she called it. Where were my books, my framed diplomas? She'd have thought my kind of *Social Register* clientele wanted a leatherbound library in glassed-in mahogany, and oriental rugs on the floor.

It did no good to explain that I was something of an anomaly in the firm, in that our principal business wasn't with individuals but corporations, or that the massive-tomed law library was a thing of the past, supplanted by the microchip and computer-accessed research services.

But this, as I say, came later. Right then, the atmosphere between us was stiff, even irritable.

"Do you always take such long lunches?" she asked as I sat down.

"Yes, as a rule."

"Why?"

"Why? Well, to enjoy myself," I answered truthfully enough.

She didn't seem to like that.

"You never called me," she said, looking away.

"No, I didn't."

"Why not?"

I shrugged. For once, an answer didn't come to mind.

"The last time I saw you," she said, "you couldn't wait to go to bed with me. Do you normally drop women so fast?"

"Only when they drop me first," I said lightly.

She didn't like that, either. I saw her jaw set firmly in profile as she gazed out the sealed and tinted windows behind me.

"But what did you think?" she said harshly. "Did

you think I was just some piece of meat that you could sling around and slap into bed?''

"I didn't—" I started to say.

"Well, but that's how you treated me: like a slab of beef in a butcher's window. Why *didn't* you call when I asked you to? That you didn't only proves what you thought of me. You probably went off and got one of your *Social Register* pieces of meat. We're all pretty interchangeable, isn't that what you think? Well, that's not who I am, Mr. Thompson, and if that's who you think I am, then . . ."

And off she went, in that vein. It was, to my astonishment, quite a performance, a full-scale Kitten rage complete with tears and recriminations. But what I didn't realize at the time was that Kitty, once she thought she'd been wronged, fueled the storm herself.

At some point I said, "I'm sorry, Kitty. But I seem to remember it was you who picked me up, not the other way around. You said you'd done it on a bet, but that turned out not to be so."

"And what does that mean?" Suddenly suspicious.

"Just what I said. You told me you'd won a hundred dollars by picking me up. Your brother said you hadn't won anything."

I'd thought it amusing. I'd run into Goldmark a week or so before, when he'd been in to see some of our Mergers and Acquisitions people. I hardly knew him— a Wall Street whiz kid, people said, and he was pointed to as a sign of the changing times—a Jew who'd made it in an all-Wasp shop—but I couldn't resist twitting him about losing a hundred dollars to his sister. Except that he'd denied it. Yes, he'd brought her to the party, and he'd told her who I was. Probably, he admitted, he'd even said something to the effect that I was out of her

league. But he said he'd learned the hard way never to
bet against his sister.

Kitty, though, failed to see the humor in it.

"So, just because he told you I lied, you believe *him*?"
she said in a bitter tone. "Now why is that? Let me
guess. Because he's a boy and you're a boy? Of course.
But suppose I insisted it was the truth. Suppose I swore
to you that he owed me a hundred dollars. What then?"

"Well, then, I'd believe you."

"No, you wouldn't. But didn't it even occur to you
that Teddy's the kind who can't ever admit he's lost
anything? No," she answered herself, tossing her head,
"it didn't occur to you. But I'll prove it. Where did this
conversation take place?"

"Look, Kitty, why make so much of it? I—"

"Where did this conversation take place?" she insisted.

I thought back. It had been around noontime. I was
on my way out to lunch, and I'd run into Goldmark in
the corridor with a group of our M and A Mafia. We'd
waited by the elevator bank together; we'd ridden down
together.

"You mean you had this conversation in an *elevator*?"
she asked. She would, I thought in passing, have made
a hell of a prosecuting attorney.

"Yes. At least I think—"

"And you'd expect Teddy to admit he'd lost a bet?
To me? In a crowded elevator, in front of a bunch of
other men?"

I smiled. From what I knew of Goldmark, no, maybe
not.

"Do you see?" she said in triumph. "You're not so
sure now, are you?" Then, before I could get her off the
subject: "What else did he say about me?"

"Nothing," I answered.

''Nothing? I don't believe it. There's no way he'd miss the chance to put me down.''

In fact, Goldmark had said something else, but under the circumstances there was no way Kitty was going to get it out of me. For as quickly as it had risen, the storm subsided in her. This, too, was very much the Kitten style, the rage boiling over and then quieting, the heat off, the planes of her face suddenly calm, the amused glint back in her eyes. Provided, that is, that she'd made her point.

''Come on, Tommy,'' she said, ''done is done. Let's have some fun now. I've brought you some business.'' I think I must inadvertently have glanced at my watch, for she went on: ''I know, you have a meeting, I saw it on your schedule. But this won't take long. I have it all laid out for you.''

She made me sit next to her on my couch while she spread her papers on the coffee table in front of us. They concerned her late husband's estate. She showed me the Petition for Probate and the appendant paraphernalia— citations, waivers, affidavits, and depositions—that accompany the filing of any will, plus the 706 (Federal Tax) and the TT-86.5 (State of New York). At a glance, they certainly looked in proper form, but she insisted on walking me through them.

Edgar Chalmers Sprague had named Kitty and his attorney as coexecutors. Nothing unusual there, although Kitty took it that way. It was her late husband's means, she said, of trying to control her even from the grave. I knew of the attorney in question, Henry Fifield, although we'd never met. He had his own small firm, and a solid reputation. Furthermore, Sprague's will was simple enough: a few specific bequests, with the balance to Kitty. The investments the executors had made seemed properly prudent: T-bills and government securities, for the most part, and a little under one hundred thousand dollars in a money market account.

"It all seems in good order to me," I said.

"Oh, that it is. Very good order. In fact, you've just described Gar to a T. No mess, no fuss, no risk."

"Well," I said, picking up the sarcasm in her voice, "there's nothing wrong with that, is there?"

"Just one thing," she said, turning toward me, her body slithering on the leather of my couch. "It's boring. It's also bad business."

"An estate's hardly a business."

"And why shouldn't it be? Why shouldn't you run it like a business?"

"Well, for one thing, it's of relatively short duration. An uncomplicated estate like your husband's, I'd guess it'd take no more than two years, three at the outside, for the tax audit, and then it can be liquidated, the assets disbursed. In the interim, the role of any executor or attorney who happens to be involved is simply to safeguard the assets. That may be boring—it *is* boring—but that's his role."

She laughed at that.

"What law school did you say you'd gone to, Tommy?"

"I don't know that I did say. But Harvard."

"I think Henry went to Columbia, but it sounds like you took the same courses. He said almost the exact same thing."

"With reason," I said. "Any good attorney would, and I understand Henry Fifield's a good one."

"I'm sure he is," Kitty replied. "I just fired him."

"Did you?" I said, amused. "But I don't think you can actually fire an executor except for gross misconduct, and even then the courts have to approve."

"I'm not actually firing him," she said. Then she

laughed again, and I saw the animated flash in her eyes. "He's willing to step down, resign, whatever it is you do. He took a little convincing, but I'm good at that."

I smiled back at her. From what her brother had said— the comment I'd suppressed—I'd have guessed she'd just made the understatement of the year.

"And that brings you to me?" I asked.

"Exactly. I want you either as coexecutor or as attorney to the estate."

"But why me?"

"Because I'm told you're the best in the business."

Flattering as that might have been, I didn't see that she, or Edgar Sprague's estate, required "the best in the business." Furthermore, I judged her smart enough to know that. But she had something else in mind.

"I want to play with the assets, Tommy. Before you say anything, let me explain. Gar never had any fun in life—no risk, no fuss, that's the way he was. But I'm in charge of the money now, and it's criminal to leave it lying there, wasting. Over a million dollars going to waste. Look, I'll show you what I mean."

She pulled a file from her portfolio, with columns of handwritten numbers on legal-size sheets, and put it in front of me. It was a summary she'd prepared of what would be hers after expenses and bequests. The bottom line showed seven figures.

"That's mine, Tommy," she said, pointing out the number with a scarlet-tipped index finger. "Mine to throw out the window if I want to. I don't, but I'd sooner do that than make nickels and dimes."

"And Fifield objected?"

"That's right. He said the purpose of Gar's will was to protect me. He said Gar would have wanted to make me comfortable, if not rich, for the rest of my life. Well, I told him I didn't want to be buried with my husband.

I told Henry—you should pardon the expression—that I didn't give a flying fuck what Gar would have wanted. Besides, I don't even need the money. I've got my own business. Gar always thought that was a joke, something to keep me occupied. Well, let me tell you something. If my projections are right, and I think they're conservative, my little pastime is going to bring down more this year than Edgar Sprague made in the last ten years of his working life.''

There was a kind of glitter, an exultation in her voice, when she talked about her business, and which transcended the bitter tinge whenever she mentioned Sprague. I should admit that, out of curiosity, I'd checked him out a little after the evening I'd spent with his widow. It turned out he'd been related to my Spragues after all, but distantly, obscurely, and was, in addition, a good generation older than the ones I knew. He'd been an executive in a large factoring company, one of those outfits that buy up receivables at a deep discount from companies in cash trouble and then, assuming it can collect them, banks a very tidy profit. The practice always smacked of a kind of usury in reverse to me, but it's certainly legal, even marginally respectable. In any case, Sprague had taken early retirement and spent the last decade or so of his life teaching in some business school. Yes, it was known that he had married—late in life, a much younger woman. Also that he drank too much, and this is what had done him in, in his late sixties.

As Kitty and I sat side by side, not quite touching but close enough for her arm to brush mine whenever she reached forward, I couldn't put her sheer proximity out of my mind. I suppose this was no accident. It wasn't what she wore, either. She had on a Chanel-type suit of black silk, the kind with the open, collarless jacket, and a high-necked blouse underneath, the color of amethyst.

She favored the gemstone, too, in her jewelry: dewdrop earrings set in gold and an antique bracelet of amethysts surrounded by tiny seed pearls, also set in gold. Rings on her fingers but no wedding ring. It was more the way her body filled her clothes, with a firm and healthy fulsomeness. Her legs, I now saw, were full-calved yet shapely. She wore more makeup than the women I was accustomed to, and certainly more perfume: that heavy, musky scent, tinged by spice. Yet in some way Kitty, so adorned, was more natural than the ex–debutante corps I frequented, who seemed intent, even as they approached forty, on looking as if they'd just stepped off the beach in Barbados.

"I want to make money with Gar's money," Kitty said beside me.

"Because money's sexy?" I asked.

She laughed at that. I had the memory of a bull elephant, she said.

"Well, I'm afraid you've come to the wrong place," I said. "This illustrious firm is so conservative when it comes to investments that we'd make Henry Fifield look like a crap-shooter."

"Oh?" she said. "That's not the way I hear it."

"What have you heard?"

"Well, that you've been involved in some of the hottest financial deals of the eighties, with a specialty in taking public companies private. I've also heard your billings last year came close to Skadden Arps's."

I assumed she'd been talking to her brother. The Skadden Arps part aside, what she'd said was true enough. It was also true, whether she realized it or not, that she'd touched a sore point.

"Be that as it may," I said, "when it comes to Trusts and Estates, we're still in the Jarndyce and Jarndyce era."

"That's *Bleak House*, isn't it?" she said, taking me

up on it. "The one where it's the lawyers who make all the money?"

"That's right," I said.

"I could never finish it," she admitted with a smile.

"Neither could I. But when it comes to estate planning, we take a very conservative investment posture."

"Even when it means the erosion of capital?"

"You mean because of inflation?"

"That's right."

"Well, we try to take that into account, of course. But yes, if we were to hit another major inflationary cycle—"

"But suppose you were only acting as attorney to an estate and the executor chose to make certain kinds of investments?"

"Risky ones?"

"Not necessarily. Say, less conventional ones."

"It would be against our best advice."

"But if the executor insisted . . . ?"

"In that case," I said with a smile, "we'd probably recommend a change in legal representation."

"Oh, come on, Tommy," she said, her lower lip protruding impatiently. "There have to be ways around it."

Indeed there were, and in idle moments I'd thought of more than one. I had, I should add, plenty such idle moments, because trusts and estates work, while it involves endless detail in the preparation and filing of documents, seldom requires more acumen or experience than is possessed by a paralegal, or even a smart secretary.

At the same time, Kitty was right in theory: in certain economic climates the kinds of investments we habitually made in behalf of our estates could mean an erosion of capital. But practically speaking, the subject never came up. Most of the estates I dealt with were considerably larger than Edgar Sprague's, and all my widows really cared about, from a financial point of view, was that the bills be paid and their monthly allowances forthcoming.

Of course, they had other needs, too.

"Let me ask you something else," Kitty went on. "How much are you billed out at? I'd guess between two hundred and two fifty an hour. Am I close?"

"Very," I said. "Actually, it's been two twenty-five, but it's about to go up."

"Whew," she said. "But how much of that is yours to keep? Including your profit share?"

Another sore point.

"I'm afraid that's none of your business, Kitty."

"In other words, you're getting screwed?"

"I didn't say that," I answered, though in fact I was. It irritated me too that she should know it, or suspect it.

"You're too discreet," she said. "But suppose an estate were willing to kick in a percentage of its profits? On top of the fee?"

"Oh, we'd have to turn that down. We don't operate that way."

"I'm not talking about the firm, silly," she said. "I'm talking about you."

"Oh? Well, I'd have to refuse that, too."

"Why?"

"Because it's unethical. Not just vis-à-vis the firm, but professionally unethical."

"Come on, Tommy," she said impatiently. "You've got to be kidding."

"I'm afraid I'm not."

"But why?"

"Because that's the way it is," I answered stiffly.

"Is that it? Or is it because your name—your father's name—is on the door?"

A third and, as far as I was concerned, final sore point. She must have seen it, too, that she'd overstepped. Her body made a withdrawing, recoiling movement into the couch.

"I'm sorry," she said. "I didn't mean to offend you."

"But you did," I answered, further irritated because she couldn't possibly have known how she'd offended me. My attitude toward my father—the Senator, as some in the firm referred to him—had by this juncture in my life crystallized into a perfect ambiguity. In fact, had Kitty understood that, she wouldn't have withdrawn at all; on the contrary, she'd have closed in for the kill.

She fell silent, her eyes still fixed on mine.

"I don't think I understand what you're after, Kitty," I said.

"What am I after?" she asked. "I thought I made that clear. I want to make money with the estate. I also want somebody who's not going to fight me every step of the way. I want a partner."

"Then I really think you've come to the wrong man."

"I don't think so."

"I do," I said.

With that, I must have glanced at my watch. My meeting had already started. She must have noticed it too, for she stirred as though to stand up. Then, catching herself, she let her body subside back into the corner of the couch, her arm draped across its leather back. She gazed at me darkly, her scarlet lower lip protruding again. Then her eyes narrowed ever so slightly, and her cheekbones stretched into the beginnings of a smile.

"Come on, Tommy," she said. "I told you I wanted us to have some fun."

There it was again, insistent as on that first night, the unmistakable invitation. In anyone else, her blatant way of offering herself, half reclining on my couch, might have struck me as vulgar, even whorish. Maybe it did in Kitty, too; maybe that's even what attracted me. But I

found myself perched again on that strange, deftly bal-
anced seesaw of irritation and arousal which she alone
knew how to manage. The previous time she'd let her
end go, dumping me hard, but this time, twenty-one
stories up in the January gloom, the seesaw dipped the
other way, pulling me forward over her.

I kissed her, felt the soft, sweet fullness of her lips,
mouth, the strong arch of her neck, as she kissed me
back. Close up, the smell of her soared through my nostrils, overpowering, dizzying, and I spread her lips with
mine, pushing my tongue upon hers in that uniquely
human imitation of sex. Then I heard, or felt rather than
heard, the quivering of laughter deep inside her, and she
broke free, pulled her head back, shook it as though to
free her mind. She pushed me a little away, her hands
firm against my shoulders, and stared at me, eyes wide,
wet, in her own version of desire.

"Come to my apartment," she said in a newly husky
voice. "How soon can you come?"

"Why not here?" I answered. "Why not now?"

"In your office?" she said, startled. "What about the
firm? What about your meeting?"

"They'll hardly miss me," I answered, truthfully
enough.

"But what about your staff?"

"It's Friday. I'm about to let them go, anyway."

"But what if someone else comes in?"

"No one will. If you want, I'll lock the door, even
pull the drapes."

She hesitated just briefly. (Out of decorum? Or because
it was a little more than she'd bargained for?) Then:

"Go take care of everything," she said, gazing up at
me.

I stood, summoning up my usual urbanity before leaving, but she called me back insistently.

"On one condition, Tommy," she said.

I looked back at her, still in that half-reclining offering posture, her arms spread, head lifted toward me, eyes now large and piercing black.

"What's that?" I asked.

"That I'm the first"—with an encompassing gesture—"here."

Even now, I can't help smiling at the scene. It was truly quintessential Kitten, how, at a moment of genuine and lustful desire, she yet dredged out this statement of quasi-virginal principle: that at least my couch, if not we ourselves, be pure and unsullied.

"You are, Kitty," I assured her, smiling. "Absolutely."

And I like to think that it was even true.

4

Doing full justice to the subject of Kitty and sex would require not only length but some considerable jumping forward in my chronology. Suffice it for now that she was open to suggestion, also that she had a predilection for certain materials and textures. Silk, for instance. (In fact, I think the most appreciated gift I ever gave her was a set of raw silk sheets, amethyst in tone, with matching comforter, ruffles, and whatever else it was that came in the set.) And leather, too, to judge from that afternoon, either against her backside or crushed under her bosom (with the drapes drawn, door locked, staff dismissed, my telephone messages unanswered on my desk). But what she really liked is, as I would discover, another story.

Better, then, to leave the subject where it left off that Friday, that is, with the two of us standing on the sidewalk outside my office building in the enveloping darkness, where, as I recall, the first tiny flakes of snow had already begun to fall, a brisk dusting which, by the time I returned Sunday night, would have coated the city white. Upstairs, while we dressed and I phoned the firm's taxi service, she'd invited me to come home with her. With appropriate apologies, however, I'd declined. As much as I wanted to, I told her, it would complicate my life beyond belief. I had, I said, a long-established date, and reservations to match, to take my kids skiing in Vermont. And I was already running late. Given the weather and the Friday night stampede for those distant slopes, we wouldn't arrive till the wee hours of the morning, which wouldn't deter Starkie and Mary Laura from routing me out at eight on Saturday to beat the lines at the lifts. The prospect of forty-eight hours in their company, I said, a good fourteen of which would be spent behind the wheel while my children either slept or squabbled, hardly filled me with anticipation, but what was an absentee father to do?

Kitty, I remember, barely heard my explanation, other than to say that she assumed even ski lodges had telephones, that I could call. I'd told her I would. It was characteristic of her, whenever I had conflicting plans to which she clearly couldn't object (increasingly rare, in time), simply to turn off. So, on the sidewalk, she kissed me back rather perfunctorily, I thought, and quickly got into the taxi, shutting the door behind her before I could— fleeing the unwanted scene, in sum. I realized, as I waited for the second taxi I'd ordered, that at least the part about complications and running late had been true. The ski trip I'd described, though, had actually taken place the week before.

This upcoming weekend—shortened, as it turned out—I was to spend not in a Vermont ski lodge but in a secluded country inn, the quaint but luxurious kind, next to a frozen lake in northern Connecticut. It was a cognac-next-to-the-roaring-fire sort of place, with large and elegantly appointed rooms, an excellent cuisine, and a graceful discretion toward its guests. My companion was the estranged wife of someone I'd gone to college with, an attractive enough creature whom I'd prefer to leave nameless, for she figures not at all in my story except, perhaps, as an illustration of the effect Kitty Goldmark had already had on me.

But one scene emerges from those interminable hours:

I am alone in the bathroom, naked, examining myself in the full-length mirror. It is Sunday morning. The snow has stopped, and the plows, I've noticed from the windows of our suite, are working the road leading to the village. Otherwise there is no sound to be heard, just a wondrous rural quiet enhanced by the muffling cloak of snow. I am scarcely one given to navel-gazing, either of the psychological or physiological type, and I doubt greatly that I'd done it since my early teenage years, but that morning I stand there anyway, contemplating Stark Thompson at forty-one.

Outwardly the same, no? But what of that still undefined stirring inside, the egg just beginning to fissure or, more accurately, the tombstone about to lift? Kitty's doing, I suppose. Certainly it is Kitty's doing that, in the course of said examination, there develops—*grows* would be better—a plump and hefty erection, for it is the first such since Friday, a lapse unusual for me and troubling enough, a harbinger of sorts.

We Thompsons, I should point out, come mainly in one variety. The Senator and I share a strong physical resemblance. We're tall and slender (although he developed late in life the pot which undoubtedly awaits me), with sandy hair receding off the temples, high foreheads, thin, fine features (a bit finer, it is said, in my case, perhaps my mother's contribution), slate-blue eyes. We have swimmers' bodies, long-limbed, with long fingers and long, narrow feet, and certain sports, particularly ones like swimming, track, racquet games, skiing, come naturally to us. In fact, the Senator liked to boast that he won the IC4A's 880-yard run while an undergraduate (a feat I once, out of curiosity, verified) and skipped the Olympic trials only because he was too busy in law school to train. He was—and still is, so he would be the first to tell you—an inveterate and incorrigible womanizer. Of which more, in due course.

Of our (apparently joint) appeal to women, what can I say? It seems to come naturally, almost like the sports. I've heard us both called handsome, and I know from my own experience that I seem to project an air—of sensitivity I suppose—which seems to inspire in women both older and younger some instinct at once to protect me and, conversely, to put themselves under my protection. From what I know of my father's many dalliances, I'd say he was more the sweep-them-off-their-feet kind, an indication of his needs for dominance and admiration, as well as—

Why is it, though, that I cannot—or could not—so much as look in the mirror that morning without evoking the comparison between us? Obviously the target of my introspection was more than my physical body. It was the old "buried alive" syndrome, my private version of psychology's most recent "discovery," the male midlife crisis. I would spare you—and myself—most of the details. Suffice it that, while I was listed as a partner at the firm, I wasn't compensated as one, nor did I share in the annual divvying up of our profits. I had my salary, a token bonus, and that was it. This had been the Senator's doing, though he'd contrived to miss the grim meeting at which Mac Coombs had put the choice to me. (As if, at the time, there'd been any choice.) Suffice it further that I was still only partially extricated from a marriage that had happened to me almost without my knowing it was happening, to a woman who seemed constantly to reappear in the various women I'd dabbled with since the divorce, such as my still sleeping companion. Forty-one, trapped, buried, while the Senator, almost twice my age, was working on his fifth marriage and none the worse for wear!

But then there was Kitty.

I walk back into the bedroom, where my companion lies peaceably on her side, her blond, shoulder-length hair curled under the collar of her nightgown. Why on earth, I wonder, do women like her wear these absurd, frilly-necked nightgowns on what is supposed to be a romantic weekend? And what, I wonder, would Kitty Goldmark bring along by way of sleepwear—other than her silken, sumptuous skin?

I turn away from the prospect of my companion with its echoes of a life (my own) not so much misspent as unspent and, still naked, gaze out the windows, over evergreens bending under the weight of snow, over undulating fields and swards blanketed by snow. This pristine vista, I imagine idly, can have but little changed from what my New England forebears beheld, and the first settlers before them, and the Indians before them. It is now, in any case, that the aforementioned erection sprouts fully, inspired not, I am sure, by my brief historical reverie, but by the sudden intrusion of Kitty Goldmark into my consciousness, and more specifically by the fantasy which had bewitched me that first night when, to my immense frustration, she abandoned me on her doorstep. For if I could not have her then, spread on the night blanket of Central Park, now in my mind I am taking her, her glorious and aromatic body slithering beneath me on a couch of Connecticut snow.

Against such powerful competition, what chance did my pale companion have?

She seemed, to her credit, if not her liking, to understand this point.

We had brunch in our sitting room, off a laden hot tray wheeled in with cheerful good wishes by the owner's wife herself. I ate little, said less. Normally, my wit would have risen gallantly to such a morose occasion and carried us, if not back to bed, at least to an afternoon's horse-drawn sleigh ride before we headed back to the city and our separate lives. But the circumstances, obviously, were not normal.

"You know, Tommy," she said, the woman spurned, eyeing me balefully over her coffee cup, "I hate to say it, but I don't have the slightest idea what I'm doing here."

"I'm afraid, my dear," I replied, "that I don't either."

We were back in the city by two. I deposited her at her door without ceremony. I'd done little, I supposed, to enhance my reputation, but what need had I of my reputation? By four, I'd crossed my new client and lover's threshold, high above the slush of the streets, and when I came after dark, violently, throbbingly, her strong arms pinning my shoulders in a shouting match of passion, I felt my own body flying, soaring, wafting, to dissolve, most deliciously, on its swaddling, snowy blanket.

5

My earliest memory of the firm was the seals. I'm talking about corporate seals, those black- or green-handled objects, too heavy to be picked up comfortably but which punched out beautiful circular emblems on sheets of paper, white on white, which you could not only see but touch, rubbing your fingers across the embossing. This was, my father liked to say, where my legal training began, as his had a generation before. On those occasions when I accompanied him to the office, which at the time was down on lower Broadway, I'd therefore be handed over to some secretary (who may, from what I later learned, have been more than a secretary, or not a secretary at all) and, seated at what seemed an immense mahogany table with a stack of watermarked bond paper, would punch out page after page of seals.

These visits—how many there were I've no idea, and it's possible there was only one—must have taken place in the late 1940s. I was conceived, so the story went, the night my father came home from the war, a full colonel, just as my older sister had been conceived the night before

he went off. This was his method, I imagine, of keeping
my mother occupied while he toured the globe with General Donovan, then later, in 1948, stood for the U.S.
Senate. He served only one term, for reasons which remained muddy in the family version but which, I realized
with some surprise years later, must have had to do with
the simple fact that he knew he'd be defeated if he ran
again in 1954.

The law firm, the family history said, needed his attention. It was growing rapidly; so were his children. But
all during my early boyhood, he was gone much more
than he was there, officially on this or that government
assignment or mission, but more likely, I now understand, as a means of getting away from work and family.
That the firm grew and prospered had to do with the work
of other people, the Mac Coombses, although I'm sure
my father's name and connections helped. At least some
of his "missions" probably did involve intelligence
work, for he belonged to that old-boy network that had
evolved out of Yale and the wartime OSS; but others,
I'm sure, involved a different kind of clandestine activity.
Either way, as far as the family was concerned, we soon
went our separate ways.

A curious incident to illustrate:

Some years ago, when Susan and I were in Rome—
vacationing in Italy was something her family *did*—I
noticed a blond woman staring fixedly at me while riding
down in the hotel elevator. She was a little on the blowzy
side, though fashionably turned out and still pretty. I was
positive I'd never seen her before, but that didn't keep
her from smiling at me with evident recognition.

When we reached the lobby, she said:

"Excuse me, but I can't resist. You're Stark Thompson's son, aren't you?"

"Yes, I am, but—"

"You look so much like him, I can't believe it. It's absolutely uncanny."

Of course the Stark Thompson she remembered would have been only a little older than I was, there in that Roman hotel lobby, but she said it was a "déjà voo" that wiped out more years than she wanted to think about. I agreed to meet her for a drink that afternoon, when Susan must have been *doing* some museum, and then she told me the story.

She had been his mistress, probably only one of them, during that period of the corporate seals. She claimed to have been a film actress, said they'd met in California. Then she'd moved to New York, where he'd set her up in a little pied-à-terre in Murray Hill. They were "together" (her word) for over a year, and then she got pregnant. It had been her doing, she confessed, though she'd never admitted it to him, and though she'd wanted to have the baby, he'd insisted on an abortion. He'd sent her out of the country; that was what one did in those days. Then, not long after she came back, they'd broken up. His doing, I gathered. She'd gotten, she said, a very generous financial settlement.

Strangely, she held no grudge against him. On the contrary, she let on that she'd known many men since but that there was only one Stark Thompson. The year she'd been with him, she said, remained one of her happiest memories—to the extent that, that afternoon in the hotel bar, her gloved hand touching my arm and a why-not twinkle in her eyes, she invited me to spend an hour or two with her the next day.

Take it as a comment on the state of my marriage that I accepted. For her, she said, giggling, it was "déjà voo all over again." Whether this meant that I resembled my father in bed as well as in the elevator I couldn't say, but when I was leaving her room on the floor below ours in that Roman hotel, she called after me, "Please give him my love when you see him, Tommy, will you? Tell him Muriel sends her love."

This, however, I failed to do.

I worked for the firm one summer when I was in prep school, as messenger, mailroom hand, and general gofer. By this time it—or we—had moved uptown, one of a series of moves that would end in the current habitat high above the Avenue of the Americas. Few people remember it today, but not that long ago the legal profession in New York was concentrated downtown: Centre Street, Lafayette Street, Broadway, and of course the Wall Street area. The northward migration of the 1950s and 1960s reflected not only the need to "follow the clients," as more and more big corporations established themselves in the glass and steel towers of midtown, but the diminished role of the courtroom in legal practice. This has since changed again, but at the time I'm talking about, courtroom skills were somehow looked down upon in the larger firms, a kind of necessary specialty but not necessarily a highly rewarded one. The accepted goal of the profession in those years was to keep the client out of court.

In any case, I spent most of that summer either perspiring on public transportation or trying to convince one Rosa Maria Castigliano, a secretary in the firm's employ, that she could do worse than accept my youthful favors. That I finally succeeded in the latter probably struck me as a heady achievement at the time—God knows I worked at it—but I found the job itself exceedingly boring, and since the cost of my commuter ticket and street-corner lunches came out of my pay, which was on the order of forty dollars a week, I doubt I retained much cash from the exercise.

As for the other family-appointed goal—for me to

"learn how other people lived"—well, yes, I guess I did learn why "other people's" beaches were jammed on summer weekends and why, in the poorer city neighborhoods, the crime rate went up every July and August. And why, conversely, the seersucker- and poplin-clad members of the firm contrived to take most Fridays off in summer, and sometimes Mondays.

This "character-building" aspect of summer work may have reflected Thompson class traditions and precepts, but for me, the question was one of simple necessity, i.e., how to scrounge together enough money to pay off the debts I'd incurred the previous school year. So, in subsequent summers, while my peers sailed and partied the eastern coasts, or toured Europe, or climbed mountains, or even in rarer cases marched for civil rights, I worked as a bartender and part-time tennis instructor at a succession of resort hotels. Even so, money was ever a near thing for me, and how to extract it from the family became a virtual obsession during my college years.

I was a so-so student at Yale. At the time, which was before they started accepting women and Orientals, it was still possible for any reasonably intelligent youth of proper background to coast through the best schools on what was called "a gentleman's average." Indeed, there was little incentive to do better. In the careers ahead of us—banking, Wall Street, publishing, advertising, the professions—the grades we'd achieved as undergraduates couldn't have mattered less. I got into the law school of my choice (or my father's choice) by acing the law boards and with a last-minute push from some well-placed old grads.

While at it, I should say that the much-vaunted events and social stirrings that are supposed to have swept the Youth of the Sixties somehow passed me by. I never marched anywhere. To hear my fellow baby-boomers reminisce today, you would think that every last one of us—how many millions?—was at Woodstock that weekend in August 1969. Except, that is, for me. I can remember the first time I smoked grass (it was in the top row of my prep school football stadium—a most daring feat at the time), but the people I knew were much more into booze and women than the mind trips of the psychedelics and the radicals.

The Vietnam War? Yes, we were well aware of it, at first as a vague menace, then a looming one. The key question was, How did we—as individuals, not as a society—get out of it? I myself, thanks to an indulgent draft board, school deferments, and, later, a high number in the lottery, managed to luck out. One or two people I knew went to Canada, although that was considered extreme. And a certain number served, none with distinction or even pride, but no one I knew with that residual scarring, emotional or physical, we've heard so much about since.

Vietnam, in fact, was much more traumatic for the Senator than for me. A confirmed Democrat, he fulminated against the naïveté of Jack Kennedy, compounded by the total and insane idiocy of that Texan, not for getting us into a war but into one we couldn't win. Maintaining (with reason) that they had wrecked the Democratic Party for years to come, he himself voted for Nixon in 1968.

I come then to my last year at law school, to two—what should I call them?—councils, neither of which, curiously, I attended. It was my father who brought me news of the first, Mac Coombs of the second.

The occasion for both meetings, as it turned out, was that I had recently made one Susan ("Sukie") Bartlett of Boston, Mass., big, as they say, with child. Or potentially big. Or so I'd been informed by Miss Bartlett, who, having missed her period, had gone to a Beacon Hill gynecologist, who, she said, had confirmed her suspicions. The event had allegedly taken place on Cape Cod in the summer home of a friend of mine, which, in January, was so cold that virtually the only way to keep from freezing was to make love, which had been our purpose in going there in the first place. Furthermore, Miss Bartlett wanted the child, because Miss Bartlett wanted to marry me. Further still, I had somehow convinced myself that I wanted to marry her back.

The Senator, when I finally tracked him down, thought I'd gone off my rocker.

"God Almighty, Tommy, you don't have to *marry* the girl!" he said with a dramatic, dismissing flourish of the hand. "Buy her an abortion, for God's sake. It'll be much cheaper in the long run. I can guarantee it, and I speak from personal experience."

The reference, I supposed, was to the fact that, having recently been divorced for the third time, he was on the one hand enjoying his freedom (which lasted but briefly) and on the other bemoaning his allegedly penurious condition. My father chronically pleaded poverty, yet I never knew him or any of his wives to suffer from want, and that omits such other Muriels as he may have left behind him with their "generous financial settlements."

We'd met for lunch at the club in New York. He was very tanned, in January, his nose peeling. It turned out that instead of ducking me (which I'd assumed) during the week of dire emergency I'd just lived through, he'd been off in the West Indies with some new playmate.

I put my case to him with all the conviction I could muster. This was my habitual posture in those years, pleading my case for money while he, usually distracted and invariably impatient, searched for the loopholes in my argumentation. In this instance, he could find none.

I loved the girl; I wanted to marry her; I needed money. At the same time, I had no job lined up after graduation. My class standing was insufficient to attract either the more prestigious firms or the clerkships the law school itself so highly touted. Besides, I'd have to spend the summer taking the cram course for the bar exam.

In the end the Senator could find nothing better than: "If you insist on marrying her, Tommy, then you're an even bigger asshole than I took you for."

"I guess that makes me a very large one indeed," I countered, channeling my anger into irony. But he couldn't budge me, and I think I succeeded not only in exasperating him but finally in boring him.

"I'll get back to you," he said as we shook hands on Fifth Avenue, he very sharp in his chesterfield and homburg. "I'm not promising anything, but I'll get back to you."

It took him two weeks, fourteen more days, for me, of an increasingly hysterical Susan. In hindsight, I'd have to agree he was right, for my marriage was to teeter for years until it finally crashed—the alleged pregnancy, by the way, which brought it about would end in an alleged miscarriage, and it took us five more years to generate a child—but at the time I'd already boxed myself in.

The two councils, then.

The Senator called me one night to tell me that the family—not he, but the family—had agreed as a wedding gift to underwrite the purchase of a house in the $150,000 range, at a cost to me of prime less one percent, but with a share in the appreciation in the event of its sale. Up until then, I hadn't even known of the existence of this family Council, which dealt with matters involving the Thompson inheritance. It was composed of senior members of the clan, my father included, and apparently its main activities were to approve the investment decisions made by the Trustee and to decide on occasional grants, usually in the form of loans, to family members in need. In my case, the family continued to profit from itself, for I continued paying prime less one percent long after I stopped living in the place, and its considerable appreciation in value over the years would, whenever it was sold, enrich the family's coffers more than my own.

As for the rest of it, the Senator said, I was to talk to Mac Coombs as soon as possible. Before I could ask what about, he'd hung up.

I went down to New York again two days later and saw Mac in his office. He was a big, gruff-looking man, which belied his urbane, even gentle manner. He too had once done a stint in government service, a feature of the firm's early days and key perhaps to its growth, but by the time I'm talking about he'd become much more of an inside man, or a "lawyer's lawyer." While people like my father roamed the world, drumming up business, it was Mac who made sure we made money out of it, and in his later years, even though it went against his own better judgment, it was he who watchdogged our rapid expansion through the absorption of, and in some cases the acquisition of, other smaller firms.

"I'm happy to tell you, Tommy," he said after we'd shaken hands, "that the partners have decided unanimously to invite you to join the firm as a provisional first-year associate. You should know that there was some discussion of nepotism—you happen to be a first for us—but we do have openings to fill and assuming you graduate and pass the bar in good order, we'll be delighted to have you."

This was the good news and so, under the circumstances, was my starting salary. Then, in a sterner but still official tone:

"I want to make clear that you'll be treated no differently than anybody else. The law, you know, is like a series of pyramids. You climb your way up the steps of one—college, law school, joining a firm—only to find that there's another one to climb. Your salary may sound good to you now—at least I hope it does, it's a hell of a lot more than I ever made at the beginning—but you'll earn it many times over. You'll work nights and you can forget about weekends. You'll be doing the drudge work we all had to do once. And when you do get to the top of the pyramid, there's no guarantee that you'll make partner, none at all. I want to make myself very clear on that point."

I didn't react to what I took to be the basic indoctrination speech. I was wondering instead why my father had interceded for me, even though it turned out he'd been absent from the partners' meeting and had abstained from the vote. Cynically, I could tell myself that dumping the problem in Mac Coombs's lap had been the simplest way of getting rid of it. But he could also have let me flounder.

Why hadn't he? Why had he made Mac, the official caveats notwithstanding, throw me a lifesaver?

I should, I suppose, have been elated. Instead, the unanswered question set off a vague malaise in me, which Mac Coombs spotted.

He sat there, a bulky figure in navy blue with rubicund complexion and slicked-back gray hair. He observed me. Then he took his glasses off, put them on the desk, rubbed at his eyes with his knuckles.

"I've known you since you came up to my knee, Tommy," he said. "I've always liked you, too, always thought you had something. I don't know if you even want my personal advice now, but in case you do, it's this."

He leaned forward, his eyes large and rheumy without the glasses.

"Don't take our offer," he said. "Whatever pressures you're under right now, find some other way to beat them. Go somewhere else—anywhere. I think it would be a mistake for you to work here."

The suggestion, I knew, was offered out of kindness. I thanked Mac for it, and if it sounds strange that I didn't ask him to elaborate, much less take him up on it, I think this was because, the way I saw things, I had no choice.

6

Kitty's father had been a furrier—actually, according to Ted Goldmark, a cutter for a furrier. I forget the more technical term for it, but Goldmark père was the one who sized and matched the skins, transforming them into the minks and sables and beavers that adorned the bodies of American women, at least until the time when the slaughter of animals for warmth fell out of fashion. By that time, though, Solomon Goldmark had already gone to his maker, having seen his children through college, Katherine through Barnard and Theodore, strange though it always seemed to me, through my own alma mater.

It took me a long time to find out this much, also to learn that there was a widow Goldmark still alive in Florida, supported by her late husband's pension and insurance as well as regular checks from her two children. Kitty's secretiveness on the subject wasn't because of their Jewishness but because her father, a devout union man, had also been something of a Marxist-socialist and even, in his youth, had played some small, undefined role in one of the plots to assassinate Trotsky.

(I learned this last from her brother. Kitty herself denied it. According to Kitty, her father had been a furrier. Not a cutter to a furrier, mind you, but a furrier.)

Why this compulsion, though, to rush ahead? Is it because it embarrasses me now, Kitten, to admit that you took me by storm? Or to recall how, captive, I waited for your summonses? And dreaded the empty, endless weekends without you?

My only competition, it seemed, was her business. Katherine Goldmark Enterprises gave parties for the well-heeled, but the way Kitty did it, she herself had to see to everything, from the design and content of the invitations to the cleanup after the last guest had toddled off. She supervised a small part-time army of waiters, chefs, bartenders, truckers, and musicians, and she did it with an almost ferocious attention to detail—the only way, she maintained, to make a profit. At the time I'm talking about, she had just embarked on her first takeover: a small catering business run by a group of Connecticut women who had been losing money steadily.

Mondays and Tuesdays usually constituted her weekends, although that's when she caught up on her paperwork. Often she'd call me midafternoon at the office, asking if I could make an emergency meeting at her apartment concerning the Sprague estate. Of course I could, did, on the run, cursing meanwhile the effrontery of the well-heeled for holding their receptions and soirées on Saturdays and Sundays. But as driven as Kitty was in her business, the moment I showed up, her telephone-answering machine went on and the outside world was cut off.

"You're my island, my darling," she'd say to me in calmer moments. "My sanity, my health. Come"—arms extended—"play island with me." But there were few such calm moments. More often we made love ravenously, violently, in every room of her apartment, on every rug, couch, chair, on the cold tile of her kitchen, in the warm, bursting bubbles of her Jacuzzi, against the windows that gave out on the park and the smoked-glass mirrors that lined her dressing room, standing, kneeling, sitting, lying. I came to know every nook, cranny, crevice, every blemish, of her lustrous body, knew them by heart with my eyes, hands, mouth, lips, tongue, and, yes, my cock. Yet never did I have enough of her. All I needed was her call, the brief chuckle that accompanied her summons, and, wherever she'd found me, I was on my way. To me, her apartment was like some airborne cave, a bewitched and magical aerie where the world got left behind. Here we did everything together: ate, drank, loved, bathed, slept, and, yes, once a month, even went over the Sprague account, the latest printout stuffed into my briefcase because I knew she would ask to see it.

At the beginning, I'd recommended the simplest method of dealing with her late husband's money: that the estate write her a check for x dollars, either as an advance against her inheritance or as a loan, and that she do with it as she wished. But she'd refused that. If she needed a loan, she said, her credit was good at the banks. What she wanted, she said, and what I'd agreed to be, was a partner. What this meant, in practice, was that I became her messenger, communicating her sell and buy orders, safeguarding meanwhile that minimum portion of the estate which it was my legal obligation to maintain. At first, the changes she'd ordered in the portfolio seemed prudent enough, Big Board securities for the most part, and in a bull market the gains she'd made did not strike me as inordinate. Still, the estate appreciated some twelve percent in the first quarter of my involvement—remarkable compared to gains made by my other clients, who might, if we were lucky, realize eight percent for the year.

The computer even congratulated us, in its way. It highlighted the Sprague gain, and our chief accountant, Arthur Prine, called me to query it.

I told him the numbers were correct.

"Christ, Tommy," said Arthur Prine from the twentieth floor, "if you could do that with every estate, we'd own the business."

"Either that or be disbarred," I answered cheerfully.

Arthur Prine, though, had trouble understanding jokes.

"What do you mean by that?" he said suspiciously.

"Not to worry, Arthur," I reassured him. "The firm's fully covered. But Sprague's a special case anyway."

"Too bad," he said. "It'd be nice to see all your accounts jump like that."

"As far as we're concerned, though, it makes little difference. We're not in for a percentage."

"Too bad," he repeated, "when other parts of the firm are."

The implied criticism, I knew, reflected the typical accountant's mentality: if one part of your business is bringing down x percent, why isn't the other? Or, if it can't, then why not get rid of it? Still, Prine irritated me. And so, from a different direction, did Kitty.

The results disappointed her. She wrinkled her nose at the papers spread out before us on the immense Chinese rug of her living room. We'd been too timid, she said. She thought we'd done better, but the numbers didn't lie, did they?

Or did they?

I remember her pointing a red nail at one transaction in the calendar listing.

"Hey, wait a minute!" she said, starting to leaf through a file folder next to her on the rug.

"What's wrong?" I said. The item in question called for the purchase of eight hundred shares of a Big Board stock. The order had been executed.

"*Here's* what's wrong!" she said, waving a small piece of paper in the air. It was a page from a memo pad with Katherine Goldmark Enterprises printed across the bottom and some scribblings above it. I recognized her writing. "You cost me a thousand dollars, maybe more, that's what's wrong!"

"Well, what's a thousand dollars between friends?" I said airily, still not seeing it.

"The *dates*," she said angrily. "Look at the *dates*!" The printout showed that the purchase had taken place on the fifteenth of March. The date noted on Kitty's memo was March twelfth. In the interim, she claimed, the stock had risen more than a point. "It took you three days to buy! Why did it take you *three days*!"

Unless a weekend had intervened, I had no idea. But a weekend hadn't intervened. I was almost positive the delay hadn't occurred in my office. We either phoned in or faxed orders to the broker immediately. But I said I would check.

This failed to mollify her, though. It turned out her file folder contained similar jottings for every transaction in the printout, and she insisted on tracing every last one.

Sure enough, she found other similar discrepancies.

"Who's the broker?" she wanted to know.

"Why, I've been using your brother's outfit on your account."

"You *what*?"

"That's right, Braxton's. Not Ted personally, of course. He's not—"

"But who told you to use *them*?"

"No one. You didn't specify. But hell, Kitty, they're

as good as any other, or as bad. They're one of the three
we use all the time.''

"Then change," she ordered. "Go somewhere else
for my account. I don't want you to ask me why, just
do it."

This was the first time I'd heard her speak with such
vehemence, the first time I'd had anything remotely resembling an order from her lips except, of course, for
those I wanted to hear. I saw the stony set of her jaw in
profile, her gaze intent, angry, fixed on the rug, and for
the life of me I didn't understand. Surely it wasn't the
money. In fact she spent freely, generously. At the time
I'm talking about, we were on a caviar and Montrachet
diet, both supplied by Kitty. But then . . . ?

She must have sensed my reaction. She bowed her
head and arched her neck several times as though exer-
cising it, then swiveled toward me, dark eyes still small,
and tossed her hair off her forehead.

"I'm sorry, darling," she said. "I didn't mean to take
it out on you."

"Take what out on me?"

She shook her head.

"I can't explain," she said, looking away.

Then nothing.

"I'm afraid that's not good enough, Kitty," I persisted.

She didn't say anything for another moment. I watched
her sigh deeply, once, twice, her bosom lifting, falling.
Then she turned back to me, her eyes wet, voice bitter.

"Oh, it's nothing a few years on the couch couldn't
fix, but who has the time? It's about Gar. Edgar Sprague.
Edgar Chalmers Sprague, my late unlamented husband."

"What about him?" I said. Other than admitting that
she didn't mourn his death, she'd said nothing about him,

and there was no trace of him in the apartment, to which, I knew, she'd moved soon after he died.

"Nothing really. He was the kind of man who kept everything under lock and key. He kept his money under lock and key, his whiskey under lock and key. That was because of the maid. He said she stole his whiskey. He locked his emotions up the same way. He even tried to lock me up."

"Hardly the easiest of tasks," I said lightly.

"Hardly," she agreed. "But let's not talk about it. It's too depressing."

"I still don't understand why you get so worked up about his money. It's as though you're trying to prove something to him."

"I guess I am. I guess I'm trying to show him what he missed out on all those years."

"But he's dead, Kitty."

"I know he's dead. But I happen to believe that the dead know what's going on, at least for a while."

"From the grave?"

"From the grave," she said.

She seemed serious about it, too. Well, I thought, people—women especially—harbor stranger beliefs. But by implication it seemed as though she was trying to rub Edgar Sprague's dead nose in it, which was not only unlike her but beneath her.

"Why'd you marry him in the first place, if I may ask?" I said.

The question seemed innocuous enough—after all, who among us hasn't made the same mistake?—but it seemed to jolt her. She was sitting on the floor on that immense sky blue rug, her back propped against the back of a couch which formed a small trysting area in front of the fireplace. I sat near her, my legs crossed. For just a second, her head went back against the couch, her eyes small and far off. *Why indeed*? she seemed to be asking herself, remembering something else, maybe, and I saw, just in that second, that bitter stony look again. But only for a second. Then her head came forward, and she turned to me with an ironic smile.

"Because I was his secretary, silly. Don't secretaries always marry their bosses?"

"His secretary?" I said. For some reason this struck me as weird. "For how long?"

"Oh, seven, eight years. From about a year after I graduated from college till shortly before we got married."

And presumably his mistress before then? But that didn't answer the question either, because knowing who he was—and who knows that better than the secretary-cum-mistress?—why, again, had she married him?

She wasn't about to answer. Maybe she even said as much, but Kitten had other ways of stopping conversations she didn't want to go on. I remember her eyes on me, flashing with sudden pleasure, appetite. Then, with raucous laughter, she lunged at me.

Thrown off balance, I went over backward. Her charge carried her with me, but only halfway up my body as, with strong, red-tipped nails, she scrabbled at my pants. I twisted, pushed at her hair, her head. "Don't!" I cried out, laughing at the same time—but too late, for she was sucking me already. I felt her jaws clamp powerfully even as her eyes sought mine, and my cock blossomed obediently, grew, thrust over her pushing tongue as though to keep from being devoured.

"Kitten, for God's sake!" I shouted, and maybe then her brother's warning flashed through my mind, or something did, for I was racked by simultaneous spasms of panic and desire. Her face, eyes, her warm red lips, were invisibly buried in me, my hands weak against her shoulders, all the strength of me sucked into her mouth, until in throbbing, spastic jerks I came, drowning her even as I drowned.

Even then she did not release me.

I felt myself go flaccid. My body flopped back weakly, spent, but still she did not release me. Her tongue and teeth held me in a wet embrace, and she pulled me deep inside her when she swallowed. Then, her head rose, her eyes glittering in dark triumph. And still she would not release me.

"Enough, Kitten," I called out. "Kitty, let me go!"

But she would not, worrying my cock now from side to side by shaking her head, and fear flooded me, an unfamiliar instinct, followed by a welling and uncontrollable anger.

"For God's sake, Kitty!" I shouted again. Then I lurched up and struck her on the cheek, a hard, angry slap.

She let go of me, fell back, her mouth agape and wet, her eyes astonished.

I hit her again, saw her flinch from the blow, heard her gasp, and her eyes went wide in obvious fear.

I pushed her back into the rug, knelt above her. Legs spreading, she reached out for me and drew me violently into her. I pinned her shoulders into the rug, riding her, my chest heaving as her body began to toss and buck with passion.

Her eyes glazed. Her head went back as far as it could, neck arched, bosom high, as though to escape me. But there *is* no escape for you, Kitten, I exulted, not now, not ever.

"Oh my God . . ." I heard her call out. "Oh . . . my . . ."

She sobbed, her shoulders trembled, and I felt her start to come in a long, unending shudder of the body.

"We can . . ."

Inspired, I felt the fire erupt inside me. Semen pulsed out of me again.

"We . . . can . . . have . . ."—gasping—". . . any . . . thing . . ."

7

Then the Sprague estate struck gold.

It came about this way.

If you follow Wall Street at all, you will remember the story of Manderling's of Cleveland. At the time it was probably the largest, certainly the oldest, of the closely held retailing empires. Though Manderling was traded on the Big Board, the family owned close to fifty percent of the voting shares, and the bylaws of the company were so written as to discourage any hostile takeover attempt. Most of Manderling's competitors—the Bloomingdales and Saks Fifth Avenues of this world—had already been gobbled up. Manderling's remained virtually the last plum. A ripe plum, Wall Street thought, because unlike most department store chains, Manderling's traditionally owned its own real estate, and these assets, some analysts said, had been vastly undervalued in the corporate balance sheet. An overripe plum, even, because there had been dissension in the family ranks. Apparently some of the have-nots, that is, the mere seven-figure Manderlings of the younger generation, were taking issue with the way their eight-figure elders were running the company into the ground, even though the ground itself was valuable.

Enter Braxton's as investment bankers and my firm as legal counsel, both of us retained "to advise the family on certain financial matters and to explore opportunities in the field of mergers and acquisitions." (I quote from the joint press release that went out at the time.)

I think, in passing, that I may inadvertently have given a wrong impression. In a strictly professional sense, my work may have set me apart from my peers in the firm, but I socialized with many of them, and a group of us, all divorced and close to middle age, found a certain camaraderie not only in shoptalk but in such diverse activities as bemoaning our alimony payments and pooling our bets on the Triple Crown races, in which activity yours truly served as secretary and treasurer. A foursome among us—usually Buck Charles, Art Fording, Phil Lamont, and I—even went to the Belmont each June, taking over the Charles family box for the outing. I was therefore well aware of our involvement in Manderling's, and when Kitty Goldmark, as executrix, began buying the stock for the Sprague account, I covered myself carefully, with letters from Kitty in the file concerning each purchase and a confidential memo from me in the same file, disclaiming any role in the transactions other than my purely formal one.

By the time the firm's involvement became public knowledge, Manderling stock was already "in play." The players were clearly betting on a takeover, and though there were inevitably a few bears—those who claimed that we and Braxton's had been retained only as a sop to the younger generation from the older, who had no intention of selling the company—the price of the shares climbed up and up, up and up. And Kitty kept buying.

In point of fact, the bears weren't entirely wrong. The company was indeed for sale. But it would never, under any circumstances—and probably this was the one point on which the Manderling clan could reach quasi-unan-imity—be sold to Jews.

Whence Braxton's, whence ourselves. For if the issue had to be dealt with subtly, nonetheless our real mission was to find Manderling's an alternative to the Spodes. A White Knight, in other words, and one of good Christian persuasion.

The Spodes were Harry Spode and William ("Buddy") Spode, father and son corporate raiders par excellence. They had made quite a splash as New York real estate developers, starting in the early seventies when Buddy came into his own. More recently, they had joined the takeover game, at least on two occasions taking control of unwieldy conglomerates and selling off the pieces for more than they had paid for the whole. In the bargain, they had been left with an oil products company, a food distribution company, a film studio, and assorted other goodies. They owned, it was said, the half of Atlantic City that Donald Trump or the mob didn't.

When the Spodes filed their intentions with the SEC, it startled the Wall Street smart money into full churn and sent the Manderlings into a panic.

Whence, as I say, Braxton's. Whence ourselves.

I knew that we had succeeded in bringing other suitors into the game, and that the Spodes had one offer rejected by the Manderling board of directors, flatly and uncer-emoniously. A second, sweetened offer was similarly rejected, though a little more ceremoniously. And one Thursday, right after lunch, Kitty Goldmark put through a sell order by phone, confirmed by messenger, on all the Sprague estate's holdings in Manderling's.

The bottom fell out the next day. At a morning press conference, a Manderling spokesman announced that, having considered several offers and found them insufficient, the company was ceasing negotiations with all outside parties. For Manderling's, it was back to "business as usual." Not to be outdone, Buddy Spode told the media that he had better things to do than try to get in where he wasn't wanted and that he and his father had already begun liquidating their holdings in the company. Just before noon, the New York Stock Exchange suspended trading in Manderling's. By that time, though, the Sprague estate had already cashed in profits of just over a million dollars.

All hell was to break loose at the firm over the weekend, and at Braxton's. Documents were reviewed by internal committees and depositions taken, not only to ascertain who, if anyone, had cost us the fat fees that would have accompanied the successful sale of Manderling's, but to make sure our collective noses were clean when the inevitable stockholders' suits began to be filed. No one, of course, thought to look into my sector, which was just as well.

Meanwhile, I had my own investigation to carry out.

I tried phoning Kitty all that afternoon. I knew she was busy until late Sunday, for her Connecticut branch had a Saturday wedding and she had some sort of anniversary brunch back in the city the following noon. I left messages for her everywhere, but it wasn't till late Friday evening that she called me back, from some Stamford hotel.

"I'm sorry, darling," she said. "I've been running all day. I'm exhausted. Let's just say good night and catch up on Sunday."

"We've got to talk, Kitty."

"We've got our whole lives to talk, my sweet. I've got to be bright and beautiful tomorrow, and if I don't get some sleep I'll never make it."

Logical enough, I'd agree now, but there was a trace of impatience in how she said it, as though she wanted to get rid of me. As for me, I wasn't in my most logical mood.

"It can't wait, Kitty."

"What can't wait?"

"What happened today. Yesterday and today."

"Tommy," she said, and now the impatience was clear in her voice, "you're starting to drive me a little crazy. What can't wait?"

"Manderling's."

"For God's sake, so I made a little money, what's wrong with that?"

"You didn't make a little money. You made a lot of money. And as smart as you are, I can't believe you made it just by looking into your crystal ball."

She didn't say anything for a minute. I tried to picture her, where she was sitting, what she was wearing. I couldn't.

"Tommy," she said then, her voice taut, "I think you'd better say *exactly* what's on your mind. Unless you've gotten so paranoid you think your home phone's being tapped."

No, I hadn't gotten that paranoid.

"I'll tell you what's on my mind. Information. Insider's information, of the kind that's now illegal, in case you haven't heard. Your timing was too good, Kitty. Nobody could have played it so right without knowing exactly what was going to happen ahead of time."

"So?"

"So we live in the age of the computer, Kitty. The Manderling fiasco—what happened to the stock—is going to be scrutinized within an inch of its life. They're going to run every transaction through their computers, every buy, every sell, and when it took place, and yours are going to pop with little red flags attached.''

''Well,'' she said angrily, ''I don't see what makes *you* so uptight about it. You've made me cover you every which way. I bet you've already checked your files to make sure.''

In fact I already had, but I didn't like being reminded of it.

''I didn't think we were talking about you or me, Kitty,'' I blurted out. ''I thought we were talking about us.''

Even as I said it, I knew I was making a mistake. Perhaps I'd wanted to antagonize her? If so, I succeeded beyond my expectations.

I'd never heard such a tearful and shrewish outburst from Kitty, not even at her angriest. How could I do this to her? How could I call her in the middle of the night (it wasn't the middle of the night, and who had called whom?) and lay these threats and accusations on her? I was supposed to be her *lover*, wasn't I? Here she was, on the verge of the worst weekend of her year, and where was the support she needed from me? The support she had every right to expect? How was she supposed to get through the weekend when the only one she could turn to in the world accused her of being a criminal? She couldn't *believe* it! Maybe it was a good thing she was finding out now who I was, sooner rather than later. And maybe it was high time somebody *did* use me, if I, Mr. Stark Thompson III, wouldn't use myself!

This last suggests that the outburst was far from one-way, but I remember little of my side of it. I did accuse her of using me. More than anything, though, I remember the sensation of blood rushing to my head, of a pounding

congestion and the feeling of something beyond anger—
is *rage* the right word?—which Kitty, and only Kitty,
was capable of arousing in me. I also accused her of
using her brother. Goldmark would have been a logical
source for her, wasn't he a senior managing director at
Braxton's? I remember her laughing me down at that.
Did I really think she was that *stupid*? Did I really think
Teddy was the *only* man she knew who knew something
about the market? Which led me to further charges
("What does *that* mean?") and her to further ripostes
("Exactly what you think it means!"). And something
about the Spodes because yes, of course she knew the
Spodes, she'd done the bar mitzvah reception for Buddy's
older son.

But beyond that? Only the sense of charge and coun-
tercharge, ugliness against ugliness, in a futile and ex-
hausting escalation. A finally unequal escalation, I should
add, for there was no way—ever—I could outrecriminate
Kitty.

And Ted Goldmark's warning, yes. I put it down now
because I remember it ringing in my head that awful
night.

"Stay away from her, Tommy" was what he'd said
that day in the office, by our elevators. "She eats guys
like you alive."

And yes, I'd thought at other times, yes, Kitty's
brother, that's exactly what I want her to do. But this
night, recoiling before her on the phone, I knew what
he'd meant.

As for Kitty and me, I do recall, quite clearly, the last
words of our exchange.

Here were Kitty's, a bitter conclusion:

"I'm going to hang up now. I'm going to take a sleeping pill—you know how I hate doing that, but what

choice do you leave me—and try, if I can, to forget that this conversation ever took place.''

And mine:

''Good night, Kitten.''

But I doubt she heard mine, for the phone had gone dead in my ear.

8

Who slept?

I can't speak for Kitty. I myself managed no more than two fitful hours. I dreamed the recurrent dream again, the one that started with my son Starkie whimpering and ended up with me waking in a sweat. But then I was up, sitting in the darkness, pacing the confines of my apartment.

I had lived there almost five years. I hadn't intended to. When I'd moved out on Susan and the children, I'd taken it because it was there, furnished, available. Two and a half rooms, in real estate hyperbole, it was really one, half of a floor-through of an old Village brownstone. An alcove kitchen, another larger alcove where—my one major investment—I'd replaced the incumbent bed with a fold-out couch. Good light from windows overlooking the backyard, a (precariously) working fireplace with bookshelves on either side, an old-fashioned but still functioning bathroom with an ineradicable rust stain near the tub drain.

Home.

That I'd stayed reflected less on my inertia than on my limited disposable income, plus the fact that, since it was in the Village, I could get away with it. People I knew thought it bohemian, a post-divorce change in lifestyle reflecting eccentricity, perhaps, but not poverty. (I knew full well, though, what Kitty would have said, and it was no accident that our lovemaking had invariably taken place in her boudoir, never in mine.)

I heard my old French clock, one of the few treasures I'd rescued from my marriage, strike its approximation of three. And four, five, six, each hour like a day marked on the wall by the prisoner in his cell, for I had thirty-six such hours confronting me, an interminable sentence. I was due in the morning to collect my children for a visit to their grandmother—no subterfuge this time—and Kitty had her stupid wedding, her asinine brunch.

Or, the unthinkable thought: Was it really over between us?

But how could that be?

We'd had a fight, that was all, wasn't it? And hadn't we had others?

But always before we'd been face to face, body to body, able to sublimate our anger in sex.

I'll try, if I can, to forget that this conversation ever took place.

God damn her for saying that!

I thought of going in search of her, even then, the middle of the night. I had no idea which hotel she was in, but how many could there be in Stamford? I'd go from one to the other, room by room, I'd wake up the town till I found her! (Was it just as well I didn't? Or too bad I didn't?) Instead, I sweated in the overheated building, my windows open to the night air of early spring, while I waited for Saturday morning and my children.

At dawn I showered, shaved, dressed, packed, and picked up my old Dodge Aries from the garage in the West Village. There was little traffic on the parkway and I pulled into the driveway a bit before nine.

My old house sat on a little over an acre, with tall trees and a sward of lawn that rolled down to the edge of some communal woods. Its sturdy New England wood frame had been repainted the year before (my expense), forest green shutters and trim against a white facade. Strange to say it seemed foreign to me, even smelled foreign, this house where I'd lived and which still sheltered my once-wife and still-children, Mary Laura and Starkie, aged twelve and nine.

Susan met me at the door, unconsciously barring my way.

"Gee, you're early," she said. "I mean, what happened, did you get a new car?" Then, apparently noticing the Aries behind me: "What's the matter, no playmate last night? You must be slipping, Tommy."

She grinned at me, revealing the space between her upper front teeth (which, so help me, I had once thought sexy). I said something to the effect that it was a beautiful day and that I'd wanted to beat the traffic.

"Well," she said, "as you can see, I've taken up jogging. Come on, get rid of your long face. I mean, the kids are still having breakfast, I'll make us some coffee. There's something I want to talk to you about anyway."

And here it comes, I thought, following her in.

Susan—I'm probably the only person she knew who was never able to call her Sukie—was tall, with straight light brown hair which she wore short, blue eyes, regular features in a long and square-jawed countenance. Why I'd once considered her beautiful I've no idea, but she belonged to that New England type that tends to age well, where the eye-glasses in their colorless frames seem to belong and the figure, always slim, knows no sag. She was decked out in a maroon sweat suit, with white towel wrapped around her neck and white Reeboks on her feet.

Mary Laura and Starkie were perched on stools in the breakfast corner, their backs to the counter, cereal bowls in their laps, watching Saturday morning TV. Mouths full, they waved to me as I entered the kitchen. I'd have thought they were a little old for cartoons, Mary Laura at least. Their mother and I, meanwhile, made small talk around the kitchen table, that worn, massive, beautiful oak piece which had come with the house and the sight of which invariably filled me with resentment.

Her coffee, as always, was too weak, and the same could be said for our conversation, except for one exchange. We'd long since been reduced to talking about the children, which, ninety-five percent of the time, meant talking about money, which, ninety-five percent of the time, ended in recriminations. But not this Saturday morning, when her mood was almost gay.

"I hear you've been seeing Helen," Susan said.

"Helen who?"

"Is there more than one, Tommy? I'm talking about Helen Charles."

There it was, like that, my unnamed companion from that weekend in Connecticut. I glanced toward the children, well within earshot, but they didn't seem to be listening.

"What have you heard?" I said.

"Just that. I mean, that you've been seeing her. I don't know her myself. I mean, I *know* her of course. Is it serious?"

"No."

"Same old Tommy," she said, shaking her head and smiling with that condescension she'd learned to affect as, I suppose, a defense against my infidelities.

It irritated me—not her superciliousness, which I was used to, but the fact that the story was around. Buck Charles was my colleague and, more or less, my friend. I hadn't seen fit to tell him of my tepid dalliance with his estranged wife. As a rule, men didn't talk about such matters. Women apparently did.

"Do you think there's a chance she and Bucky will get back together again?" Susan asked.

"I've no idea," I said. In fact, knowing Buck, I doubted it. He was enjoying his freedom too much.

"It's so hard," Susan went on. "I mean, it's so hard to build the trust back after all that's gone on. And what's a relationship without trust? But I think Helen would like to try."

Was she telling me all this to make me feel bad? I wondered. I asked if I was supposed to carry a message back to Buck. Of course not, she said. But she went on about the Charleses anyway, in that same soap opera vein, and I felt the unmistakable urge to tell her about another relationship I knew of, one involving a woman she didn't *know* but who, even as she rattled on, was no more than fifteen minutes away. Because as I stood in that kitchen, somehow repelled by its very odors, Kitten rose up in my mind, in full fume, as it were, and the horrible irony of the moment, as of that whole endless weekend, was that in the midst of their chit-chat—hers, my mother's later, the children's throughout—there was no way I could banish Kitty for very long.

I didn't, needless to say—I mean, tell Susan (to use her abominable syntax). Instead I gathered up the children, and off we went to grandmother's house, the three of us abreast in the front seat, Starkie in the middle.

I'd been accused—what noncustodial father hasn't?—of being neglectful of my children. All in all, the charge seemed fair enough. In part it was because I had no good place to take them. There was no room for the three of us in my apartment, and where spend the night? In some anonymous motel? On occasion I took them out for the day, and we'd have lunch and go to a movie or, in summer, to the beach, and then sometimes out to dinner. Once each winter we'd go skiing. Twice a year I took them over to their grandmother's. The truth was, though, that we never had a great deal to say to each other. The further truth was that the children, Starkie particularly, still harbored the ridiculous fantasy that somehow, some-day, their mother and I would get back together. Viz. (in the car, driving west through the beautiful rolling back roads into New York State but away, I kept thinking, from Kitty):

"Do you like Helen Charles?" This from Mary Laura. I guessed that she'd overheard after all.

"Helen?" I said. "Yes, I do. She's a nice person."

"Oh." Pause. "Well, how much do you like her?"

"I don't know. I don't know her all that well. I'd say she was a nice person."

"How nice?"

"Hey," I said, "what is this? Some kind of inquisi-tion?"

"Well, you're going out with her, aren't you?"

"No. Actually I have gone out with her. But not now."

"Oh."

Silence.

Then Starkie: "Do you like her better than Mom?"

Mary Laura saved me the trouble of answering. She jumped all over her brother for asking such stupid ques-tions.

Silence.

Then Starkie again: "But you're not going to *marry* her, are you, Dad?"

A huge sigh from his sister.

"No, Starkie, I'm not," I said.

But there was a flip side to it, at least from their point of view.

"Did Mom tell you?" Mary Laura said a few miles later. "We're not supposed to be back early tomorrow."

"What does that mean?"

"Didn't she tell you?"

"No."

"Well, she said she doesn't want you to bring us back till late afternoon at the earliest."

"Is that what she said?"

"Yes." Then, while I did my slow burn: "She has a date."

Mary Laura's tone was scornful. Maybe she was jealous, or fearful, or whatever it is daughters are in such situations. Or thought *I'd* be jealous, for all I know. What drove me up the wall, though, was that Susan should decide arbitrarily when I'd be permitted to bring the children back. As if I had nothing better to do. Presumably this was what she'd wanted to talk to me about, not Helen and Buck Charles. Presumably, in her inimitable way, she'd "forgotten" and had left it to her daughter to deliver the message.

As soon as we got to my mother's, I was on the phone to her. I endured her I-have-the-right-to-my-own-life peroration, punctuated by tears, until finally we reached a compromise. I could bring Mary Laura and Starkie home at three on Sunday. If she wasn't there, they could fend for themselves.

Why do I torment myself, though, with the details of that dreary and irrelevant weekend? My mother, even in my earliest recollections of her, had never harbored any particular liking for me. I was simply one of her children. She had remarried again, this time a career Navy officer, now retired, a sawed-off, crew-cut, blazer-clad man, whom I found offensively vulgar. For instance, that evening after dinner, by the gaslit fireplace, he said to me:

"Y'ought to get married again yourself, Tom—only to somebody with money this time, eh? That's what I did, and look what it's got me!"

At this he reached out and gave my mother, who was standing next to him, a swat on the rump, something less than a slap but more than a pat. I watched her push his hand away, feigning disapproval but laughing at the same time.

I suppose, though, that there's no accounting for people's tastes. My mother was a tall, handsome, and still elegant woman, and one of very considerable independent means. She and her commodore lived well enough, in a rather sterile ranch house on a bluff overlooking the Hudson, with a couple over the garage to take care of their needs (I don't recall my mother ever cooking anything more complicated than a soft-boiled egg), an apartment in Palm Beach for the winter, trips to Europe on the *QE 2*. And he, her third husband, made no bones about the fact that she was paying for it all. Indeed, he seemed to boast of it, as of the fact that she'd once been married to my father. "A great figure in his day," he invariably chimed in when my mother—equally invariably—asked after the Senator.

With effort I could summon a few other details of that visit. (My older sister was there for dinner, and her husband.) But what we ate, or did, or talked about, or where the children were, or why finally I was there to begin with, are questions I can't answer.

Someone must have noticed my distractedness. "What's wrong, Tommy?" I remember being asked, and replying, "Why, nothing. Nothing at all." Nothing indeed except that I lusted after Kitty haplessly, hopelessly,

with a schoolboy's ardor and, at the same time, a schoolboy's rage. For I knew she had used me, exploited me,
and the two visions of her, as the object of my passion
and the exploiter of my passion, drove me from ardor to
anger, anger to ardor, until by Sunday morning, after a
fitful, tossing night, these had themselves given way, like
the thesis and the antithesis of the old Hegelian equation,
to a new and pervasive emotion.

Yes, she had used me, and yes, I had been forewarned:
She eats guys like you alive. But didn't the two together
suggest that, having already gotten what she wanted from
out of me (the million dollars' profit in the Sprague estate), she might already be moving on?

How did I know she'd been alone when she called
Friday night? How, for that matter, did I know she'd
been in a hotel in Stamford? Or at a wedding in Connecticut on Saturday? Or at a brunch in the city today?

I didn't know any of these things! Yet I *had* to know.
Yet I *dreaded* knowing.

Dread. Not jealousy, dread. With lassitude and helplessness for companions. In other words, by Sunday I'd
managed to convince myself, however irrationally, that
I'd already lost her. And rather than rushing to confirm
this awful fate, I found myself contriving ways to post-
pone it.

In this respect I had some unexpected help from Starkie.

Overnight, he'd developed a stomachache. No fever,
maybe something he ate, but no foolin', Dad, it really
hurts. Toward noon, he threw up, and then fell sound
asleep. I decided to let him sleep and went for a walk,
alone. It was mid-afternoon by the time he woke up, a
little pale but seemingly recovered. Only then did he, his
sister, and I hit the road.

It was already dark when I deposited the Aries in the

garage near West Street and walked the few blocks to my brownstone. My one room was dark as well, and empty, small, uninviting. I had no answering machine, no way of knowing if she'd been calling me.

All the way home from Connecticut, I'd rehearsed what I would say. Now, telephone in hand, the words I'd committed to memory seemed suddenly flat, wrong. Yet I had myself believing that my future with Kitty, if I still had a chance for one, would hang on what I said and how she heard it.

I took a deep breath and punched out the number.

And got her answering machine.

"This is Kitty Goldmark speaking . . ."

The familiar sound of her voice—or was it the fact that she wasn't home?—shook me so that, having heard the beep, I let the message space on the tape run through without being able to utter a word.

All right, where was she if she wasn't home? I myself was late, that was true. I'd said I'd be home by four-thirty, five. Was she really not there? Or could she not be answering in order to punish me?

I waited some time—an hour, less. There was nothing in the house to eat but I decided I wasn't hungry enough to go out. Besides, if I went out, I might miss her call.

But the phone didn't ring.

I punched her number again, got the answering machine again. This time I'd prepared an amusing message, something along the lines of "Do you happen to know a lovelorn lad named Tommy? If you do, he'd be delighted to hear from you." But at the last minute I scratched it and simply said: "It's Tommy. Eight o'clock, Sunday. I'm home. Please call."

This was just the first of many such messages those next few days: Tommy at four o'clock, Tommy at noon, Tommy at midnight, Tommy round the clock. Of course,

I remembered that she sometimes left the answering machine on when she was home—and why. But this realization only sent all those other emotions I'd maundered over the weekend long—lust, anger, dread, whatever—flying out the door, chased by a now rampant and biting jealousy. It was this that sent me to her building the next night, where her doorman turned me away because there was no answer on the intercom, and to her office the day after, where a startled receptionist tried to convince me—legitimately in this instance—that Ms. Goldmark was out.

But she hadn't disappeared off the face of the earth. And I knew it by the next afternoon.

9

The payoff.

It came in an envelope marked "Personal & Confidential," delivered by messenger Tuesday while I was out to lunch. The messenger apparently had been Ms. Goldmark herself. The payoff was in the form of a promissory note payable to yours truly upon the distribution of the Estate of Edgar Chalmers Sprague. As I calculated, the amount represented exactly twenty percent of the estate's gain through the acquisition and sale of Manderling stock.

No letter, no message, nothing except the financial instrument itself.

I put it back in the envelope. More than once that dismal afternoon I took it out again. It occurred to me to frame it and hang it on my wall, like those first dollar bills you sometimes see hanging in grocery stores and bars. Instead I cut it into pieces, neatly with a scissors, which pieces I put into a fresh envelope addressed to Katherine Goldmark and marked "Personal & Confiden-

tial,'' which envelope I personally delivered to Central
Park South that evening.

No letter, no message.

Done.

It was the beginning of May. The city had come alive
with the sounds and smells and colors of spring, but in
the midst of it, I felt as though somebody had died, and
furthermore that the somebody was myself. And no
amount of analysis of what had happened, or hadn't, or
how could it have gone wrong so fast, or why, or whose
fault, could assuage my chagrin.

And then my phone rang at home, early Thursday
morning. It was Kitty. Her voice low and choky.

"This phone call may be the biggest mistake of my
life," she began without preamble, "but I want to see
you."

She'd caught me in the midst of shaving. I was standing
naked, the receiver in my hand.

"I think there's been a terrible misunderstanding," I
said back. "I—"

"I don't," Kitty interrupted tersely. Then, her voice
softening: "But I'd like us to talk about it."

She said she was free for dinner that night if I was.
Yes, I was free. (Free, I remember thinking, for the rest
of my life.) I suggested we go to La Banquette. She
rejected that idea. She suggested an Italian place down
off Grand Street. I didn't know it, but what difference
did that make? Did she want me to pick her up? No, she
would rather meet me at the restaurant. At what time, I
asked. Seven-thirty? Seven-thirty it was.

And that was that. No time for me to ask why she'd
felt compelled to insult me with the promissory note. Or
to tell her I'd missed her sorely in spite of everything.
Or for her to reply in kind.

Just soap dried on my face.

I tried to cut that day short by going home early from the office. I was too keyed up to work, too keyed up to do anything. I remember showering again, shaving again, and worrying about what to wear. I admit to changing, at least once. I ended up settling for the same suit I'd worn the day of the Christmas party, midnight blue, with suspenders, tie, and matching handkerchief. For luck? Yes, for luck. And deciding to walk to the restaurant so as to clear my head, then deciding against it lest I be late, and hailing a taxi. And so arriving early.

No, Signora Goldmark hadn't yet arrived, but I was la Signora's guest? Yes, then, by all means, they would seat me at la Signora's table.

For Little Italy, where the gastronomic decor ranges from Neapolitan modern to Sicilian garish, the restaurant had an understated, even sedate elegance. I was led downstairs to a table near the kitchen, where, it turned out, favored diners were seated and served not off the menu but from the chef's suggestions. In cuisine and style, with its brick arches and white damask napery, gleaming cutlery and crystal, it seemed to have been lifted in toto from one of the northern Italian cities, and the service matched—friendly yet unobtrusive and consummately professional.

Leave it to Kitten, I thought. To judge from the flurry at her entrance, she was a well-known client.

She was late. I was already halfway through a bottle of Gattinari when I saw her surging toward me among the tables, talking breathlessly even as I rose, in a spate of apology and frustration, something about having been detained at the office and then she hadn't been able to find a taxi. All breathless, as I've said, and she could barely manage to kiss me on the cheek.

"Sit down, Kitten," I said, smiling and holding the back of her chair. "It's okay now."

She looked different to me. She wore silk as usual, but not black, instead a print, predominantly red and pink, with huge, vaguely oriental flowers splashed across it in black outlines, high-necked, and a black-lined jacket of the same outer material. She wore the cuffs of her jacket sleeves casually turned up and rather less jewelry than usual. The overall effect was to make her seem older and younger at once, older perhaps in that the outfit was more daring and high-style than her habitual look, younger in the carefree touch of the rolled-up sleeves and the fact, too, that she had on less makeup than usual. Younger too in the look she gave me at the words I said when she sat down, a wide-eyed glance as though to say: *Is it really okay now, Tommy? But how do you know?*

I was dazzled by her, I admit, and if I've dwelled on the older-younger idea, it is because I experienced two Kittens that night, neither of them precisely new except in combination. The one was as firm and direct as ever in saying what she wanted—out of me, herself, us, life— but beneath her forthrightness ran an undercurrent of . . . what should I call it? . . . The ingenue? The schoolgirl? It was as though, underneath, she needed someone to approve of her. *Is it really okay? Please tell me it is.* This came out less in her words than in a glance, a pause, a hesitation.

As for me, I'd never found it easy to tell a woman exactly what I was thinking, but with Kitty, that night, I tried. I had missed her terribly. The week since I'd last seen her had been a torture to me. Up till then, I probably hadn't let on to myself how much I needed her. If the experience had taught me one thing, though, it was that, whatever happened or didn't between us, I couldn't stand her avoiding me.

"It's true," she said, eyeing me. "I *have* been avoiding you. I didn't want to see you. But do you understand why?"

"Not really. I assumed you were upset. I think you also may have felt a little guilty."

"Guilty? Over what?"

"Over the fact that you actually did use me."

Her eyes widened. She stared at me a moment, then shook her head angrily, her dark hair flying.

"Then you really *don't* understand," she said. "Not anything."

"Then maybe you'd better explain," I said softly.

"I don't know if I can, or where to begin. But I'll tell you this much. All this talk about being used, that's just the professional in you, the Wasp lawyer who's scared to death of getting his hands dirty. Where's the real you in it? Where's Tommy?"

Not knowing how or what to answer, I said nothing.

"How *dare* you say I used you?" she went on. "To the extent that I did, I could have used any lawyer in town. And for every item, every single transaction in the estate, I covered you in writing. But is that all I am to you, another one of your widows who's *using* you?"

"You know that's not true, Kitty."

"Well, that's what it sounds like. For the rest of it, what *am* I to you other than a piece of meat? I know, I know, you say you *need* me. But do you know what that *need* feels like in here? It feels like it's you who's using me, like I'm just somebody you're fucking on the side— no mess, no fuss. And above all, no responsibility."

"You know that's not true," I repeated.

"Come on, Tommy, why won't you just admit it?" she said. "It's not such a terrible thing, using somebody for sex. People do it all the time. Besides, we're good at it."

I knew somehow, out of some instinct, that if I agreed with her, I'd never hold her in my arms again. Anyway, I wasn't using her. Maybe it was true with other women, yes, but not with Kitty. And I told her so.

"Then how on earth could you have accused me of being a criminal?"

"I didn't—"

"Oh, come on, Tommy. If we're going to end up nowhere, at least let's be honest with each other."

"What the hell do you think I'm trying to be?"

"Look," she said, smiling faintly, "let's suppose I did break some stupid law. I'm not saying I did, but *if* I did, and if I made some money by doing it, and you went along innocently, not knowing, with a paper trail to prove you were only carrying out instructions anyway . . . then what's the big deal?"

What came to mind immediately was that I was still, at least in theory, an "officer of the court." But to say so would have acknowledged her point about uptight Wasp lawyers. And to bring up her attempted payoff would, I suppose, only have corroborated it.

"Jesus," I said, feeling trapped. "What do you want of me, Kitty?"

"I think I told you that already, my dear, maybe even the first time we met." She looked at me firmly, head on. "I want a partner. I don't want a lawyer—I can buy that anywhere. Or sex either—I imagine I could buy that, too, if I had to. But the feeling that somebody's in it with you, no matter what. And that means somebody who's not going to head for the hills at the first sign of trouble."

Underneath the directness of her words was that suppliant tone again, an element of plea. Or what I took for plea.

"That sounds like a proposition," I said, half in jest.

"It's not," she answered, shaking her head. "What you want in life and what you get aren't always the same."

"Meaning that I've already failed the test?"

"Meaning that . . ."

But she stopped, head slightly tilted in that appraising, examining way she had.

"Look, Tommy," she said. "I'm going to tell you something you may really not want to hear, but if that's so, so be it. I once married a man who chased me for years before I accepted. I was Gar's secretary—I told you that—and he wanted me so badly, it was like a joke. He said he'd do anything, I could have whatever I wanted, et cetera, et cetera. I always said no—as nicely as I could because I thought he was a nice man. And then, one day . . ." Here she hesitated, and her eyes flicked away, as though she was reminded of something else. "And then, one day, I found myself saying, 'Why not?' I won't go into all the reasons, I'm not sure I understood them myself. I said 'Okay, he loves me, I'll do it.' I think he was even more surprised than I was. So we got married—went downtown, took out a license, and some minister friend of Gar's said the right words, and that was that.

"Well"—with a heavy sigh—"I think it took me a week or two—no more—to realize that I'd married a dead man. Dying, as good as dead, dead. Not physically—in those days he even enjoyed sex, on occasion, and the heavy drinking came later—but in every other way. I lived with him all those years, but it was like living with a corpse."

"Why are you telling me all this now? Are you saying I'm like him?"

"No." Then she smiled at me. "You're a lot cuter, for one thing."

"But . . . ?"

"But," she agreed, eyeing me directly. "My point is that I see too much of him in you. There are ways in which you *are* dead, Tommy, with your life only half over. You don't need me to tell you. Your career, the way it's worked out, is pretty much going nowhere. One failed marriage, children you don't particularly care about. Not enough money, I'd guess, though you try to hide that. Already you drink too much. It's not that you don't have any fun—you're witty, lively, sexy—but it's all dabbling. You dabble with women, for instance. You even dabble with me."

"I wouldn't call that—" I began.

"Call it what you will," she said, cutting me off. "It's dabbling. No risk, no responsibility, no ambitions. It's as though you'd already given up—dead in that sense—even before you started."

Up to this point, I felt no great pain. After all, I'd long since been giving my "buried alive" speech to pretty much anyone who listened, and if it hurt a little to hear it from Kitty's lips, I couldn't argue with the appraisal. Except in one respect.

"There's one thing you're leaving out," I said.

"What's that?"

"You."

"What about me?"

"That I'm hopelessly in love with you."

"Oh, that," she said. "For that matter, I'm in love with you too, Tommy."

"Then . . . ?"

"But that's only dabbling, too."

"It's not dabbling as far as I'm concerned," I blurted out, feeling myself go hot under the skin. "For God's sake, Kitten, what do you want from me? Do you want me on bended knee?"

"Not now," she said, smiling with her eyes. "Not that it's a bad idea . . ."

"I'm sorry, Kitty, but I'm serious!"

"Stop shouting, Tommy"—still smiling. "I'm serious too."

"I *won't* stop shouting if I'm shouting. What the hell do you want from me?"

"It's not what I want from you. It's what you want for yourself."

"That's too easy, damn it! Too facile by far! I don't want anything *for myself*, I want you. For God's sake, are you telling me I have to *earn* you?"

Again she had that ability to bring me to the point of explosion, as though everything inside me was about to burst through, spill over, the dam giving way, or the crust of the earth, or the membrane of air that holds the thundercloud together. Nobody had ever had that power over me before. I see myself standing in the restaurant, raging down at her. In my imagination, the place is empty, except for Kitty—empty chairs with bare white tablecloths and crystal gleaming in the blazing light and all staff gone. And Kitty, eyes alight, skin flushed a deep and dusky red, the red of her lips and the red of her nails around a wineglass, the smile still there but trembling now, as though the emotion I'd let loose had kindled her, too . . .

But no, not at least in her tone. I remember she said it mildly:

"Yes, if that's the way you want to put it. Yes, Tommy, I want you to earn me."

"Then for God's sake tell me *how*!"

And so, in due course, she did.

There was more to it, of course, and if I've tried to give it the coherence of a single-threaded argument, in order to illustrate my conquest of Kitty and Kitty's of me, there were sub-arguments too, in the restaurant and after. One, I recall, was over the check and who should pay it. (Kitty prevailed.) And the "payoff" came up, too. Why had she sent me the promissory note? (To compromise me? No, to close the books on me.) And why had I sent it back in pieces? (Because I felt compromised? No, because I'd felt the jilted lover.) I mention these only to point out the weird emotional climate of that night, when the merest spark could ignite us instantly and, by contrast, the most horrendous accusations could go unchallenged. We talked, we fought, we walked, we rode, we made love. Maybe there was a full moon. We must have eaten in the restaurant, but I've no recollection of it. All this, I should say, was Kitty's triumph, for if she was in her element, I was, in an emotional sense, clearly out of mine.

I do remember quite vividly how it ended.

We were making love on her living room rug, Kitty astride me, her hair falling over both our heads, like a curtain.

"Tell me now," I said up to her.

"What?"

"Did you in fact break the law?"

I heard her start to laugh, a deep, uncontrollable sound not only of humor but of her own helplessness when she had what she wanted.

"Yes, you silly," she said, her arms now shaking and losing strength. "Of course I did."

PART
TWO

10

Wanda Russell had been a great beauty in her day, and you could still see it, despite the fact that she was past seventy, drank too much, took too many pills, and tinted her hair blue. Round-faced and heavy-set, she said the secret of her looks was that she had never been afraid to take on weight. Most of the debs of her year, she said, those who were still around, looked like so many scarecrows, dieting all the time, going to spas. Wanda wanted to be thought of as outspoken, outrageous, and jolly, and she liked to tell people that she still enjoyed sex. She was also a widow, rich, and, I suppose, lonely.

Wanda Russell became, by a couple of days, the first client of Stark Thompson, Attorney-at-Law, P.C.

As I was careful to document, the move was strictly Wanda's idea.

"Congratulations, Tommy, darling!" she'd said heartily when I'd called to announce that I was leaving the firm. "Where are you going?"

I'd told her I was planning to open up on my own.

"Superb!" she'd said, using a favorite word of hers. "I want to be your first client."

Elated, I'd nonetheless counseled her against making any rash decisions. The firm, after all, had served her and her late husband for a long time, and well, I said.

"Nonsense!" she'd retorted. "They're nothing but a bunch of old windbags, Mac Coombs and your father and the rest of them. They'd have retired long ago if they didn't have old fools like me to pay their fees and young ones like you to do their work for them. I could use a breath of fresh air, Tommy. I want you to take over *all* my affairs, not just the estate."

"I can't tell you how flattered I am," I'd told her, "but please don't do anything yet. Once I've actually left, I'll be glad to come up and discuss the prospects with you. If, that is, you still want me to."

"Horseballs, Tommy," she'd boomed back at me. "You just go in there and tell them Wanda's leaving with you. Or I'll do it. But you count on me, as long as I'm the first. I insist on being your first client. I assume I'm the first one you've called . . . ?"

I'd assured her on both counts, and if I fudged a little on whom I'd called first, I don't suppose that mattered. Wanda Russell was too excited. She even promised to get rid of her blue rinse for the occasion. (I had often teased her about that in the past, telling her she was too young for it. To which she'd invariably replied that I might not like it but—with a wink—there were those who did.)

The process of opening up on my own turned out to be as easy as Kitty had predicted. The minute I announced my departure from the firm, she'd said, my blue-haired widows would flock to me like bees to the rosebush. And not, needless to say, for my skills as an attorney but for my other "services"—as confessor, psychotherapist, and general hand-holder. I was careful to point out to one and all, orally and in writing, that a large firm offered resources and services I couldn't hope to match and to recommend that their decision be made carefully. As it happened, few were as impulsive as Wanda Russell in turning over all their legal affairs, and several balked when I explained that my fee structure would, if we were successful, cost them a good deal more money than they had been paying the firm. In the end, though, over half the clients I'd dealt with came along with me, on my terms. This, along with new business, meant that before my first year was out I had to expand my offices in the new tower on Fifty-sixth Street by buying out my neighbor. All of which, as will become clear, had the practical consequence of putting me ever more in Kitty's debt.

That I was so meticulous in the paperwork—to the point, I imagine, of pleading the firm's case a lot better than the firm itself ever did—exasperated Kitty to no end.

"*Do* it," she'd say. "For God's sake, Tommy, just *do* it, and then you can futz with your papers all you want to."

The Yiddish *futz* (for fuss, I suppose? Or fidget?) had, the way she used it, the connotation of fussbudget, of Dickens and the clerks on high stools with paper cuffs and green eyeshades. As I explained to her, though, I had good reason to "futz." For one thing, if the old unwritten rule among attorneys—"Thou shalt not steal thy neighbor's clients"—had long since gone by the boards, there had been too many recent cases of Lawyer X suing Lawyer Y over fees and clients and alleged tampering. I wanted a complete paper trail if and when the firm ever woke up to the fact that I'd pretty much single-handedly decimated their Trusts and Estates practice.

More serious was a second consideration. Anyone active in trusts and estates has a so-called fiduciary responsibility and that responsibility, at least in a formal sense, is watched over by the courts. Even the fees I charged were, theoretically, court-approved. All this may have come about historically to protect innocent widows from being gouged and swindled out of their inheritances, but the practical effect had been to make professionals in the field archly conservative.

"But that's just the point, Tommy," Kitty said. "What you're selling them is just the opposite. You're going to be their partner. You're actually going to make them money, and you're going to do it together!"

"But making money involves risk, doesn't it? Taking some gambles? The possibility of losses?"

"Not the way we're doing it, love."

"And I suppose you want me to tell them that?"

"Not in so many words, Tommy, of course not. All I want you to do is convince them that you're smarter than the next guy. It'll be easy, you'll see."

Finally, there was my fee structure. In essence, I made nothing if the estate in question failed to appreciate more than it would have in the hands of a bank or fiduciary trustee. If, for example, a million-dollar estate failed, in three years, to grow beyond $1,158,000 (that is to say, at a five percent annual increase), then whatever work I had done would have been at my expense. If, however, the estate outperformed the index, then I'd be cut in for an escalating percentage of profits, which could—and actually did in one or two cases—reach fifty percent.

There's nothing new or, strictly speaking, illegal about the contingency fee. In dealing with the rich and their inheritances, though, it's just not "done." And needless to say, I'd never have done it myself had it really involved the high risks I had to warn against so carefully in my client agreements.

Kitty was right, though: *Like bees to the rosebush*. The reasons nonetheless remained complicated. After all, Wanda Russell could have lived the rest of her life with her money sewed into her mattress and never have known want. What possible difference could a few million more or less have made to her? Did it let her boast to her friends about her net worth? Or was it greed? Or stinginess? Or whatever that secret ingredient is that moves some people to accumulate wealth upon wealth?

None of the above, with Wanda. In fact she spent money freely and never, to my knowledge, kept track.

I even asked her about it once, obliquely. We were in that room of her Park Avenue apartment, a cluttered hymn to Victoriana, which she called her office. It contained a secretaire—a massive mahogany antique—but also tables set in little groupings of chairs and settees, and heavy drapery, tall oriental screens, and palms growing out of ceramic tubs. I'd gone up to review the quarterly results with her—a particularly successful quarter, too, because several oil stocks had gone haywire at once in a takeover war, and we'd been riding every one.

"Well, I get a kick out of it, Tommy, don't you?" she said, pointing with a bejeweled finger to her bottom line. "It's exciting, it's fun. It makes me feel like we're a pair of evil geniuses plotting the fate of the world."

Fun, then? Excitement? The sense of riding a fast track in a world that was otherwise slowing down?

Or (Kitty's old pronouncement): Money is sexy?

But Kitty herself had a different version.

"It's you, my love," she maintained. "The partnership, remember? '*You and I, Wanda, we're going to make money together*,'" mimicking my voice. "It's the *pair* that counts, the *pair* of evil geniuses. Do you think for a minute that if you were thirty years older, with false teeth and prostate trouble, she'd still get a kick out of it? Believe me, darling, she'd rather do it with you even if it meant losing every penny.''

"What do you mean, 'do it with me'? I don't have to sleep with her, do I?''

"You screw any of them you have to, sweet. All of them, if you want to. But nobody under fifty, remember? Any female clients under fifty and I'll put a padlock on you.'' Then, smiling, her eyes alight: "On second thought, better make that sixty.''

Witty, I thought. But she meant it too.

Ironically, having set out to "earn" Kitty and having turned my life on its ear with her encouragement, I saw rather less of her than before. Further irony, I found myself working harder than I ever had. For one thing, I was obliged to hustle for new business. For another, we now required a far more sophisticated knowledge of investing than I'd ever gained at the firm, because there was no way (as Kitty, for once, agreed) that we could repeat the model of the Sprague account, where all available resources had gone into, then out of, Manderling stock. To try to do the same on this large a scale would surely have attracted the attention of anyone investigating insider trading. Rather, we had to "launder" our coups within much broader investment programs, which, for additional security, we decided to spread as widely as possible in the marketplace. I therefore spent considerable time allowing myself to be cultivated by traders and brokers, that Wall Street breed whom, I think, I'd always looked down on slightly even though I'd been to school with a number of them. In addition, there was all the traditional, or Dickensian, work to do—the records, the endless court filings, the tax reports and negotiations with IRS auditors—which drudgery, having done it for long enough, I was happy to dump on an associate as soon as I could afford one.

Kitty's capital floated me at the beginning and paid for the office expansion, as well as the condominium I moved into the following fall, within walking distance of both my office and her apartment. All such transactions were duly recorded in our files, not only, she pointed out, in case anything happened to me but as an utterly reasonable justification for her fifty percent share of my profits. But her real value to the firm lay elsewhere.

The information came in sporadically. Weeks, sometimes months, would go by, the markets rising, falling, and nothing from Kitty, to the point where I'd ask her if she'd lost her source. But then, one day: "Start buying X. Go slow for now. I'm not sure, but I think something's going to happen." Then, as little as a few hours later but sometimes several weeks: "Go now, Tommy. Buy. Up to your limit."

Invariably we beat the professionals to the upswing. I once did a study that showed we were never first—presumably our source himself had beaten us to it and/or our source's source—but always well before the stampede of buyers that always preceded announcement to the public.

And the same at the selling end. While we seldom stayed in for the final round, we never got caught in a bailout situation.

It bothered me, I confess, that she would never tell me who her source was.

"Why is it so important for you to know?" she'd say. "Why make such a big deal out of it?"

"Because it bothers me. It's got to be somebody you're pretty intimate with. How do I know you're not sleeping with him, too?"

She'd make a tsk-tsk sound and shake her head exaggeratedly.

"You don't know, do you? Does the idea make you jealous?"

"You know it does," I'd say hoarsely.

"And you know that excites me, making you jealous, the idea that you could be jealous. Here, Tom, show me how jealous you are, for God's sake."

Other times she'd ask me what made me so sure it was a him. Or just one person, for that matter. In fact, I wasn't. I tried over and over to connect her "crystal ball" to a single source by tracing the principals involved in the deals we made money on—the investment banks, the law firms, the proxy houses, the buyers, as well as the underwriters of junk bond issues—but I could never do it. Some of our coups seemed even to have bypassed Wall Street—the oil deal, for one, and then a variety store chain on the West Coast whose stock suddenly started to jump after we'd bought in.

"It's strictly business," Kitty maintained. "Look, suppose there was just one person, who knew certain things before the rest of the world did. Put yourself in his or her shoes. What would you do? You can't get away anymore with using it yourself, not even trading overseas. Sooner or later they'd catch up with you. The next best thing is to seed it, let it seep into the market through other people's money. If you control the people carefully, you control the risk, and if you can get enough capital working for you, you'll make as much money in the long run as you would have on your own."

This was as close as she came to admitting she was paying for information.

"You make it sound like some kind of irrigation system," I said.

"That's exactly what it is. And what makes Stark

Thompson, P.C., an ideal conduit is that, while you control a very large investment pool, it's broken up into a number of smaller accounts, each of which trades independently through different brokers."

"Meaning that it'd be pretty hard for anyone to link up all the pieces?"

"Exactly."

There was, maybe, one other reason for her secrecy. It came out oddly. All that summer I'd worked on convincing Kitty to go away with me just for a weekend, but summer was the hot season in the party business and I couldn't budge her. Finally, when I found out she had a hole in her schedule several weekends after Labor Day, I simply showed up with the plane tickets in my pocket and determined that there be no arguments.

Surprisingly, she put up only token resistance. She was tired, she admitted. Maybe she could use a weekend on a beach, in the sun. She'd never been to the Caribbean either. What would the weather be like? What should she wear? And though I half expected an eleventh-hour cancellation, even after I picked her up at her office, our luggage already in the trunk of the car that would take us to JFK, she came along docilely enough.

September is a lovely, if chancy, moment to visit the West Indies. The summer crowd has gone, the high season won't start for several months, the hotels are half empty. The chanciness, of course, has to do with the weather, and I'd experienced it both ways: a glorious hot sun one year, but forty-eight hours of torrential downpour and gale-force wind another.

This time the weather cooperated, but clearly my past "experience" unsettled Kitty. She wanted to know how many other women I'd brought to that hotel, that island, the Caribbean in general. She asked me repeatedly how she looked in her bathing suit and wouldn't venture out

without a floppy-brimmed straw hat to protect her from
skin poisoning. The water was a problem, too. She was,
she said, a mediocre swimmer, and even though you
could wade a good fifty yards out and still be in water
up to your waist, how could I be sure there were no
sharks?

Mostly we sat under a thatch umbrella at the hotel's
beach bar, watching the gently lapping surf, the coco
palms bending gaily under an eastering breeze, the occasional pelican making a strafing run across the bay.
Kitty sipped at some nonalcoholic concoction in a hol-
lowed-out pineapple while I stuck to the local rum and
lime. The food, she had to admit, was first rate—dolphin
and flying fish, simply prepared but elegantly served, and
a steamed mélange of local vegetables tinged with a spice
or spices neither of us could identify, and the glorious
tropical fruit which somehow tastes different in the Caribbean than anywhere else in the world.

We slept in what was just about the most romantic
setting imaginable—a separate thatched cottage just off
the beach, with a terrace where breakfast was served and
where, at night, you could watch the white sand veritably
light up under a shining moon. But we didn't make love
the first night. Kitty didn't like the night sounds she
couldn't identify, or the slow-turning ceiling fan over our
heads, or the fact that there were no windows, only shutters. She couldn't help herself, she kept saying, she felt
strange, out of her element. And the questions kept coming: Who were you here with before? What did she look
like? What did you do all the time besides fuck? I fielded
them as gracefully as I could, stressing the athletic (the
tennis, the snorkeling, the sailing—all true enough), saying (truthfully, too) that that was all another time, place,
another life, retreating meanwhile into an increasingly
rummy haze.

I remember thinking, though, on the deserted open-air dance floor that second night, that I'd had about enough. We'd dressed for dinner, I in a white dinner jacket with red accessories, Kitty resplendent in gold shoes and a glittering sequined outfit, pants and overblouse, but it was all I could do to coax her into dancing.

She said she couldn't dance.

Of course she could dance.

Then she said: "Who else have you danced with, on this floor, to this music?"

We were the only couple on the floor. I remember stopping her, holding her firmly, staring down—angrily, I guess—into her sullen eyes.

"No one, as it happens," I said acidly. "Not one damn living soul. But maybe now you've an inkling of how you make me feel sometimes."

"What do you mean, how I make you feel sometimes?"

"Like when you won't tell me where we're getting our information."

She stared back at me, uncomprehending. Then, as quick and violent as a tropical storm, she burst into tears—hysterical, convulsive tears—and how this was the first time we'd ever gone away together and now she'd wrecked it, ruined it. Then she pulled me by the hand off the floor and down the moonlit beach, stumbling in the sand on her heels, all the while going on about how she couldn't help herself, she hated all those other cunts I'd been with before, all those pinched Wasp cunts with no hips, they enraged her, she hated them, she'd scratch their eyes out, she'd . . .

Somehow we got to our cottage. Somehow we got to our bed, or near it, Kitty still sobbing, raging, I, intoxicated now by her jealousy, pulling at her trousers until strands of sequins peeled off onto the woven straw rug.

"I've ruuu-ined it. I've ru— Oh, my God, *Tommy*!"

The next day, under the thatch roof of the beach bar, her hat on the table and her sunglasses perched among the black curls of her hair, she made the remark that prompted this idyllic recollection in the first place.

"But if I told you who my source was, Tommy," she said, "how do I know you'd need me anymore?"

11

One of my first needs, in setting up on my own, was a new team of brokers. This was no knock on the people we'd used at the firm—indeed, they were the very model of what I wanted: stable, reasonably competent, unimaginative—but the fact that I'd used them before ruled them out. I wanted no eyebrows raised, no questions asked. I also wanted a surplus available, so as to be able to move my accounts around the trade.

In one sense this was the easiest of my tasks. True, I had no use for the Gucci hotshots, those ambitious young MBAs Wall Street continues to attract, who are out to make seven figures before they're thirty and eight before forty. But for every one of them, there were still dozens of what I wanted, wearers, if you will, of traditional brogues from Church or Brooks, those sturdy, hail-fellow account execs of Ivy League background who were happy as not to have me do their work for them and collect their commissions on my trading.

"Thatch" Thatcher (Harlan Russell Thatcher Jr.) was, I suppose, my ideal broker in every respect save one. A heavyset specimen with a taste for blue blazers and kelly green trousers, he had known me since prep school, where he'd flunked out. In fact, I think he was the first of his line of Thatchers not to have played football for Harvard, which, whatever his family thought, hadn't fazed Thatch in the slightest. Thanks to his connections and his general, round-faced bonhomie, he'd found his niche in stocks and bonds, which was where I'd run into him again when I was still at the firm. Married and the father of three, active among the Colgate alumni and in his church and yacht club, he was the ideal customer's man—genial, outgoing, and almost painfully eager to accommodate. He'd been very successful at it, too. By the time I'm talking about, he ran his own virtually autonomous unit within a large brokerage house, with a couple of those MBAs on his staff to, I suppose, keep him from making any truly flagrant blunders. He was my one holdover from my time at the firm, and I'd have given anything to get rid of him—for the very reason I couldn't. He was Wanda Russell's nephew.

God knows it wasn't for want of trying. Hardly a meeting went by without my recommending to Wanda that we ought to make a change.

"Oh, Gawd," she'd say with a sigh, "what's the boy done now?"

Thatcher himself gave me ammunition from time to time—either he'd been slow to execute an order, or he'd been off on the golf course when I needed him, or his commissions were too high. All true, if not critically important. And Wanda, shaking her head and sighing, would say, "But he's such a nice kid. How could we do that to him?"

"He's hardly a kid anymore, Wanda, and this is business. He's costing us money. Besides, he's not going to starve."

Another, deeper sigh.

"Why don't you let me talk to him, Tommy?"

"Please don't"—having had the experience before.

"Well, you do it, then. But I want to give him another chance."

The best I was able to do, in time, was to wean away from Thatcher his aunt's other interests. But the Russell estate remained sacrosanct, this despite the fact that Wanda routinely referred to her late husband as a mean son of a bitch who'd tried to squelch her all his life, and her husband's sister (Thatcher's mother) was cut from the same cloth. Whereas Thatcher himself, whenever I confronted him, bent with the wind and came up more eager to please than ever.

Under my pressure, he did cut his commissions, and when I pushed him harder invariably found another fraction of a point to give me, saying, "We're losing money on the account as it is, old man, but if they'd let me, I'd do Aunt Wanda's work for free. You know that." At the same time, he courted me assiduously, inviting me to those intimate high-level seminars his company held for big investors, offering me tickets to sporting events and Broadway openings, and worse, with his wife's participation, trying to fix me up with this or that eligible woman.

This last had become something of a problem for me. While I could, and did, turn Thatcher down much of the time, I couldn't turn all my Thatchers down all the time. Part of my success did involve socializing, party-going. In addition, I was single, and I still bore the reputation, from the days before Kitty, of being both eligible and available. At the same time, Kitty insisted on keeping our relationship private.

"They're not my kind of people," she said.

"For God's sake," I'd retort, "do you think they're mine?"

"No, but you know what I mean."

"No, I don't."

"Look, Tommy. This is business. *Your* business. And we've agreed to keep my involvement in it strictly at arm's length. I don't think we should be seen together so much, that's all."

"Are you saying we can't mix business with pleasure?"

"Something like that."

"But that's nonsense, Kitty."

"No it isn't, not when there's so much at stake."

"But I can't always go alone."

"I know that." Then, with a slow wink: "But remember, love, nobody under sixty."

The "stake" Kitty referred to turned out to be Safari Mining and Drilling. Safari was a sleepy Louisiana company not even quoted on the Amex, much less the Big Board, and at the time Kitty told me to start buying, Thatcher himself had never heard of it. The thing about Safari was that, years back, it had acquired drilling rights to very considerable undeveloped oil and gas reserves. Most of these were underwater, in Gulf of Mexico tidelands protected, and in some cases owned, by the federal government.

Then, at hearings in Washington that fall into energy preparedness, several key congressmen reopened the old what-if question: What if the war in the Middle East took a new and bloodier turn? What if the oil fields of Saudi Arabia were set afire by terrorists? What if OPEC decided to shut off its wells? What, finally, were we doing to develop our own natural resources?

At its height, the bidding war for Safari involved four major companies. Safari stock, which had been trading in a range between 11 and 13, rose rapidly through the 20's (at which point Wanda Russell's buying was complete), then the 30's, and once the battle settled down to two serious competitors, it reached 52. What was stranger still was that the competitors' stock rose proportionately. Normally in a takeover situation the reverse happened, under the theory that the bidders would be overpaying, expending capital, diluting earnings, and so on. But articles began to appear projecting Safari's earnings into the twenty-first century and quoting experts who said that, even at 52, it was the last true bargain in the energy business. Then another scheme emerged, orchestrated, it appeared, by good old Braxton's, who had been called in by Safari's principals to advise them, to take the company private. Now you began to hear predictions that $70 a share would be the ultimate price, and not an unfair one at that.

I had originally, out of prudence, bought Safari only for the Russell estate, but all my accounts had invested in the companies bidding for it. All had made substantial paper profits. All (on Kitty's instructions) had cashed in, Wanda included, a few points short of the top but a good week before the bubble burst.

Overnight, it seemed, the congressional environmentalists woke up, and they switched the media focus to the negative side of the story: Was the government going to give away still another slice of our national heritage to big business? With all that that meant in the destruction of the ecological balance in the Gulf and the loss of how many miles of national coastline? Safari became, overnight, another Santa Barbara Channel issue, and the politicians in question stampeded, claiming they'd been misquoted, that their concern for our strategic reserves was surely legitimate but that they'd never meant to permit Safari to begin drilling right away. Whereupon a

White House spokesman (allegedly quoting the president himself) said that under no circumstances would the administration permit the interests of the many to be sacrificed to the greed of the few.

Thatcher called me the same day to congratulate me.

"Hey, big feller, you sure must be doing something right!"

"What do you mean, Thatch?"

"I mean Safari. S-A-F-A-R-I. I didn't think you knew what you were doing when you bought it. Hell, we'd never even heard of the company down here." Thatcher had a way of referring to his office as though it was in the catacombs of Wall Street even though he was actually a few blocks south of me. "And I sure as shooting thought you were wrong when you unloaded it. I even said so to Aunt Wanda, but she told me to mind my own business."

"So?" I said, though I already knew. "What's happened?"

"You haven't heard? Come on, Tommy, it's all over town. You can't sell Safari at any price. It's so bad people are practically giving out certificates on the street like handbills. Some pretty heavyweight people are pissed as hell. But not Wanda. Come on, how'd you know to get her out?"

"I didn't," I said. "Just lucky. But I've got a rule of thumb, Thatch."

"What's that?"

"Greed doesn't pay. It almost always makes sense to quit while you're winning."

"No kidding? But that's what I always try to tell my clients: You don't lose money when you're cashing in profits."

"You've got it, Thatch," I said.

I tried to get out of the conversation then, but he wouldn't let me go. Had I talked to Wanda yet? No I hadn't. Well, she'd be calling me, she was going to throw a party.

"She says we've made her a fortune," Thatcher said. "That means you, Tommy, not me. She's hell-bent on celebrating. Besides, she says there's somebody she wants you to meet. Says you've been single long enough, that it's not fair to women. Well, you know how Wanda is when she gets the bit between her teeth."

That I did, and in case I'd forgotten, Wanda called that same day.

"I won't take no for an answer this time, Tommy," she boomed at me. "I'm calling it the Safari party— that'll be the theme—but it's in your honor. I'll schedule it whenever you're free. And don't tell me you're busy *all* the time, you won't get away with it."

"I'll be glad to come, Wanda, but on one condition."

"What's that?"

"That it not be in my honor."

"Come, come, Tommy, you're too modest by far."

"No, I'm dead serious."

"I can hear that. Goodness. Well, it doesn't matter. I'll drink a silent toast to you anyway, young man. Now when do you want me to schedule it?"

We set a date. Then I tried to talk her out of the safari theme—did she really want everybody to know how rich she was?—but to no avail. Then I asked her if I could bring a date.

"Aha!" she exclaimed, bursting into rumbly laughter. "You're too clever for words, young man." Then, subsiding: "I gather you've already talked to my nephew?"

"Yes, I have."

"Well, that's too bad. Of course you can bring anyone you want, but there's still somebody I'd like you to meet. In fact, she says she already knows you."

"Oh? Who's that?"

"Never mind. She's a superb young woman, and she remembers you vividly."

"But Wanda, that's not fair," I protested.

To no avail, however. The more I argued with her, the more she scolded me for trying to deprive an old lady of a little fun. I got no further with Thatcher. He called frequently in coming weeks. His aunt, he said, had become a legend in his office—their only client, it turned out, who'd made a killing on Safari, and they'd had several who'd been scorched. Of course, people in the know knew who was behind Wanda's success. How? Because he'd told them. And not just about Safari but the string of winners I'd put together that year. People were intrigued, he said. In fact, one of his senior VPs had suggested they ought to hire me. Did I think that was such a crazy idea?

"Is that a joke, Thatch?" I asked him. "Or a feeler?"

"It's more than a feeler, old man. I think you could write your own ticket here."

"Thanks," I said. "I'm sincerely flattered, Thatch. But no thanks, after all."

"Well, that's what I told them you'd say. You can't blame us for trying. But if things ever change, old man, you only have to pick up the phone."

The offer may have flattered me, but it also brought on the jitters. Kitty herself agreed that it was time to let Wanda's accounts lie fallow for a while, but that was easier said than done. Wanda had already started to ask what we were going to do for an encore, and for every Wanda and her nephew there were my other blue-haired heiresses, and their brokers and advisers.

"What did you expect?" Kitty said. "You've made yourself a rich man, and you're making them richer. Did you really expect them *not* to notice?"

"No, not really. But the more visible I am, the more likely it is that somebody will put two and two together."

"What somebody?"

"The SEC, for one. Thatcher said he'd heard rumors that Safari was going to be investigated. A lot of important people got burned, and apparently they're more than a little annoyed about it."

"I don't blame them, do you? Nobody likes to lose. But suppose they do investigate? Suppose they even found you, which is unlikely. After all, you're still a fairly minor player by Wall Street standards. But supposing they did? Then what?"

"Exactly," I said. "Then what?"

"Then you'd just tell them what you told Thatcher. You got lucky, that's all. It stood to reason that Safari was going to be a hot acquisition someday, you just got lucky on the timing."

"And lucky in the sell-off, too?"

"Not lucky. You yourself said it: it's just that you're not as greedy as the next guy."

All true enough, and whether or not people believed it, there was no way on the face of it that I could be charged with a crime. Still . . .

"The link stops with you, Tommy," Kitty said. "Now maybe you'll understand why I've wanted to keep us quiet."

"You mean so that you wouldn't be investigated, too?"

She shook her head, protruding her lower lip. I remember she was examining her fingernails at the time, holding them toward her, knuckles bent in a half fist, then outward, palms down, fingers together. I also remember what we were wearing or, more accurately, weren't wearing. We were lying on her bed, on the silk sheets I'd given her.

"Well," I said, still not satisfied, "why do we have to, then?"

"Have to what?"

"Have to keep us quiet. Why is it that every time we run into somebody I know or you know, you always flinch, as though you wish you could make yourself disappear? Or me disappear?"

"I didn't know I did that," she said.

It had happened more than once—in a restaurant, at the theater, in a store. Kitty invariably seemed to duck.

"Well, you do," I said.

She didn't answer right away. She gave up on her fingernails finally and turned toward me. Her head was propped on one hand, her legs together, her full breasts sagging a little.

"Look, my darling," she said, "there's no law that says you have to do this forever. You can quit anytime you want to. Who knows? Maybe you've already gone as far as you want to?"

"That means quitting you, too, doesn't it?"

"I didn't say that."

"No. But I haven't *earned* you yet, have I?"

This started her giggling.

"Oh, God, Tommy!" she said, her breasts shaking prettily. "You've got the memory of an elephant! I wish to God I'd never said that."

"But you did."

"Well, in that case I take it back."

She began tracing a line down my flank with her fingernail. Then she reached for me. But something made me pull away.

"Seriously," I said. "What would happen if I did quit?"

"I don't know. But why do we have to decide that right now?"

We didn't, of course. It wasn't the first time, either, that the idea had occurred to me: that one day the joyride would end, and for any number of reasons. But I think this was the first time I acknowledged to myself that I didn't want it to.

"You still haven't answered my question," I said.

"What question?"

"Why is it that you flinch whenever we run into someone we know?"

"I'm sorry. I'll try to change."

"But don't you see the point, Kitty? I want us to stop living like hermits. I want the whole world to know about us. You say you love me, you say I'm the grand passion of your life, you say you'd rather kill than lose me. But why is it that we've been together almost a year and still live apart?"

This last was another sore point. In fact, in the early days of our relationship, no matter how long we made love into the night—and there were times when, reaching the sidewalk on Central Park South, I'd found the sun already up—once it ended, it ended. Time for me to go. We'd gotten past that eventually, but I remember Kitty's agitation that first time when, stripped of her makeup, her hair mussed, her eyes a little crusty from sleep, the warm and sour smells of love enveloping us in her tousled sheets, she awoke to find herself still in my arms.

Of course there was another answer besides the business one, and for a moment, lying on her silk sheets, I thought she was about to tell me. Instead her expression lightened and, lips curling in a sly smile, she said:

"All that's going to change now, anyway."

"What does that mean?"

"Well, we'll be going to the same party, for one thing."

"What party?"

"Your friend, Wanda Russell. The Safari party. We've already started work on it."

"For Wanda?"

"That's right."

"But how did that happen?"

"Easy. Word gets around. She came to us. It just so happens we're the best in the party business nowadays."

"But why didn't you tell me?"

"It came up in such a hurry, there wasn't time," she said, tracing her fingernail along my flank again. "Besides, I thought you might object."

"Object? Why would I object?"

"I don't know," she said, giggling softly as, finding my cock, she began to tease it alive. "It's mixing business with pleasure. And for you to be seen, in public, with your secret woman . . . ?"

It was already too late for me to object, too late to pull back or do anything other than what she had in mind, insistently. And it was only afterward that—quintessential Kitten—I realized she'd still managed not to answer my question.

12

Take a Park Avenue apartment, even one as considerable as Wanda Russell's, and try transforming it into an *Out of Africa* encampment. No mean feat. Yet Kitty had managed it, in November, with thatch and tenting in the party rooms, bamboo and peacock feathers, camp chairs and wicker, a staff, male and female, togged out in khaki shorts and shirts, with sandals on their feet and topis on their heads. The music was Olatungi style, complete with bird calls and jungle night sounds against a muffled drumbeat, and the drinks and food were served on bamboo trays, in gourds and calabashes. The overall effect definitely "said" safari, and when you stopped to think about it, the throngs of guests in their costumes didn't look any more out of place on Park Avenue than they would have on the plains of Kenya.

I went with a certain amused anticipation, for I'd never been to a Kitty Goldmark production, and when I stepped off the elevator into Wanda's transformed entrance hall, to the distant tom-toms, Wanda herself met me, resplendent (I can think of no other word) in a floor-length gown

115

of figured African silk, her blue hair coiffed high in a
beehive effect and her arms outstretched.

"Ah, welcome, dear Tommy!" she called out, sepa-
rating herself from some other guests. "Welcome to *your*
party, darling!" She pulled me to her in a massive embrace, whispering, "Because it *is* your party, nasty boy,
even though you wouldn't let it be." Then she took me
by the arm and in her normal voice said, "Come on, I
want you to meet everybody—and one person in particular."

I complimented her on her outfit and on the decor.

"Kitty Goldmark," she said. "She's absolutely superb. Do you know her?"

"We've met," I said.

"She's the only one to go to these days. Very much
in demand. I was lucky to get her."

And so, I remember thinking, was I.

I knew Kitty had been there almost the whole day,
supervising operations, but I failed to spot her as Wanda
patrolled me through the rooms, pausing to chat, pausing
to introduce me. I knew, or knew of, many of the guests.
They represented, one might say, the *tout* New York, at
least the *tout* New York of a certain moneyed kind. The
men, playing it safe, wore mainly British Colonial, but
most of the women had gone Evening Safari, or tried to.
To behold them, you'd never have supposed that it was
New York and late autumn, unless, that is, you spotted
their furs on the coat racks in Wanda's vast pantry, which
had been stripped for the purpose. As indeed her whole
apartment seemed to have been stripped. Where had
everything gone?

"Kitty Goldmark's solution, darling," Wanda explained. "The vans came yesterday, they had it cleared
out by noon today. It's all parked somewhere in Long
Island, New Jersey, wherever they do such things.

They're supposed to bring it all back tomorrow, but I'm thinking maybe I'll keep it this way awhile, what do you think? Oh, *there* she is! Come on, Tommy, tell me you're *not* surprised!"

I failed, though, to recognize the tall, stylish woman who, turning from a group under a thatch bar, now strode toward me, smiling, hand outstretched. I'd like to say it was because I'd been looking for Kitty, but it could also have been an old anxiety actually come to pass: that someday I'd fail to recognize women I'd once slept with.

"I told you, Wanda," the woman said, gazing at me with a glint of amusement at my embarrassment. "I told you he wouldn't remember me."

"Oh, you're *terrible*, Tommy!" our hostess boomed. "You really are! *Terrible*! And I understand the two of you once spent a remarkable weekend together!"

"Not true," I said, recovering. Her voice had tipped me off. "Cabo San Lucas, how could I forget? How are you, Martine?"

In my defense, the remarkable weekend had taken place some years before. Also, the last time I'd seen Martine Brady, she'd been wearing no more than a tank top and shorts, and her hair had come halfway down her back. Now the hair was cropped short across the cheekbones, a little darker than before, I thought. Wide brown eyes, long lashes. The same lanky model's figure: broad-shouldered, small-breasted, narrow in the hips. She wore a low-cut, bright red waistcoat, double-breasted with brass buttons, and a cream-colored evening skirt which followed the lines of her legs almost to her ankles. But it was the voice I remembered, low-pitched, cool, with a timbre when she laughed that prickled the nape of my neck.

"Oh, I'm fine, Tommy, but I haven't been fishing in ages. How about you?"

I laughed at the private joke, and Wanda, mission accomplished, drifted off into the throng.

The joke brought the rest of it back to me. I'd been in Los Angeles on business, and we'd met there by design. We'd flown down to the bottommost tip of Baja, California to a fledgling resort called Cabo San Lucas, with a dirt landing strip, a couple of new hotels, and where the main attraction was supposedly the best big-game fishing within striking distance of the West Coast. All weekend, we'd talked about going fishing; except for meals, though, we'd barely left the hotel room.

I remembered how it ended, too. Martine had been fairly recently divorced. When, on the flight back to Los Angeles, I'd admitted that I was still married, if not very happily so, her carefree mood had shifted suddenly to ice. She'd said something to the effect that she didn't have time for men who couldn't make up their mind what they wanted or where they belonged, and the minute we landed at LAX we'd gone our separate ways.

Normally I'd have been intrigued to run into her again. But these weren't normal times, and even as we talked I found myself craning my neck in search of Kitty.

I asked Martine if she still had the sombrero I'd bought her, a woven-straw affair, which, I recalled, had looked marvelous on her. With a smile, she told me she'd chucked it the minute she'd left me.

"But I wouldn't do that today," she said, laughing.

"Why not?"

"Oh, I'm more practical. A little older, a little wiser. Maybe a little more cynical, too."

"How cynical?"

"Well, let me catch you up in a hurry. I've been married again, divorced again. In fact—surprise, surprise—he's here tonight. Small world. Thatch said he ran into him somewhere, brought him along. You know

Thatch, don't you? He said he didn't think I'd mind. Well, I do mind, but it's too late for that, isn't it? You probably know him, anyway. Thorny? Bobby Thorne, the investment banker?''

"No, I don't think so.''

"We're still on speaking terms, more or less, but I wouldn't have come if I'd known. Except that I wanted to see you again. I understand you've made Wanda a ton of money?''

"Well," I said, "a pretty small ton.''

"Oh? That's not the way I heard it, Tommy. Anyway, I could use some help in that department myself. You see, I've become a woman of, as they say, independent means. Thanks to Thorny. The truth is, I hit him pretty hard.''

We'd been walking slowly through the party, balancing drinks as we talked, or rather as she talked and I scanned the crowd. She still had, I noticed, that blithe, even offhand way of talking about things most people considered private. Such as divorce settlements. And she was, I thought, very definitely under sixty.

"He even looks like a son of a bitch, doesn't he?'' Martine said, pointing out her ex-husband, a tall, good-looking fellow in a double-breasted navy blue suit, standing with a group of men. Square jaw, ruddy complexion, and a streak, or shock, of white running diagonally across his otherwise black hair. "The streak, by the way, is natural. He's had it since his twenties, though he likes to say I gave it to him. Makes him devastatingly handsome, don't you think? Come on, Tommy, let me introduce you. I'll have some fun with him.''

Martine linked her arm through mine as we approached the group. Thatcher was among them; the others I didn't know. Thatcher wore bush garb, complete with multi-pocketed khaki shorts.

"Well, here comes the hero of the day," Thatcher called out when he saw me. "Come here, Tommy. Meet Bob Thorne, the only other man at the party who made a killing on Safari. No pun intended."

Thorne and I shook hands.

"Hardly a killing," he said, laughing. "Nothing like what Thatch says you pulled off."

"Thatch is given to exaggeration," I answered.

Our eyes met briefly. Thorne was a big man, a little taller than I, with large hands and a firm grip. I imagined him thinking: *How did you find out about Safari*? Then Martine came between us, gave Thorne a quick kiss on the cheek, and, holding his arm and turning to the others, said:

"Hi, I'm Martine Brady. I used to be married to this one, can you imagine? I'm glad to hear he's doing so well because a piece of it's mine. Hello again, Thatch"—breaking from Thorne to kiss Thatcher. "Gee, Thatch, I didn't tell you before, but you look positively fetching in those shorts. Banana Republic?"

I saw them all hesitate at her first remark—was it supposed to be a joke?—to be saved by her second. Thatcher, it seemed, was a fair butt, and the men broke into laughter. Then Thorne and I stood briefly side by side while Martine played the group, at once outrageous and teasing, which combination had the simultaneous effect of throwing them off balance and titillating them.

"Well, Thorny," she said, turning back toward her ex-husband, hands now at her hips, "are you ready to kiss and make up yet?"

No answer from Thorne. Perhaps he knew her too well.

Martine cocked her head provocatively, as though measuring him.

"Poor Thorny," she said. "I hear she's already ditched you for somebody else."

"That'll be enough of that," Thorne said abruptly.

"Enough of *what*?" she retorted. Her voice flared suddenly, as though she intended the whole party to hear. "Enough of *what*, I ask you? The son of a bitch leaves me for Kitty Goldmark, everybody knows that, and then she dumps him, too. What's the matter, Thorny, was she too smart for you? Or didn't she like it when you—"

Stunned, I didn't even see Thorne step forward until it had already happened. He slapped Martine hard across the cheek. I heard it. I was aware of her recoiling, face white, mouth open. Somebody—Thatcher, I think—stepped between them, blocking Martine, who stormed behind him.

"That'll cost you, Bobby! That's public humiliation, and everybody saw it!"

Everybody, meanwhile, tried to move away at once. Thorne himself turned on his heels, while Martine let Thatcher lead her away.

I stood in the eye of the storm, immobilized, my confusion compounded by the fact that Kitty had apparently seen it all. I'd just caught sight of her when Thorne let it fly. She was talking to somebody in the next room, but her eyes were on me, Thorne, Martine, her mouth ajar.

Small world indeed. And I stood there like a fool, the proverbial stuck pig, with that awful flushed sense that the *tout* New York was watching to see if I squealed.

But of course nobody was watching me. Why should they have been? Nobody knew about me. Nobody was *allowed* to know about me.

Whereas: *The son of a bitch leaves me for Kitty Goldmark, everybody knows that . . .*

Was that why Kitty wanted us secret? Because of Thorne?

And how many others of us, Thornies and Tommies,

was she playing at the same time? How many of us were out there, buying and selling Safari for her?

I went after her, but she'd disappeared from the cluster in the next room. Angry and hurt, I circled the party, ducking past people and palms, to end up in the kitchen, where I ran into Wanda Russell, herself awhirl in the midst of traffic.

"Ah, there you are, dear boy"—reaching out her arms. "I've hardly seen— But you look pale, Tommy, is something wrong? Can I get you something?"

"I'm all right. Have you seen—?"

"That dreadful Thorne person. Did you hear what he did? He slugged Martine right in public! Punched her out! At *my* party!"

"I was there too, Wanda. But—"

"I told her she should sue, that everybody would testify. Just wait till I get my hands on—"

"Have you seen Kitty Goldmark?"

". . . that nephew of mine. He— What did you say?"

"Have you seen Kitty? Kitty Goldmark?"

"Well, yes. She just left."

"She *left*?"

"That's right, just now. Poor thing, who can blame her? She was exhausted, utterly. Nobody has any idea what it takes to do an evening like this. And now it's absolutely ruined."

"I'm sorry, Wanda," I said. "I'm not feeling well myself. I . . ."

But she wouldn't hear of it, wouldn't let me leave. Instead she steered me back through the swinging kitchen doors and into the party, chattering about Martine now, poor Martine, bad luck in husbands, still quite a catch, stunning woman, and it wasn't until she caught sight of Thatcher, and relinquishing me, started to berate him for having brought Thorne, that I managed my own uncer-emonious escape.

I remember standing in the dark outside Wanda's build-ing, where the limousines waited in long, double-parked formations for the guests to emerge. I turned down a few cruising taxis. I was stone sober, and though there was a chill in the November night, I sweated inside and, pulling off my tie, opened my shirt collar, my jacket, my overcoat to the air. In truth I dreaded a new con-frontation with Kitty, but I saw no way to avoid one.

Unless Martine Brady had invented it?

The son of a bitch leaves me for Kitty Goldmark...

But why would she have?

I walked south slowly to Fifty-ninth Street, then west toward Kitty's. Past the GM building, the Plaza, twin symbols of the once richest city in the world, and along the narrow strip of luxury bordering the south edge of the park. There was another New York we all knew about now, where people slept in cartons, on sidewalk heat grates, in subways and train stations, always with their hands out and badgering us for money. More of them clearly than us, and making your way among them was like walking a gauntlet. Who knows why I thought of them that particular night? They were little enough in evidence on Central Park South. Was it perhaps some awareness that my new connection to luxury could sud-denly become tenuous and that, having severed with the firm, I now needed Kitty a lot more than she needed me?

When I reached her building, I went straight upstairs, for by now I was well known to her doormen and had a key of my own. The apartment, though, was empty. It looked neat, even unlived in, except for the bedroom. Some signs of disarray there: probably she'd come home just before the party to change. I lingered among the familiar objects: the silken bed and brocaded comforter, the spindly-legged chairs and table near the window where we sometimes ate breakfast, the antique dressing table with the lovely curved mirror. The Boucher prints on the walls in their gilded frames. Then I retreated to the living room and gazed out the windows over the darkened expanse of the park, where little rows of light marking the roadways meandered into the northern dimness. I poured myself a drink but left it standing.

At some point I punched out my own home number. After three rings, my answering machine, another recent improvement, came on. Knowing she wouldn't pick up even if she was there, I started talking through my own recorded message:

"Kitty? Are you there? It's me. Please pick up if you're there."

Nobody picked up.

I thought of going home anyway, dismal though the prospect was. Instead I fell asleep on the couch facing Kitty's empty fireplace.

It was after two when I awoke to the sound of a key in the front door. I sat up, momentarily disoriented, then stood stiffly. Through the mirror above the mantelpiece, I saw Kitty standing at the other side of the room.

I glanced at my watch.

"Gee," I said, "I'm surprised to see you."

"Why's that?"

"Well, I heard you were exhausted. When I didn't find you here, I thought you'd gone to sleep someplace else."

"If that's meant to be funny, Tommy, I'm too tired for jokes."

"It wasn't meant to be funny. Not at all."

"Then please say what you mean."

"Just what I said. It's past two in the morning. I heard

you left the party exhausted. I'd like to know where you've been between then and now.''

She'd been holding on to her purse, with her coat slung over her shoulders. Now she dropped both on a chair.

''I think maybe you'd better go home, Tommy,'' she said quietly.

''Go home? Now there's a good answer.''

She said nothing. Head down, lips tight, she crossed the living room toward the back hall. Then, turning to me:

''Stay if you want to, then. I'm going to bed.''

I went after her, following her into the bedroom.

''You can't do this to me, Kitty,'' I called after her. ''You can't abandon me and then just show up in the middle of the night and go to bed. Just like that. I *demand* an explanation. You went off with Thorne, didn't you?''

She started to undress. First the high heels, kicked off, then her gown, up over her head. I'd watched her undress countless times, but now the sight of it infuriated me.

''Why won't you tell me?'' I challenged her. ''Thorne left the party at the same time you did. Quite a coincidence! *Now* where are you going?''

In bra, half slip, and stockinged feet, she'd started for the bathroom.

''I told you,'' she said, a tremor in her voice. ''I'm going to bed. I've got another terrible day tomorrow. First I'm going to take my makeup off.''

''I won't accept that!'' I shouted abruptly, seizing her by the arm.

Head down, she tore free of my grasp. For a second, her hair swirling, her head lowered, I saw the Kitty of almost a year before, that first night outside her building. But when she looked at me, there were no tears.

''You're making me crazy, Tommy,'' she said, her voice now shaking as though she was fighting for control of it. "You don't *own* me. I don't know where you got the idea that you did."

"*Own* you? Who's talking about *owning* you?"

"You are. Just listen to yourself. You *demand* an explanation, you won't *accept* this or that. But you don't own me, Tommy. Nobody owns me."

"I'm not talking about ownership! But I have certain rights. I *love* you, for Christ's sake!"

"You're hardly acting like it."

"Neither are you! We're supposed to be *partners*! Partners in love, partners in business."

"As far as business goes, I never said it was exclusive."

"You *what*?"

"That's right," she said, her eyes unwaveringly on mine. "You don't make me enough money for it to be exclusive."

The statement dumbfounded me, not just the fact of it but the utter calm with which she said it. For a weird moment, I felt as though I didn't know her at all.

"So you gave Thorne Safari, too," I said finally.

"I didn't say that."

"But you did give it to him, didn't you? And you were with him tonight, weren't you?"

"I didn't say that either."

"And I don't give a goddamn what you didn't say! You were with him, weren't you?"

A rush of anger seized me, and the impulse to hit her made me ball my fist. She must have seen it too. She didn't flinch, but she lowered her head, neck bowed, as though she knew what was coming.

"Well, weren't you?" I repeated. "Weren't you with him?"

"Don't push me, Tommy," she said softly.

"Then *answer* me, goddamn it!"

She looked up at me, jaws set, her eyes just beginning to water. I saw a trace of that pleading look I'd seen before, like that part of her inner self she couldn't hide in her otherwise implacable facade.

"Please don't push me," she said again.

"Then answer me, Kitty. Answer that one question."

She looked away. I saw the sharp granite planes of her profile, the straight lines of her nose, cheekbones, her jaw. And then back again. The plea gone.

"The answer is no," she said. "I wasn't with Thorne."

"Then where the hell were you?" I exclaimed, uncomprehending.

"I think we've said enough" was her reply.

And mine, like an explosion I was incapable of stopping:

"And I think you're one cold-hearted bitch."

She stared at me for a split second, then without a word turned and went into the bathroom, shutting the door behind her. I stood staring at the closed door, immobilized for the second time that night. I was, I think, quite literally afraid to move, afraid that, if the frozen scene were to shift however slightly, something terrible would inevitably follow.

How long she was gone, I can't say. When she came out, she was wearing her familiar blue silk floor-length robe, tied by the sash with the tasseled ends. Her face was uncommonly pale, scrubbed clean, and the lines around her eyes showed fatigue clearly.

She seemed surprised to see me still there. She stopped and stared at me a moment, then looked away, as though thinking, and walked on past me. I heard her sigh deeply behind me. Then:

"Sit down," she said tonelessly. "I'm going to tell you a story."

I remember glancing at my watch.

"Never mind," she said. "I know it's late. But you asked some questions, didn't you? Well, I'm going to give you some answers. So sit down, please."

She had one of those Madame Récamier chaises longues in her bedroom, half chaise, half sofa, covered in the same brocaded material as the comforter. I sat on the edge of it while she stayed on her feet, pacing about while she talked.

"Once upon a time," she began, "there was a young woman. She was very young, very inexperienced, and like most young women she wanted to be independent. She'd had boyfriends, plenty of dates, but nothing serious, and she was in no hurry on that score. She was a college graduate. She had a job, an apartment she shared with two roommates. She was taking graduate courses at night, had enough credits already for her M.A.

"And then one day she met a young man with a beard, a very good-looking young man. A little shy, serious. He wanted to be a concert pianist. In fact, he already was one, but the kind of music he played, by contemporary composers, wasn't much in demand. Oh, he could play Chopin beautifully, Beethoven, Liszt—any one of the classics—but what he really cared about was music by people nobody outside the music schools had ever heard of. Sometimes he played pick-up piano in cocktails bars. Sometimes he worked in a bookstore. He had little money, lived with next to no furniture, ate poorly, and practiced on an old piano—it was a Knabe—that needed a new soundboard he couldn't afford.

"And the young woman, against the better judgment of all her friends, fell in love with him. Who could say why? Maybe it was because he told her he didn't have time for serious involvements and she took that as a challenge. Or maybe because she thought he needed her.

Or because she wanted to find out what was underneath the beard. Who knows?"

I smiled at the line about the beard. I'd heard Kitty say before that only men who had something to hide wore beards. But she didn't smile back or so much as look at me, only continued to pace while she talked, occasionally picking up some object and putting it back down, and her voice held the same monotone.

"Anyway, she ended up moving in with him. She got a better job, quit school so as to take on freelance typing. She was a very good typist. She even borrowed the money—it cost thousands of dollars—to get his piano rebuilt. She worked for him, cooked for him and his friends, cleaned house for him, even cut his hair for him. When he finally had his first New York recital, she was the one who paid for the program and, when the recital hall lost money, negotiated his way out of paying his share of the deficit.

"They lived this way for several years. There was never a question of marriage. He didn't believe in it, for one thing. Also, he said he needed to feel free to sleep with other women, whether he actually did or not. Anyway, his career was what counted. He worked hard at it, too. He practiced morning, noon, night, weekends. Finally, after she helped him find a new agent, he began to be in some demand. His kind of music meant college campuses, mostly. He also had two small tours in Europe and played in several group recordings, which sold poorly.

"Then one year, his agent organized a tour for him on the West Coast. He'd be away for over two weeks, giving concerts from Orange County all the way up to Seattle. In the past, she'd always gone with him when he traveled, but this time she couldn't. He went alone. They talked on the phone almost every night. The con-

certs were a success; yes, he missed her, too; the reviews
he'd seen had all been good.

"When he came home, he'd shaved off his beard.
Should that have tipped her off? Well, it hadn't. He'd
shaved it, he said, because he felt like it. How did she
like it? Though she didn't say so, she thought he'd looked
better with the beard.

"Anyway, things went back to normal. Yes, maybe
he was on the phone more than usual, but he'd always
talked a lot on the phone to his friends. She hadn't realized how much he was calling, or where to, till she got
the next phone bill.

"Then one day . . .

"He'd been back about three weeks. She'd gone to
work as usual. Nothing special about the day. She'd asked
him to do the shopping for dinner and take some clothes
to the cleaner's because she'd known ahead of time that
she was going to have to work late. Anyway, when she
got home, late, she felt something funny, some kind of
premonition . . .

"He wasn't there. Not only wasn't he there, he was
gone. Not only was he gone, but he'd cleaned the place
out. Every item, every stick of furniture that wasn't specifically hers, gone. Even the piano was gone.

"She found out later that he'd sold the piano and the
furniture to a dealer for cash.

"No note, no telephone call. After years, nothing.

"None of his friends knew what had happened. Or if
they did, they weren't telling. His agent didn't know,
either. She even thought of calling the police, but to say
what? That he'd disappeared and she was afraid something had happened to him? And that whoever had done
it had taken all his stuff too, including his piano?"

She stopped talking then and, looking about for a place
to sit down, finally chose the bed, the edge. She pulled

the halves of her robe together and held them, hands making fists on her thighs, and gazed not at me but past me.

"She lived there alone," she went on, "not changing anything. Waiting, she told herself. Finally—it was around six months later—she found out what had happened. He'd had a girlfriend in Los Angeles. Maybe it was somebody he'd met on the West Coast tour, or maybe he'd had her right along. Either way, the minute he'd arrived back in New York, he'd known he had to go back. He couldn't help himself, he had to go back. He couldn't hide it any longer, but he couldn't tell her either. The only thing to do was make a clean break with his past, all his past, her, everything. And that's what he did. A very clean break."

She stood up abruptly as though she herself couldn't stand listening to it anymore, and shook her head slowly, side to side, exhaling deeply. When she spoke again, it was to me, and the third person had been dropped, and her eyes had gone small.

"Do you know how I found out?" she asked me.

I shook my head.

"He told me himself," she said contemptuously. "He called me. Collect, if you please. It was about six months after he cleared out. He said he wanted to apologize. He knew I'd understand. He asked my forgiveness. He'd done what he had to do, that's what he'd thought at the time. But it had all been a terrible mistake, the mistake of a lifetime. From three thousand miles away he was on his knees, begging my forgiveness. Was there any chance I'd take him back?"

She was standing near me, the robe pulled tight around her body, looking down at me.

"What did you do?" I asked.

She shrugged.

"I hung up on him," she said. "The next day I moved out of the apartment. A couple of months after that, I married Gar Sprague."

No matter that she'd answered none of my questions, I wanted suddenly to tell her a lot of things: that all men weren't like that, that *I* wasn't like that, that I didn't even know how to play the piano. Et cetera, et cetera. Failing words, I wanted to take her in my arms. But there were moments when, no matter how well I thought I knew her, I found Kitty utterly unapproachable. This was one of them. So I simply sat there on her Madame Récamier sofa until she said quietly:

"I think I'd like you to go now."

And so I did.

13

Ah, Kitten, you told such good stories. The only match for you might have been my own father, and even there I'd be going on hearsay, for though his reputation as a raconteur was widespread, I myself had been little exposed to that side of him. To him, as I'd learned over the years, I was little more than an intermittent nuisance. I'd seen little of him after I joined the firm, not surprising since he was absent from the office for long stretches, and when I left, he was conspicuously missing among the wellwishers, leaving it (again) to Mac Coombs to express the formal regrets and official Godspeeds. As with my professional life, so with my private. I don't recall his ever expressing an opinion, either way, on my divorce from Susan, and I'm pretty sure Mary Laura and Starkie would have failed to recognize their own grandfather had they passed him on the street.

Under the circumstances, I was not only startled but a little suspicious when, a few days after Wanda Russell's party, he called to invite me to lunch. I tried to beg off under the pressure of work, but he wouldn't hear of it.

There were several matters of some urgency he needed to discuss with me. Besides, he wanted to find out first-hand if all the rumors he'd been hearing about how well I was doing were true.

He picked me up at my office a little after noon, impeccable as ever in a gray winter coat of some cheviot material with a black fur collar and the inevitable black homburg. Perhaps he'd slowed up some, but for a man his age, whose lifespan almost matched the century, he seemed remarkably fit, like one of those spry elder-statesman types who, long after everybody thinks he's dead, appears on the front pages of the papers on this or that mission to Moscow or Peking. He took a cursory look at my premises to satisfy his curiosity, and then we were off to the club.

"I understand you're on the way to a very considerable success," he said, toasting me with a very dry Gibson. "You know, it's remarkable how some men—and you seem to be one of them—can benefit from a radical change. I've known any number of great success stories, but in some cases you'd never have guessed it if you'd known them in their younger years."

An interesting comment, I thought, for a father to make about his own son.

"Point of curiosity," I said, "but how do you know I'm on the way to a very considerable success?"

"Oh, I have my sources," he said. Then, laughing drily, "You forget, some of the people you're making money for are clients I brought into the firm originally. For instance, did Wanda Russell ever tell you I once had an affair with her?"

"No, she didn't," I said, thinking at the same time that there were, it seemed, precious few women above a certain age whom the Senator hadn't had affairs with.

He told me about it. She'd been splendid in her youth,

he said. There had even been a moment when he'd thought they might get married, but he'd chosen my mother instead. A good thing for Wanda, too, she liked to remind him, because marrying him would have kept her from Jack Russell's millions.

"She was quite a hot number in her day," he reminisced. "Don't think I was the only one who thought so, either. But then she lost it, don't we all? The only moral of the story, Tommy, is: Don't get old."

This brief, wry play for sympathy, if that's what it was, reminded me that he, at least, had tried to avoid getting old by trading down in wives. The incumbent, whom I'd never met, was still somewhere in her thirties.

It took him but a short time, and a second Gibson, to get to the point of our meeting.

"The truth, Tommy?" he said, eyebrows raised, knife and fork poised over his Dover sole (grilled on the bone). "The truth is, I'm tapped out. Amazing though it may sound, this will be the last meal I'll eat here unless I can come up with some way to meet my arrears."

He stared at me, cutlery still aloft, as though awaiting my reaction. Surprise? Commiseration? Condemnation? In point of fact, I didn't know how to react. His finances had always been a mystery to me. As far as his club bill was concerned, I suppose I'd have thought that would have been the firm's responsibility, if I'd ever thought about it, which I hadn't.

"I see you don't believe me," he went on, undaunted. "But the truth is that you're looking at a man—your own father—who's almost eighty years old, is drowning in debt, and doesn't have a nickel in his pockets."

He went on, while we ate, to review his obligations, summarizing, as it were, the balance sheet and income statement of Stark Thompson Jr., which he drew with imaginary strokes of his fork on the tablecloth. Yes, he held some assets, but everything was leveraged to the hilt, he said, and even if he cashed in, he still wouldn't net enough to pay off his debts, much less have anything to live on.

"Add it all up," he said, carving a bottom line on the tablecloth, "and you've got a negative net worth. Right now, even as we speak, I'm legally bankrupt. In fact, that's one of the options I'm considering: to declare bankruptcy and let the vultures worry about it. Now that would be a first, wouldn't it? A Thompson declaring bankruptcy? At seventy-nine?"

Oddly, the idea didn't seem to devastate him at all. On the contrary, togged out in an elegant business suit, with silk tie and matching handkerchief, he ate and drank with gusto even as he described his ruin. I tried to imagine what I would have done in his shoes. Without success.

"But what about the firm?" I said. "It's had a run of very profitable years, hasn't it?"

"Ah, yes, the firm. Not as profitable as it should be, mind you. Growing too fast. Too many partners, and the overhead's horrendous. I've warned Mac time and time again. But you see . . ." Here he hesitated, looking in his lap for his napkin, then spotting it on the floor and leaning to pick it up. "Well"—dabbing at his mouth—"what happened there, Tommy, is that they reduced my participation a couple of years ago. I didn't like it, mind you—after all, my name's still on the door—but some of the younger partners felt I wasn't pulling my weight anymore. I couldn't altogether blame them, either. I haven't been all that active in recent years. Still . . ."

This I hadn't known. They'd pushed him to retire, he

said, and he'd fought them, but in the end he'd had to agree to a much smaller slice of the annual pie.

"But the real killer," he said, "is that Braxton's just upped my margin requirement. Can you tie that? After all these years? Hell, Charlie Braxton and I went to school together! I was an usher at his wedding, I was toastmaster at the party when he took over from his old man! When this first came up—that was a while ago— I blew my cork. I went to Charlie. I told him I was going to pull every last penny out of Braxton's and not just *my* last penny. And they backed off. But now they're saying they can't cover me anymore, and I think they mean business this time. The market makes them nervous. Hell, who isn't nervous about the market these days? Present company excepted, from what I hear."

He looked at me, eyebrows raised, leaving an opening for me to comment. I had nothing to say.

"Anyway," he went on, "they've given me until the end of the week to cover, else they're going to start selling me off. And that, sir, given the sorry state of Wall Street right now, is likely to be the final nail in my coffin."

Again the pause, the opening, but again I didn't take it.

"I think what really happened," he said, "is that they've heard how precarious I am. How, I don't know, but word gets around. Probably the only person who doesn't know by now is Karen." Karen was his fifth wife. "I haven't had the heart to tell her. She thinks we're going to Europe in a couple of months to celebrate my eightieth birthday. How am I supposed to tell her I can't pay for the plane tickets?"

We finished lunch and walked into the library for coffee. It was a splendid old room, hung with some fine portraits of illustrious members past, mostly from the nineteenth century, and a small but apparently very valuable collection of rare books and manuscripts in glass cases. We sat at right angles to each other in high leather armchairs, and since my father wouldn't or couldn't bring himself to ask the question, I finally did.

"What brings you to me?" I said.

"Well, you're family, aren't you? My only son and heir?"

"In a manner of speaking," I said, but if he caught my irony, he didn't show it.

"I need a loan, Tommy. A bridge loan, really. I think I can hold Braxton's off with as little as sixty thousand dollars cash. Say seventy thousand to be on the safe side. Then something on the side to take care of a few nuisance situations, like my arrears here. Five thousand dollars ought to take care of it, but ten thousand would make me comfortable. With ten thousand, I could even float the plane tickets. Eighty thousand dollars, then, in round numbers. And short term, mind you. Just to tide me over. A bridge loan."

Later I might ask myself: a bridge from where to where? But on the spot, in those elegant surroundings, with the Senator tapping a new cigarette against his thumbnail the way they did in the years before filters, I was totally at a loss. Didn't he realize that not very long before, in my state of shabby gentility, eighty thousand dollars would have represented over a half a year's salary to me? Why had he come to me, anyway? Was it that he'd tried everywhere else and been turned down? And what of that sacred Council which managed the family hoard and to which I still sent a monthly check on the house my children lived in?

How much he read of my embarrassment I can't say— embarrassment for him that, at his age, he had to turn beggar, embarrassment for myself that I'd been put in the position of turning him down. But he must have seen something.

"You're too much of a gentleman ever to have said it, son, but I know you don't think much of me as a father. Maybe you've done better at it than I have. I've tended to lead my own life. On the other hand, I think it's safe to say that I've always been there when you needed me. It was I, remember, who got you into the firm in the first place, even though there was an unwritten rule against nepotism. Once you were there, there was obviously precious little I could do for you. In fact, I never expected you to stay so long. I thought you'd leave as soon as you got your bearings. Anyway, that's water over the dam. I'm delighted by your success and not at all surprised. But now it's my turn to ask you for help."

"I'm sorry," I said stiffly, thinking what water over what dam, "but if you're claiming some kind of indebtedness on my part, I don't accept that."

"Who's talking about indebtedness?" he said airily, gesturing with his cigarette. "You don't owe me anything, son. I want us to put this on a very businesslike basis—a formal loan agreement, market rate of interest, and so on. Beyond that, well . . ." He paused, for effect, presumably, and because he seemed to enjoy holding on to something just a moment longer. "I've something to offer you in exchange. By way of inducement, so to speak."

"What's that?"

"My place on the Council," he said. "I mean, the family Council."

"Oh?"

"That's right. As you probably know, the way we used to do it, a member kept his place on the board till he died, and then the senior member of his branch of the family automatically took over. But several of us are getting on in years, and we're considering stepping down now and appointing our own successors. It may come as no surprise to you, but the Funds hasn't been doing that well lately from an investment standpoint. Not that we're actually losing money, of course, but there's growing sentiment that we're out of touch, that we need to bring in younger people who know how to make money in today's world.''

He talked as though I knew much more about it than I did. The Council existed, yes; he himself, I'd gathered, was a member; its role was to manage the so-called Funds, i.e., the Stark-Thompson fortune. But to what end or purpose, or how they went about it, I had no idea.

"I'm afraid I don't quite see where the inducement lies. I mean—"

"I shouldn't have called it that, Tommy. The eighty thousand dollars? That's a straight business transaction between us. The board's more of an honorary thing. Of course, there are certain material advantages I can't really go into. The only one who has to do any real work is the Trustee, whom we choose from among ourselves, but he's very well compensated for it.''

"Who's the Trustee now?" I asked.

"My first cousin Corky. I guess that makes him your second cousin, doesn't it?''

Corcoran Stark, whom I vaguely remembered from one or two family reunions during my childhood, had to be a few years senior to my father.

"Not to worry," he went on with a smile. "Corky's the first one to want out. I wouldn't be at all surprised if you proved the most likely replacement for him. Apropos, though, in case you've been wondering if I've applied to the Funds myself, in re my, uh, small personal problem . . . ?"

"The thought's crossed my mind," I replied.

"Well, the answer is that I haven't. It's a little awkward, you see, since I still wear a director's hat myself. Then, too, it's really not our kind of thing . . . awfully small potatoes . . ."

But neither too small nor awkward, I remember thinking, for you to hit up your own son.

To my astonishment—but why should I have been astonished?—he stood then, brushing some imaginary crumbs from his lap. It was as though the interview was over and its outcome a fait accompli, as though all he'd had to do was explain the situation and, utterly reasonably, he'd walk off with a check for eighty thousand dollars in his pocket!

I was tempted, to be sure, to refuse him on the spot. But seething as I may have been inside—hell, I was burning! At his *presumption* among other things!—I still couldn't bring myself to do it. I told him the best I could do was take his request under advisement. He accepted that readily enough—"Who in his right mind these days would keep eighty thousand dollars lying around in loose change?" But, he reminded me, there was a small urgency involved, he ought at least to know where he stood by Friday.

Would he hear from me before Friday?

Yes, he would hear from me before Friday.

We shook hands outside the club. He thanked me most courteously, even formally, then wheeled and headed east, erect under the homburg, his stride nimble for his years, even jaunty, and never would anyone passing by have guessed that here was a man who didn't have a nickel in his pockets.

In any case, that Friday morning a messenger from the

firm showed up at my office to pick up the check and the loan agreement, which called for a five-year payback at prime.

That was your doing, Kitten. I must give you full credit.

I even remember the conversation, also the transformed atmosphere in which it took place.

What should I call the atmosphere? Thaw? Détente? Honeymoon?

Whereas, that night after Wanda Russell's party, I'd finally gone home, alone, beset by persistent anxieties, Kitty had apparently undergone a profound sea change. She herself, when she called me the next afternoon, ascribed it to her having revealed so much of her past to me. It was something she never talked about, particularly with men. Too painful, she thought. After all, it had been years out of her life. The fact that she'd told me about it scared her a little. At the same time, she wanted to see me. Wanted to see me very badly.

The same change affected our lovemaking. Gone, at least temporarily, was that desperate rapacity, in its place a gentler and mutual attentiveness. And we talked incessantly, talked about everything, talked even about Thorne.

Yes, she'd had an affair with him, but to all intents and purposes, she said, it had been over by the time she and I had met. At least over for her. The night she'd picked me up at the Christmas party was, she said, an anomaly—it wasn't like her, picking up a total stranger, not her style at all. But she'd used me at the time, used me shamelessly, as her means of escaping from Thorne.

He wasn't, she said, a very nice man. Not nice at all. Their business relationship had survived the affair. It hadn't worked the way ours did. Essentially she'd sold him information on a restricted-use basis, for a flat fee. But that, too—the business relationship—was over.

So Thorne wasn't her Deep Throat?

No, Thorne wasn't her Deep Throat.

But she'd given him Safari, hadn't she?

No, she hadn't. In fact, she'd been as surprised as anyone to hear that he'd made money on Safari.

Then where had he gotten the information?

He must have bought it elsewhere. Given the heavy volume of trading in Safari, we'd hardly been the only ones who knew about it.

"Well, then," I said, "that leaves the million-dollar question, doesn't it? Who *is* our source?"

"Darling . . . my darling Tom," Kitty replied, "I still think that's best left unanswered. I wish like anything I could convince you it doesn't mean I don't love you, or love you less. I'll tell you this much. We're part of a group, a network. I buy us certain information, and we exploit it. If the crunch ever comes, isn't it obvious that the less any one link knows, the better?"

"What you're saying is that I could give you away but not the person above you?"

"That's right. But remember, darling, that cuts both ways."

"Meaning?"

"Simply that 'the person above me,' as you put it, could give me away but not you."

I hadn't, in point of fact, thought about it that way.

"You know," I said, "there's a way of making that link even tighter."

"I don't see what you're saying."

"No?" I raised my eyebrows. "Think about it for a minute. What's the one way you and I could protect

ourselves from ever giving each other away? Perfectly
legal, mind you. It happens all the time.''

She hesitated, then started to laugh. Then stopped and
gazed at me wide-eyed, chin propped on her hand.

''I assume that's a joke, Mr. Thompson,'' she said,
''and not a proposal.''

''It's not a joke,'' I answered.

She looked away then, her hand half covering her
mouth. Eyes averted, unblinking. That chiseled expression, which someone who didn't know her would have
taken for anger or hurt. But when she turned back, her
dark eyes were wet with tears.

''You're quite wonderful, Tommy,'' she said, study-
ing me. ''The problem isn't you; it's what's in me. Underneath this tough exterior, you see, hides a very timid
woman. But I love you for asking, and in your funny
way.''

It was in this climate that we discussed my meeting
with my father. I had long since told Kitty what the
relationship consisted of, and didn't, but she still didn't
see anything unusual in his having come to me for money.
That's what parents did, she said, when they had nowhere
else to turn.

''But he had somewhere else to turn,'' I pointed out.
''He had the Funds, so called.''

''I wouldn't be so sure that he didn't go there.''

''What makes you say that?''

''It would have been the logical thing for him to do.
But the family, at least to judge from your own experience
over your house, would have insisted on some form of
collateral. It could be that he has none to offer, couldn't
it?''

Yes, it could, I thought. It could also be that the Council had turned him down.

''But then why did he lie to me about it?'' I asked.

"Come on, Tommy. Would you really have expected him to grovel at your feet? A man like that?"

Hardly, I thought.

"Look," she went on, "it's your decision, not mine. But it's not so uncommon for children to help their parents out financially, even when there's no love lost between them. Who do you think has taken care of my mother all these years, in Florida? Teddy and me. Yet she begrudged everything she gave us when we were little, and I'm not just talking about money. I had more to do with bringing up Teddy than she did. You can say we're suckers—a part of me does every month when I write out the check—but I'd rather do that than know she's destitute."

"Anyway," I said, "I don't happen to have eighty thousand dollars to throw out the window."

"Oh yes you do," she said blithely. "In fact, you already threw it out the window once, remember? It was more like one hundred twenty-three thousand dollars. You cut it into little pieces and sent it back to me. But it's still yours."

"I don't agree with that."

"Don't agree, then. But I've no objection to your taking the money out of the firm. Who knows? He might even pay it back. Or his seat on this Council of yours might turn out to have some value."

"Yes, and if pigs had wings—"

"I've heard of worse investments. Besides, from what you tell me, the Senator's a proud man, and proud men have a way of doing terrible things as a last resort."

"Meaning . . . ?"

"Meaning that they've been known to kill themselves."

"That sounds pretty melodramatic to me. I don't think he's capable of it, either."

"You're probably right. But knowing you, darling, I'd hate for you to have to live with it in case you were wrong."

Still, I dillydallied over it. Among other things, I found it hard to believe that I *was* his last resort, even though he repeated same when he called me again, to find out what I'd decided.

I put him off one more time. But when I told Kitty, she landed on me.

"Frankly, I think that's cruel, Tommy. If you're not going to do it, you at least ought to have told him so."

"All right. But let me ask you this seriously: Given all the givens, what would you really do in my place?"

"I thought I'd already told you that. I'd give him the money, and I'd do it exactly as he wanted you to—as a loan, with interest and payments. And his place on the Council. I'd even push him to make you Trustee."

"I doubt he has the power to do that."

"No, but you know what I mean."

"And then hope for the best?" I said.

"Yes, hope for the best."

I still didn't know entirely why I did what I did. But I did it.

True to form, I heard nothing from him. The loan agreement was returned to me signed, and the check passed through my bank account. A few months later, however, I received a formal letter from the Stark-Thompson Family Council, announcing my father's resignation and inviting me, with suitable congratulations, to their next meeting.

14

The trouble came between, in two parts.

I'd been expecting the first for some time: a letter from Susan's lawyer, referring me to our divorce agreement, which called for a renegotiation of child support and alimony in the event of a "drastic" change in my circumstances. Such a change having apparently occurred, for which the lawyer offered me her personal congratulations, I was invited to come forward and renegotiate in good faith.

I wondered how and where Susan had gotten her information. I, in turn, had been working on information of a different sort. The divorce agreement also stipulated not only an end to alimony should Susan remarry but a reduction in same should she take up "seriously" with another man. I decided not to answer the lawyer's letter until the private investigator I'd retained delivered his final report.

Part II came in the form of a phone call, then a visit, and totally out of left field.

The phone call:

"This is Henry Angeletti, Mr. Thompson. In Mr. Thatcher's office? I'd very much like to see you personally, if you could spare me some time."

I think I mentioned that Thatcher had several young MBA types working for him. Henry Angeletti was one of them, a tall and lugubrious analyst whose hair had already receded halfway back on his skull even though he couldn't have been more than thirty. I knew him only slightly, for Thatch kept client contacts to himself.

"What's the problem, Henry? Is your boss out on the links this week?"

"Who? Mr. Thatcher? Oh no, he's in his office. This is more in the line of a personal matter."

I noticed that he spoke in low tones, as though he was worried about being overheard.

"What is it then, Henry? You're not looking for another job, are you?"

"Oh no, not that. It's more in the nature of a personal matter. But it's important that I see you."

I looked through my calendar and, in order to get rid of him, suggested a date some two weeks off. This, though, failed to satisfy him. It was a little too urgent, he said. He knew I would agree when I saw him. Finally we settled on 5:30 the next afternoon, but no more than half an hour, which he thought would be long enough, and then I put it out of my mind until 5:25 the next day, when there he was, stooping a little in my doorway, in an ill-fitting brown three-piece suit yet carrying a handsome leather briefcase which might have been Dunhill but looked at least Crouch & Fitzgerald.

At his overture we shook hands. His palm, I remember, was sweating. So for that matter was his forehead even though it was almost winter. He lifted his briefcase to the corner of my desk, opened it with both thumbs, and extracted a thick computer printout bound in blue. This he centered on his side of the desk, lining it up, and then he folded back the blue cover, creasing it with his thumbs to keep it from flipping forward.

There was, it turned out, good reason for him to be sweating. He was carrying a bomb, and, when I found out what it was, I had the presence of mind to turn on my concealed tape recorder.

For the next half hour, perhaps more, Henry Angeletti walked me through the printout. It was his work, he maintained, his work alone, though he had had help gathering the data. On that score, all he'd say (with a self-satisfied smile) was that if you had the right connections on the Street, asked the right questions, got the right access codes, then you could do the rest by telephone, computer talking to computer. The real work, he said, was in sifting through masses of data, manipulating it till it made sense, then drawing the correct conclusions.

He knew only one or two other people who could have done what he'd done, and he himself, he claimed, had almost given up more than once. I'd almost been too clever for him, he said, the way I'd put other people's money to work for me, spreading their accounts among the brokers, then shifting them periodically from house to house. But Safari, he said, had been my mistake. Safari carried my signature loud and clear. In fact, without Safari he never would have thought to look in the first place.

"What went wrong with Safari?" he asked me at some point. Then, answering himself: "I guess you didn't count on it creating so much talk on the Street. Or did you think nobody was watching?"

I don't recall answering.

What Henry Angeletti claimed to have tracked were *my* trading activities over a three-year period, by account and by stock. (I've italicized *my* for reasons which will become apparent in a moment.) He had done it by using my Safari "signature," that is, my pattern of buying and selling, complete with dates and numbers of shares and computer-generated graphs to prove the pattern. The companies he had traced (all involving takeover situations) went from Safari back through Jumping Judy Stores to Manderling's, but then beyond to several I'd never so much as bought a single share of. Similarly, the account list included every last one of mine—the Russell estate, of course, but also Fallowes, Boyd-Rogers, the Lancaster trust, and so on. But these were intermingled on a much longer roster of names, some of which were evidently estates but others partnerships and corporations. Dummy corporations, Angeletti claimed. He admitted he hadn't been able to link every account to me—in many cases I'd covered my tracks too well—but the "signature" was always mine, and this he insisted on demonstrating, case by case, graph by graph.

Endowed as I was with a pretty fair poker face, I doubt I showed the gamut of my reactions. At first, I simply didn't know what the hell he was talking about. As far as my so-called Safari signature went, which was the key to his investigation, I had deliberately limited my dealings on Safari to Wanda Russell. But the more Angeletti went on, mixing things familiar to me with others I'd never heard of, the more the truth dawned on me. I couldn't believe it; then I couldn't *not* believe it. Somehow, by some quirk, or accountant's zeal, or crazy luck, Angeletti had stumbled onto the whole network. The signature he kept talking about clearly wasn't mine alone. Neither, needless to say, were the profits he claimed for me. By the time he got there, though, I realized that I was gripping the arms of my chair so hard that my knuckles showed white.

"By my calculation," he said, head down over the

printout, index finger rapidly descending a row of figures, "and I'm sure I've missed some things, but by my calculation, you have grossed, minimum, over a three-year period, just under a hundred and eighty million dollars in profits."

A hundred and eighty million dollars. $180,000,000.00. I have no idea whether I thought it in words or digits.

I became aware that he was looking up at me, his narrow face in a half and expectant smile, a little like some hotshot student who, having completed his oral report, now awaited the professor's gold star.

"Well, Henry," I said finally. "What, if anything, do you really expect me to make of all this?"

"Make of it? Well, nothing more than what I said. That over a three-year period you made an incredible profit."

"So? Assuming that's true, which is a very large assumption, I also assume you didn't come here just to congratulate me."

No, he hadn't, though he did think congratulations were in order. He was filled with admiration for what I'd accomplished. How exactly I'd done it would be interesting too, though less so to him probably than to some other people.

Such as?

Such as the U.S. Attorney, the SEC, the NYSE. He even mentioned the congressional subcommittee that, because it involved national resources, had announced hearings into the Safari affair.

"And yet you've come to me," I said.

"Yes."

"First?"

"Yes, first."

"Why?"

"Because, like I say, I admire you for it. Also because you've got a great deal to lose by being exposed."

The heart of the matter, in sum. I suppose, in this era of greed and suspicion, the shakedown can come in any shape or form. Henry Angeletti was as unlikely a practitioner as I could imagine. Yet there he was, unblinking, eyebrows up, leaning forward, telling me what he wanted.

It could go one of two ways, he said. Or one of three, actually, because I could always buy his disks outright. But he'd already rejected that solution, because it would mean I'd have to trust him not to make a duplicate set, and why would I do that? A better way would be for me to give him a percentage of my profits, a sort of finder's fee. It could be a very small percentage, one I wouldn't even notice. Say as low as one percent? The best of all, though, from both our points of view, involved no money. He wanted my information, that was all. The same information I was using myself, as soon as I got it, and that way it wouldn't cost me a nickel.

In spite of everything, I found myself laughing inside at the thought that, somewhere in all of us, even the Henry Angelettis, there flickers the entrepreneurial flame. Outwardly, though, I maintained my poker face. It seemed, moreover, a good time to raise Henry's bet.

"You mean you want to go into business for yourself?"

"Yes. But only in a small way. Nothing like your scale."

"My information in exchange for your silence, is that it?"

"Yes."

I stared at him, unsmiling.

"I don't know, Henry," I said, "but it sounds like blackmail to me."

"Blackmail? Well . . ."

"What do you think would happen if I took all this to Thatcher and told him everything?"

"To *Thatcher*?" His eyebrows rose again, this time in incredulity. "You wouldn't do that."

"Why not? After all, I'm his aunt's attorney and one of his most valued clients. Thatch probably wouldn't understand half of all your stuff there. I doubt he'd even try. But if I pushed him on it, I bet I could have you out on your ear within an hour. Do you disagree?"

He didn't answer.

"I'm not saying I'm *going* to do that," I went on. "Or anything like that. It might well not be in my best interests. But it's something you should think about, Henry. And as far as the SEC et al. are concerned, the threats you made—"

"They weren't threats," he interrupted.

"Well, I'm glad to hear that. They certainly sounded like threats to me."

As an attorney, I went on, I found all the work he'd done, the material he'd developed, purely conjectural. Presumably I'd made a great deal of money for my clients in the stock market. Presumably I'd done it because I had information, presumably privileged or insider information, presumably illegal. But where, in all these presumptions, was the evidence? He hadn't produced a single shred of evidence to support his claim, and lacking evidence, what did he think the agencies investigating the market would make of it? The way I understood it, they were already overworked and understaffed, with dozens of leads they didn't have the manpower to follow up on. What made him so sure he'd even get a hearing?

He said nothing. I was about to remind him, furthermore, that attempted blackmail is a felony, but when I saw him swallow hard, his Adam's apple bobbing under

a paled and narrow face, I stopped short—not out of
sympathy, needless to say, but I sensed a risk in cornering
him.

"Look, Henry," I said, "the truth is that I find the
work you've done absolutely brilliant, if a little quirky.
Naturally you want to be compensated for it. It could be
that I'll want to do something for you in that direction.
It could also be that I'll decide to do nothing. There's
no way, though, that I'm going to give you the answer
today. The best I can say right now is that I'll take the
matter under advisement."

Angeletti seemed relieved to hear this. He stood up
awkwardly and fumbled with the printout, getting it back
into his briefcase.

"When will you decide?" he said.

"I'll call you Monday."

"No," he said. "I'd rather call you. I'll call you Monday."

"Good," I said.

And then he was gone.

And then I, suddenly rubber-legged, sat down again
in a state of semishock.

I was due to meet Kitty. I couldn't bring myself to
move, though, and when my phone rang a little later, I
let it ring. Any way I looked at my situation, I felt vulnerable. A hundred and eighty million dollars. It did no
good to tell myself that Angeletti had made a mistake,
that I was responsible for only a piece of it, or that he
could clearly be bought. As far as the meeting itself went,
I thought I'd performed reasonably well. At least I'd
conceded nothing and had bought us time. But who was
us? Me? Me and Kitty? Me and Kitty and who else?
Furthermore, at the risk of damaging Angeletti's frail
ego, was he really the only one in the world who could
perform the same analysis? How did I know that there

wasn't some other gnome, tall or short, sifting data on his computer screen in some rabbit-warren office, spotting a connection here, a correlation there?

Because he worked for Thatcher, Angeletti had focused on me. Maybe someone else, tracking from a different starting point, would discover the links elsewhere. But what did that matter? In this day and age, the first one caught saved his skin by implicating another, and the second implicated the third, the third the fourth, the fourth the fifth, until the chain stopped and one or more went to jail. Which line of reasoning led to another question I still couldn't answer definitively: Who, if anyone, knew about me besides Kitty?

Even so, the full impact of what had happened didn't hit home until, having closed the office and ridden down in the elevator, I reached the street outside my building. It was dark out, and in that brief lull between the workaday crowd and the night people, the sidewalk was largely deserted. High banks of blackened snow, strewn with debris and garbage, hid the gutters, limiting the traffic on the street to a single file, and a cruel wind swept the canyon from west to east. Like most of us, I'd always tended to suppress potential danger, so that while, yes, I had been aware of risk from the time of Manderling's and the Sprague estate, and while, yes, when I left the firm, I'd known full well that I was crossing a line, I'd never let myself believe I'd ever be confronted, cornered, caught. Somebody else—not me. But that night, making my way toward Kitty's in the crusted, icy slush, the forces of the city, which I'd always thought indifferent to me, now joined in open and watchful hostility, and the gusting winds that chased me toward the park hissed at my head in scornful mockery, and the people I passed, strangers all—didn't they already know, hadn't they already seen

the headlines? LAWYER FINGERED IN PROBE, SENATOR'S
SON.

Kitty and I had planned to go to the theater that night.
Instead we stayed home and listened to the tape recording
I'd made.

One thing became clear as a bell: unless he was a very
accomplished dissembler, Henry Angeletti had nothing
on me, or anyone, beyond the half-right, half-wrong in-
ferences he'd drawn. It didn't seem even to have occurred
to him that anyone other than I had been dealing with
the same "signature."

But who else *had* been dealing? That was the key
question.

Kitty claimed she didn't know.

What about Thorne? I asked.

Thorne, possibly.

But only Thorne?

Unlikely.

Then who else?

She didn't know. She claimed, though, that she was
going to find out.

Beyond this, I couldn't budge her. No, she wouldn't
tell me who else was involved in the network. Didn't the
very fact that Angeletti had bungled his analysis prove
her point, unpleasant though it had been for me to have
to confront him?

But what, I asked, if someone else, not Angeletti,
followed the "signature" from another direction?

That, she said, was just what she had to find out.

"You know, darling," she said to me, "I have to hand
it to you. You handled him beautifully."

"That and a dollar will get me on the subway," I
answered.

"But you don't take subways anymore, remember?"

Besides, she said, we had until Monday, I had gained

us that, and long before Monday, she promised, we would know how to deal with Mr. Angeletti. Meanwhile, I should stop worrying about it.

"My poor darling," she said, putting her arms around my neck. "You're a wreck. Come. Why don't you let Kitten take care of you?"

And so, in her inimitable way, she did.

It would be easy to say, in hindsight, that we should have quit right then, that night, quit while we were ahead and taken the money and headed for the hills. The Costa Rican hills, for instance, or those of Brazil, or any place where life was cheap and extradition treaties nonexistent. But the subject never even came up. And given who we were, I suppose it would have been as easy to stop the clocks of the world, freezing time, while the two of us lay enswathed in each other's arms, in the warm womb of Kitty's bed.

The next night she had a party to organize and I my every-other-month poker game. I almost didn't go, but the prospect of an evening alone daunted me more than the company of Buck Charles et al. As someone observed, my game lacked its usual "intrepid" style. True enough. I simply couldn't concentrate, folded early and often, and managed to duck out before the last round.

I went home to my apartment, a new and antiseptic four-room condo which had cost a small fortune, and there I found Kitty ensconced in a comfortable chair, her legs tucked under her, watching some movie on television.

A rarity, that she be there at all. Most of the time I myself used the place only to change clothes.

"What are you doing here?" I said.

"Waiting for you."

"But I thought you had a party?"

"I didn't go. I sent Bettina instead."

Bettina was her Number Two in Katherine Goldmark Enterprises, a frowsy redhead whom Kitty swore by. Still, Kitty herself always at least put in an appearance.

"But how long have you been here?"

She shrugged. "A while."

I bent over, kissed her.

"How was the poker?" she said.

"Boring."

I slumped into the matching chair next to hers.

Presently she pushed the off button on the remote, then stood, stretched—in her stocking feet, I noticed—and leaned over me, her hands propped on the arms of my chair, hair down and almost brushing my face.

"Well?" I said. "What did you find out?"

"In a minute," she answered. "I want to kiss you properly first."

This she did, licking my lips apart with the tip of her tongue, then, as was her way, opening her mouth wide to me. I reached to pull her to me, but she backed off. Still propped on the arms of my chair, she now stared at me, lips still a little separated, eyes intent on mine.

"I need your help," she said.

"Your wish is my command, lady," I replied, smiling up at her.

She shook her head.

"It's not a joke, Tommy," she said. She seemed to be measuring me, as though to give herself one last chance to decide if she'd misjudged me. Then: "There's someone we have to get rid of. I promise you, it's the only way. You're going to help me kill him."

"Who?" I think I answered, and I must have named somebody outlandish because I remember her repeating that it wasn't a joke.

No, clearly it wasn't. That much was evident in her

impassive expression. Her cheekbones glistened in the light, and her eyes, dark and penetrating, kept me from turning my head one way or the other.

"Who?" I said again, staring back at her.

"Robert Thorne," she answered.

15

I guess he didn't have much of a chance, not once he'd agreed to meet her. He had a house way out on the North Shore, and that was where Kitty went that Saturday afternoon with, of all things, a picnic hamper in the back seat of her rented car.

A last supper, you could say, for Robert Thorne.

I carried it downstairs for her and put it in the car. Also a large tote. It was mid March, gray and newly cold, freezing cold. We got into the car together in full view of the doorman and drove off eastward where, a few blocks later, Kitty dropped me off. Then she, the woman I loved, went off to seduce another man, and I went into the movie theater off Third Avenue. I've no idea what was playing. I walked out again after a while, went into a bookstore on Third Avenue, bought nothing. From that time until I picked up my own rented car at an all-night garage in the Village, I have no recollection.

Oh, yes: what I was wearing: The old alpaca-lined great-coat, one of my few remaining relics of the past, and a heavy seaman's sweater she'd given me with buttons across one shoulder. I remember stopping on the Long Island Expressway to take the coat off and driving the rest of the way with the window down. Alone. The radio loud against the wind noise.

I, in my way, had no more of a chance than Thorne. Not after that night in my apartment.

The way Kitty explained it, someone else in the network had sold Thorne Safari. She claimed not even to have suspected it until the night of Wanda's party. Thorne had apparently been made to pay through the nose, and with no controls over what he did with the information, he'd gone haywire. Many of the accounts I hadn't recognized in the Angeletti meeting were, according to Kitty, traceable to Thorne. The limited partnerships, the dummy corporation—all Thorne's.

Worse, she'd learned that Thorne was already under investigation, for other matters as well as Safari. Worst of all, she was convinced that, under pressure and given the chance to make a deal, Thorne would crack. Would name names, sources, transactions. Kitty Goldmark included.

He had to be stopped; it had to be done fast.

But Jesus Christ, she was talking about murder! And not only meant it but had it already planned!

What I actually said was: "For God's sake, Kitty, that's murder!"

I must also have said something like: "People like us don't do things like that," because I remember her glaring down at me, lips tight.

"*People like us*?" she said. "What does that mean? Who do you think we are, anyway? We've already crossed that line, dear heart. We could go to jail for what we've done."

"Yes, in theory. But you've always assured me that it can't be traced back."

"Well, maybe I was wrong. I'm sorry, but maybe I was wrong. Don't you understand? If Thorne gives them the network, the parts he knows about, anyway, and then they investigate all the other transactions in Safari? That's how they'll find you, too, Tommy. Angeletti in reverse. They'll back into it, whether they link you directly to me or not."

"I can see that," I answered. "But does that justify murder?"

"Would you rather go to jail, Tommy darling? Would you rather wreck your life? Our life? Or is it that, deep down, you think that somebody will get you off in the end?"

I'd never known her tone to be so cutting. I fell silent, but my silence only fueled her sarcasm.

"What makes you so *moral* all of a sudden? This isn't prep school, you know. You haven't just been caught cheating on some test."

My reflex, when faced with that kind of bigotry-in-reverse, is invariably to fold up my tent. But this was Kitty, this was the woman I loved...

"There has to be another way," I said as calmly as I could.

"There isn't, believe me."

"No? Why can't we buy him off?"

She shook her head.

"It's too late for that. Besides, I know the man."

I tried to visualize Thorne. *Devastatingly handsome*, Martine Brady had called him at Wanda's party. The shock of white hair. I'd also gotten the impression, from something Martine had said, that he liked beating up on women. Beyond that, nothing.

But what unholy difference did it make what I knew of him?

None whatsoever. All irrelevant, totally irrelevant. Kitty herself made that abundantly clear.

"There's no choice," she said. "Believe me, I've looked. *We've* got to deal with it, and we've got to do the dirty work ourselves."

"Even when the dirty work is murder?"

"Even when the dirty work is murder."

I was having trouble taking it in. At the same time, I felt myself slipping, sliding, and no place to grab on to. No place except Kitty, who stood before me, staring me down.

"You're going to do this with me, Tommy. There's no other way."

"And what if I refuse?"

"You won't refuse."

"Why not?"

"You don't need me to answer that."

"Maybe I do," I said.

"Very well," she answered implacably. "We're either in it together or we're not. If we're not, then it's all over between us. You and I are finished."

A long time later I might wonder where she got the strength. But all I could think of on the spot, all I could blurt out, was:

"What the hell is it that always makes you so goddamn *sure* of me?"

No answer.

Maybe she wasn't always so sure. That night, at least, I think she had simply steeled herself to run any and all risks.

But I felt a bitter reflex, the need to strike back at her even in defeat.

"Let me ask you this, Kitty. Suppose I do refuse after all, and suppose we do break up. What makes you so sure I wouldn't turn witness against you, too? Just like Thorne?''

For a split second I saw the hurt surprise in her eyes. Then she ducked away, shaking her head.

"You wouldn't do that," I heard her say.

"Oh, no?" I persisted. "And why the hell not? Wouldn't I logically do it to save my own skin? And hadn't you better kill me too, just to make sure?''

"You wouldn't do that, Tommy," she repeated.

"Why not? Tell me why not?''

"Because you love me too much," she said hoarsely.

At this she turned fully away, neck and shoulders bowed, and I could see her body shaking despite her efforts to control it. And then, so help me, I took her in my arms.

Kitty had given me precise instructions, including a map and an elevation sketch of the house. I was to be there by midnight and park on the side of the road outside the property, where I'd have a full view of the house. Possibly I'd hear shots. Either way, I was to wait for a light to go on in a particular second-floor window, signal that the deed was done. If the light hadn't gone on by one in the morning, it would mean that, for whatever reason, she had failed. In that case I was to go home.

I arrived a little after eleven. The light was already on in the upstairs window. What I hadn't expected was that there were lights on throughout the ground floor, too. The house, a rambling turn-of-the-century affair with a wraparound veranda, resembled some sort of cruise ship in the night, perched on a bare bluff overlooking the Sound, and at a glance you'd have thought a party was going on, unlikely though that would have been at that time of the year. In any case, I was clearly too early. I debated whether to drive on and return later, but I was afraid of losing my way on the winding road. Instead I parked as planned, turned off the motor and the headlights, and hunkered down in my seat, my eyes on the house.

At some point, without my noticing it at first, the lights started to go off downstairs, one after the other, as though someone were walking through the rooms. Then darkness below, but the single light remaining above.

A car passed in the opposite direction, its headlights swerving over my head. Then nothing, quiet. The wind sound, that was all.

Could she already have done it?

At eleven forty-five I got out of the car into the freezing air, put my coat on, and walked up the curving driveway, shifting from gravel to the lawn when I heard my own footsteps. I was now in almost total darkness, but my vision had adjusted sufficiently to make out the shape of two cars parked beyond the porte cochère. One was Kitty's, I assumed, one his. Slowly I went up the front steps to the veranda, listening, hearing nothing except the wind and some distant tinkling sound. I saw a pinpoint of green light next to the front door, an alarm system, the alarm off. Then, suddenly: abrupt movement. The door open. Kitty's voice, impatient, from the darkness.

"For God's sake, where have you been?"

Her voice sounded like a shout in the silence. I started to say something, but she cut me off.

"It's done. I've been waiting for you for almost an hour. Come in."

She touched a light switch, illuminating the staircase directly in front of me, a dark wood affair that doubled back on itself.

"Where is he?" I said.

"Upstairs. Come on. We're wasting time."

In the upstairs light, I saw that her face had taken on a waxy pallor. Later she admitted that she'd thrown up. Her victim lay naked on his bed, face down, head wrapped in a towel with the ends tucked in, and the murder weapon lay on an empty pillowcase on the floor.

She'd gone there, I knew, intending to shoot him. Instead, she'd quite literally clubbed him to death.

For God's sake, though, he was almost twice her size! How had she done it?

In his sleep, she said.

I could think of only one way she'd have gotten him to sleep. I pictured them, or half pictured them (as though through the fingers of my hand, spread across my eyes), and Kitty then sliding from the bed noiselessly and lifting the weapon above her head with both hands . . .

"I couldn't move him without you," she said. "We have to get his clothes on first, anyway."

I hesitated before touching him. I'd never seen a dead man close up who hadn't been prepared for viewing, and never a victim of violence. Bloody violence, too, for when we inadvertently pulled the towel free from his scalp, there was a fresh ooze of blood. His body felt heavy, deadweight. Together we propped him into a sitting position, where I held him, maneuvering his arms, while Kitty dressed him. White button-down shirt, V-neck cashmere, blue blazer. No tie. Then flat on his back while we did the underpants and trousers. Gray flannels. Ragg socks. Cordovan loafers.

Kitty debated about an overcoat, then decided that he'd have gone out without one.

I struggled under his weight, carrying him downstairs and outside while Kitty led the way. She opened the passenger door to his four-door convertible, and I deposited him inside. Then we returned to the house to clean up.

Blood had soaked through the sheets on his bed, and a little had even worked its way under the rubberized sheet that covered the mattress itself. I bundled the sheets and the pad and stuffed them into Kitty's tote, an enormous carryall, while she scrubbed at the mattress. The weapon went into the tote, too, in its pillowcase shroud, all for me to dispose of the next day. Kitty decided to turn the mattress, and I remade the bed while she wiped the room clean of fingerprints. Downstairs in the kitchen she repacked the picnic hamper, putting Thorne's dishes and glassware into the dishwasher. She filled the soap receptacle, then closed the door and turned the machine on.

I loaded the tote and the hamper into the trunk of Kitty's car. Then we met by the front door, and she worried as to whether to lock the house, putting the keys in Thorne's pocket, or to leave the keys in the inside alarm lock and the system off.

"What would you do?" she asked me.

"It would depend on where I was going," I answered.

"To an assignation," Kitty said.

"How long will I be gone?"

"At least till morning."

"But I'm coming back? And my usual habit is to leave the house open?"

"That's right."

"Then let's leave it open."

And so we did.

There was, however, one small problem. When I got behind the wheel of Thorne's Cadillac, I called out to Kitty for his car keys. She didn't have them. As carefully as she'd planned every step, she'd forgotten about

Thorne's car keys, and the fact that she'd overlooked them threw her into a temporary panic.

"For God's sake!" she shouted at me. "Look in his goddamn pockets!"

I managed to, awkwardly, but found no keys.

Then Kitty, cursing, ran back into the house.

I sat in the dark for a moment. Then, perhaps because I'd done the same thing myself, I started running my hands into various possible hiding places until, sure enough, I found them. They were tucked into the overhead visor on the passenger's side.

I retrieved Kitty. We drove off, she leading the way in her car. The spot she had chosen was one where the cliff line jutted out into the Sound. There was no guardrail around the curve in the road, just a wide place beyond the macadam shoulder where cars could park, and steps cut into the face of the cliff where you could make your way down to the rocky inlet.

Following her signal, I parked beside her. A strong and icy wet wind blew into our faces, and distantly, it seemed, you could hear the sound of water crashing onto rocks. Kitty had the rest of it precisely planned, down to the positioning of Thorne's car. From a spouted metal can he carried in his trunk, we doused his upholstery with gasoline, front and back, including the convertible roof, and opened his gas tank cover. Then, cumbersomely, we propped his body behind the steering wheel and fastened the seat belt. Kitty called to me to get the towel off his head. It was stuck to his skin, and I had to tear it free. Then, reaching in, depressing the brake pedal with my left hand, I turned on the headlights, then the ignition, and with my right hand shifted the transmission into drive. I released the brake pedal, jerked my body free, slammed shut the passenger door, and General Motors engineering did the rest.

The car seemed to hesitate, just for a second, when it reached the edge. Then it continued forward, in slow motion. Over. Gone.

Kitty had said there was a risk it wouldn't ignite, in which case we'd have to climb down the cove. It did, though. We heard the sound of one explosion. Then heard, and saw, a second and larger one.

"Done," Kitty said beside me.

She drove us back to Thorne's house. Totally dark now, its shape even darker than the background sky. I got out. In the dim interior light of her car, I saw Kitty adjust the rearview mirror so as to examine her face, and she fluffed her hair, pinched color into her cheeks. She reminded me again of the side street in the city where I was supposed to park and wait for her to pick me up.

"I love you, Tommy," she said, reaching one hand toward me. "I couldn't have done it without you."

I drove back to New York with the windows wide open despite the cold, and still I couldn't get the reek of gasoline, Thorne's gasoline, out of my nostrils. I parked as agreed, and within thirty minutes Kitty pulled in behind me. We drove around to her building, where, in view of the night doorman, we unloaded the remains of our outing, and Kitty carried them upstairs while I returned her car to its rental garage.

It was after four in the morning by the time I got back, closer to five. Kitty had a CD playing—something Mozartean, I'm sure—and a drink ready to hand me. She had already showered and changed her clothes. Her hair was wet.

"I don't know how it's possible," I said, "but I feel wide awake."

"Me too. Are you hungry?"

"No," I said, sipping from my drink. "But I want a shower."

I stood in the stall in her bathroom, jets as hot as I could stand beating down on me. My clothes were piled in a heap outside. I wanted to destroy them, incinerate them, along with their smell of gasoline. I imagined in the hot steam that if I could erase the smell, I could erase the night, too, like a dream that, no matter how vivid, you can no longer summon to memory the next day. But when I got out of the shower, the pile of clothes was still there and the gasoline fumes now seemed to cling to the wet towel I held in my hands.

Kitty was waiting for me in the bedroom, stretched in her silk robe on the Récamier sofa. She was listening to the music. Her dark hair, still damp, had begun to form little ringlets as it always did when she didn't blow-dry it.

A faint smile on her face.

"Better?" she said.

"A little."

"Are you hungry now, poor darling?"

"No." I couldn't, though, remember when I'd last eaten.

"Well, I am," she said, reaching for me.

"Please, Kitty," I said. "I'm not sure I'm up to it."

"Oh yes you are. Let Kitten show you that you're up to it."

She laughed, a low chuckle, and rose to her knees on the sofa, holding firmly to my stem while she began to lick its underside.

I felt heat, nauseating heat, spreading in my stomach, and the fumes in my nostrils, and her wet hair crushed in my fist.

She fell back, her robe open, her hands pulling me firmly, inexorably, inside her. She was right: I was up to it. But when she came, her nails digging into my back, her voice in its raucous, rhythmic cry, I was, I think for the first time, genuinely afraid of her.

In time, though, that too passed.

PART
THREE

16

We were married the following June.

It was an outdoor wedding, held on the lawn of our new house under a *chuppa*, one of those four-pole canopies which, in Jewish practice, is held over the bride and groom, supposedly to symbolize the happy home-to-be. Kitty had found a rabbi who had agreed to officiate over a mixed union and in fact waxed quite eloquent about these two "strangers" (presumably a Jew and a Christian) who had chosen to join in the joyful and sacred mysteries of marriage.

Over a hundred people attended, but representation on my side was sparse. My mother sent regrets and a gift. For the second time in my life my father, newly returned from Europe, told me I was a fool for marrying. She simply wasn't our kind, he said. (He sent no gift.) My children were there, over their mother's and Kitty's objections. So were Art Fording and Phil Lamont, both lawyers and among my oldest friends. So—finally and to my surprise—was Mac Coombs, now slowed of gait and in the process, I'd heard, of being pushed out of the

firm himself, but still able to kiss the bride and squire
her around the outdoor dance floor.

It was, in any case, Kitty's show. She said she had
always wanted to be married in June and outdoors, in a
long white gown with a lace veil and a bouquet of orchids
in her hands, and the men in morning suits, and a string
quartet to play the Handel. And so it came to pass, on a
warm and lovely Sunday, with her brother to give her
away and her mother, a rather crabby old woman, in
attendance with, as they say, a hundred or so of Kitty's
closest friends.

Why, one might ask, did we marry? The stormy passion of our "courtship," if that is the word, had not
abated, and in fact the Thorne affair had locked us into
each other more than would any prayer or sworn vow.
Why bother, then? Kitty said she needed the respectability of marriage. There was a part of her, she admitted,
that craved the normalcy of the hausfrau. Having proved
that she could succeed in the business world, and though
she had no intention of giving up her company, she yet
wanted something else out of life. Something more. Even
that there be people in the world who knew her as Mrs.
Thompson instead of Ms. Goldmark. Beyond herself,
she wanted respectability for us, too, wanted us to be
Mr. and Mrs. Stark Thompson openly.

"In other words," I remember saying to her sotto voce
as we greeted our guests, "I've finally earned you."

"And I," she answered back, laughing up at me with
her eyes, "have just married an elephant."

Of course, in hindsight, Kitty had other things in mind
as well. As for me, if I took to telling people flippantly
that it was just in the genes (people, that is, who could
appreciate my father's marital record), the truth was even
simpler: I wanted Kitty. Therefore, I wanted what Kitty

wanted. And if that included the bonds of matrimony, so much the better.

The Thorne affair—that was how we referred to it—had put an end to the network's activities. For the time being, at least, we were shut down, even though, as far as anyone could tell, we were clean on the various on-going Safari investigations. The paper trail that had led people to Thorne ended in the North Shore cove. While my own activities might still be investigated independently, there was no way I could be linked to Thorne, no reason I couldn't stonewall, and this because, as Kitty pointed out, she hadn't budged on revealing the network to me. Knowing could only harm me now, she said, and, in theory, put other people at risk. There would be no benefit to anyone, she said. And the only response I got from her, when it was announced that Mr. Henry Angeletti had joined Braxton's as an associate managing director, reporting directly to Mr. Theodore Goldmark, was: "If you want to know, why don't you ask Teddy yourself?"

I will come back shortly to my new brother-in-law.

The police investigation into Thorne's death brushed against us and then, like the shadow of a cloud on a windy day, moved on. The authorities, it seemed, were no closer to determining whether suicide, accident, or foul play had been the cause, but in the course of following leads, a Suffolk County detective visited the offices of Katherine Goldmark Enterprises. Why? For two reasons. One: Thorne and Kitty Goldmark had once been romantically linked. Two: Thorne had paid Katherine Goldmark Enterprises considerable sums of money on several different occasions, going back months, even years, before his death. But Thorne, it turned out, had been a great party giver, and Kitty's catering services, which had been properly billed in each instance, did not come cheap. In addition, Kitty pointed out to the detective, the romance between them, such as it had been, had long since ended.

In fact, the Thorne affair had other, potentially more troublesome consequences for me. My success with my blue-haired ladies had brought me new clients, which had meant expanding my practice, hence my staff, and both new and old clients now expected repeat performances from me. Wanda Russell, for instance, embracing me after the wedding ceremony, said, "What's happened to us, Tommy? It's been so quiet since Safari, I'm positively bored!" As I explained to Wanda, and others, opportunities of that kind didn't come along every day. I counseled patience. No one complained—for the moment. But I foresaw the day when I would have become just another estate manager, no more or less effective than the rank and file but with the single difference that, while the rank and file charged the same management fee in good times and bad, I profited only when my clients profited.

"So?" Kitty advised. "Start charging a fee like everybody else. Only make yours larger."

Knowing my Wanda Russells, though, I postponed that day.

Another adverse financial situation could, however, no longer be postponed. Despite their efforts, the agency I'd hired to investigate Susan had come up virtually empty-handed. Our divorce agreement had scarcely precluded her from seeing other men, even sleeping with them, and while we knew she had a steady lover, we couldn't prove anything resembling "cohabitation." Meanwhile, her lawyer had started to press me to renegotiate. Meanwhile, Kitty and I had decided to get married.

"Settle it," Kitty advised me. "Don't show them financial statements if you don't want to, but make them an offer, knowing that whatever you offer won't be enough. But do it now.''

"You mean because we're going to get married?"

"Exactly."

"But she and I have been divorced for six *years!*"

"It doesn't matter. The minute she hears you're remarrying, she'll feel scorned all over again and the price will go up. And if you insist on having your children at the wedding, though I still don't see why, then you'd better be generous.''

In the end, against my own better judgment, I was more than generous, but when I told Susan I was remarrying and that I was going to invite the children to the wedding, I ran, as Kitty had predicted, into a wall.

"Who's the lucky woman?" Susan asked acidly over the telephone.

"I don't think you know her. Her name's Kitty Goldmark.''

"Oh, I've heard of her. I mean, she's the woman who does parties, isn't she? But isn't she Jewish?"

"Yes, she is."

"Well . . ." Pause. "Well, you'll never cease to amaze me, Tommy.''

"I want the children to attend."

Another pause. "Well, I don't think it's a good idea."

"What the hell does that mean?"

"Just what I said. I mean, it's traumatic enough their father marrying someone else, but, I mean—"

"I think they're old enough to decide for themselves whether they want to come or not.''

"Well, I don't."

"Look, Susan," I said, trying to control myself and only half succeeding, "we've just completed a negotiation that has turned out to be pretty generous for you. Do you want to continue to get your checks on the first

of the month? Or do you want to have to go to court to
get them?''

"You bastard.''

"Maybe I am, but I want the children to come, if they
want to—and without your poisoning the well.''

And so they did.

Why was it important for me that they be there? Good
question, the more so when Kitty, to put it in its brutal
form, clearly had no use for them. And my link to them,
as described, had been at best tenuous for some time.
Still, for a man who was burning most of his bridges, in
fact already had, the few that remained seemed worth
preserving.

So my children attended the wedding too. And felt, I
thought, awkward and out of place, knowing no one. But
they were there, and heard their father blessed in Hebrew
and in English, and saw him dance with his bride, their
new stepmother, to the corny old Berlin tune "Always"
(the string quartet having by then been replaced, or aug-
mented, by the instruments of a swing band), and they
stayed until Kitty tossed her bouquet, when I saw them
off in the chauffered car I'd hired for the purpose.

We had decided—Kitty's one departure from tradition—not to go off on a honeymoon. The timing was
wrong for Kitty's business. Then, too, she hated the
custom of the bride and groom leaving, thereby aban-
doning their wedding guests to their fate. It was *her* party,
after all; she wanted to be there when the last one went
home. So, after Mary Laura and Starkie left, I wandered
back across the lawn, looking for her among the dancers
under the striped awning and the people sitting at the
shaded little tables that dotted the grounds. And, not
finding her, made my way toward and into the house.

We had bought what the real estate people called a
center-hall Colonial, a large redbrick affair of Georgian

inspiration, with tall white columns and white trim and shutters. It had been constructed in the 1920s. The gardens were of English style, lovingly tended, and included a trellised and slate-paved rose arbor, which was in full, glorious bloom for the wedding. Kitty had chosen the place and had virtually stripped the interiors. Few of our old possessions adorned the main rooms, which, though they had been tastefully redecorated, still had that new feel and look, that smell of paint, stain, wax, which only a few seasons of living would dispel. For myself, I liked it well enough, but I scarcely felt as though it belonged to me, or I to it.

I walked in on what I assumed was a family council. More row apparently than council. Ted Goldmark had just shouted something as I entered—some taunt or gibe, I gathered, for his face was twisted into a sardonic smile, and Kitty, having burst into tears, rushed past me in the doorway, head down. She glanced briefly in my direction, without apparent recognition, then ran on up the center staircase, tripping on her gown as she went.

"What's going on?" I asked, but Goldmark had already turned away and Kitty was on her way up the stairs.

I caught up with her on the second-floor landing.

"What's going on?" I repeated, taking her by the arm.

"*Nothing's* going on!" she said hoarsely.

"Hey, wait a minute. This is *me*, remember? Your lover and admirer and brand-new husband?"

This didn't make much of a dent. Kitty turned toward me, her face small in a grimace of tears, and her expression told me that having to deal with me, too, right then, was more than she could handle.

"It's nothing, Tommy. Family. My brother's a son of a bitch. What else is new? Just leave me alone now, please. I just want to be left alone."

"But what did he say?"

At this she pulled free of me, not for the first time in our relationship, and stumbled off in a blur of white to what I thought was our new bedroom, where she slammed the door behind her.

I retreated down the stairs, shaking my head, and found Ted Goldmark pouring himself a Scotch at the bar in the living room. For some reason this irritated me.

"What happened between you and Kitty?" I asked him.

"Oh, nothing. Nothing, really. What did she say?"

"She called you a son of a bitch."

"Is that all?" he said, laughing. "Usually she calls me worse. Look, Tommy," he said, "I don't have to tell you this, but she's a very emotional woman. I think probably the wedding's gotten to her. Can I pour you one?"

He gestured with the bottle of Laphroaig. I shook my head.

"What do you mean, 'The wedding's gotten to her'?"

"Oh, you know," he answered with a shrug. "Women cry on their wedding days. And she had one bad marriage. I myself advised her against it, but you know Kitty. A long time ago anyway, and that sure doesn't mean she doesn't love you, old man. I *know* she does."

Goldmark, if it needs pointing out, was the kind of man who'd never miss an opportunity to impress you somehow—in this instance, I suppose, with his knowledge of brides in general and his sister in particular. I'd once thought it was the short-man syndrome: he was only a few inches taller than Kitty. Or because he was, after all, Jewish in an all-Wasp outfit. Until quite recently, remember, Wall Street had had its Kuhn, Loebs and its Lehmans on the one hand and its Paine Webbers and Smith Barneys on the other, and ne'er the twain shall meet, and the fact that Goldmark had reached the topmost echelon in a place like Braxton's still brought everything he did or said into a kind of limelight—a fact he himself seemed to relish.

He was known in his trade as a shark. Depending on who said it, that could be taken either pejoratively or complimentarily. He was considered good-looking: he had a mass of curly black locks and dark, busy eyes to go with his quick, glib manner. I'd heard him called both a workaholic and a skirt-chaser—when he appeared in public, it was always with some new model on his arm— but I'd also heard some speculation that he was gay because, now in his mid thirties, he'd never married.

Facing him there, in my new and as yet unlived-in living room in our matching morning suits with boutonnieres, I felt a keen antipathy. By my quick calculation, when "he himself" had advised Kitty against marrying Sprague, he'd have been in his teens. And here he was, reassuring me that Kitty loved me and sipping my Scotch as though he himself owned the place.

"There's something I've been meaning to ask you," I said.

"Shoot."

"How come you hired Henry Angeletti?"

I watched him for a reaction but saw only the characteristic half smile.

"Henry?" he said. "Well, he's an excellent recruit for us at Braxton's. And he was pretty much buried, working for good ole Thatch."

I could guess without asking what Goldmark would think of Thatcher.

"Is that the only reason?"

"Sure. Henry's brilliant, hard-working—what more do you want? But why are you asking?"

"Because Kitty suggested I should."

"Oh?" His eyebrows raised.

"Yes. I asked her if she thought it had anything to do with Safari and certain other related matters. And she said if I wanted to know I should ask you."

"Did she really?" The eyebrows again.

"Yes, she did."

He seemed to think over his answer before giving it. I understood, I thought, why Kitty had contrived to keep us apart, and why she never spoke of her brother without a certain edge to her voice.

"Look, Tommy," he said smoothly, "you're a very smart man. You don't need me to tell you that. And you've just married a very smart lady. I'd have thought both of you were smart enough to understand that sometimes it's better not to dig into things after the fact."

"Let sleeping dogs lie, so to speak?"

"Exactly."

"Like one hundred eighty million dollars' worth of sleeping dogs?"

He frowned at me over the rim of his glass, not answering.

"And Thorne, too?" I said.

"Poor Thorny," he said coolly, his eyes still on mine. "But done is done."

He'd have done well, I suppose, to leave it with that epitaph. After all, it wasn't he who'd pushed Thorne's car into the North Shore cove. But Goldmark, as I've said, couldn't resist an opportunity to impress.

"Anyway," he went on, "I understand congratulations of a different kind are in order."

"What for?"

"The Stark-Thompson Funds."

"Yes? What about it?"

"Well, I hear you're going to be named Trustee."

"Oh? Where'd you hear that?"

"I've got my sources," he said, smiling.

I couldn't say which antagonized me more: the fact that he knew (and I didn't) or the way he told me.

"I'm sorry," I retorted. "That's not good enough. I want to know where you heard it."

"Hey, hey," he said, holding up his hand in a stop-sign gesture. "Don't forget that we at Braxton's handle a piece of that business. I hope we'll hold on to it in the future, by the way. But there's no need for you to get into such a sweat, old man. It's quite an honor. And more than that, it's big bucks time for you. Corky Stark's become a very rich man doing it."

The truth, and I'll come to it, was that the family Council had put the question off. More to the point, the only person I'd so much as mentioned it to was Kitty, and it struck me as inconceivable that she'd have discussed it with her brother. It was, I judged, none of his damn business.

We were interrupted then. Some guests were leaving, friends of Kitty's. I told them I didn't know where she was, and in the course of their well-wishing, I saw Goldmark lift his glass to me in a silent toast and walk away.

I didn't see him again that day. Kitty reappeared shortly thereafter, pale of mien and unaccountably irritable toward me, but she joined me in seeing off our guests, flashing smiles and exchanging embraces amid the white columns of our front entrance. At some point I invited her to take a last turn with me on the dance floor, but she declined. She said she didn't feel up to it. Then the band packed up, at dusk, and the last of the guests were gone. The cleanup crew wouldn't come until the next morning. And we were alone.

The one room in the house Kitty had decided to leave untouched was our master bathroom. It was, she said, simply too extraordinary and too kitsch to change. An enormous affair in pink marble, heavily mirrored, with floodlamps embedded in floor and ceiling, its pièce de résistance was a great circular hot pink tub, big enough for two or more, with a Jacuzzi and an entire, as it were, control panel, and one of those rolling trays that spanned the tub like a bridge and was long enough to hold a small library in addition to soaps, sponges, oils, lotions. Kitty had said that, provided she could wear tinted glasses to subdue the pink, she could imagine spending the rest of her life there, soaking, and it was there that I found her, after I'd taken a last shirt-sleeved stroll around our empty and shadowy grounds.

The latter act, I suppose, constituted my own male version of brides bursting into tears at their weddings. Grooms, too, feel a sense of foreboding, however unfocused, at the finality of what they've just done. On the one hand, I felt I knew Kitty more intimately than I ever had any other person. Or ever would, for that matter. On the other, there were times when she seemed a total stranger. This last, I confess, held the upper hand in my consciousness that evening when I patrolled the grounds. Yes, the conversation with Goldmark had unsettled me, and yes, the new house unsettled me. But beyond these was Kitty, my co-conspirator, now become, if you will, my co-conspirator till death do us part. Yet all I could see of her was that empty expression, devoid of recognition, when she'd rushed past me in the doorway to the living room, crying, and burst up the stairs.

I found her, as I've said, in that great garish tub, stretching back, a towel wrapped around her head like a turban, and resting against one of the steps just out of the water. Her eyes were half closed, and her pearly skin seemed to undulate gently under the water.

She opened her eyes briefly at my intrusion, then let the lids fall again.

"I'm just exhausted," she murmured. "I don't think I've ever been so exhausted."

"I know," I answered. "Who was it who said that all the great ceremonies of life—christenings, weddings, funerals—are really for the guests?"

"I don't know," she said languidly. "Just let me lie here a few more minutes, darling, and then I'll be with you."

For once, though, this wasn't good enough.

"There are a few things we have to talk about first," I said.

"Like what?" Vaguely, as though half hearing.

"Like what your brother said to you today that set you off."

No answer at first. Then:

"I told you. It was family business. Stupid. I overreacted, that's all. What exactly are you getting at?"

"I don't know exactly what I'm getting at. All I know is that he acted today like he owned the place. He made you cry, and he patronized the hell out of me."

"That's Teddy, all right. That's just the way he is."

"Does he know you killed Thorne?"

Her eyes opened wide then, and the murmur was gone from her voice.

"Are you kidding?"

"I don't think I am." I couldn't, in fact, quote Goldmark to her. It wasn't what he'd said— *Done is done*— but the knowing manner in which he'd said it. The all-knowing manner. "I've got to tell you, Kitty, there's something I've never understood. On the one hand, you always said there was no way anyone could touch us, over Safari or anything else, as long as I stonewalled. But on the other, you said we had to kill Thorne because he threatened to bring down the whole network, us included. Well, who runs the network? It's your brother, isn't it?''

"The network's done, over."

"All right. But who *ran* it? He did, didn't he? It stands to reason, Kitty. With his position at Braxton's, he had access to all the information, but he couldn't use it himself, could he? So he decided to take a piece of other people's action, people like Thorne, people like you and me and God knows who else. *He* was the only one whom Thorne made vulnerable, not you and me. Did we kill Thorne for him, Kitty?" I held up a hand, stifling her retort momentarily. "Did he *order* you to do it?"

Evidently that was a mistake, saying it that way. She sat up abruptly in the tub, covering her breasts with an involuntary gesture. A gesture of vulnerability, I guessed, and it was true, although I'd never realized it before that minute, that as sensual and physical as our relationship was, Kitty clearly preferred to do her toilette alone. It was in fact rare that I'd witnessed her naked, in a bathtub.

"I think you're being paranoid, Tommy," she said angrily, "but there are two things you just said that drive me right up the wall. No," she said, for I'd started to answer, "you listen to me. You keep saying *we* killed Thorne, when the truth is that *I* did. You helped me after the fact, which puts you on the hook too, and if you're having second thoughts about that now, well, that's too bad." She interrupted herself, standing now in the tub and gesturing. "Hand me a towel, please." Then: "But the second thing is this: nobody *orders* me to do anything. I don't take *orders*. I don't take them from Teddy, I don't take them from you, I don't take them from anyone."

She stood there, her skin aglisten, chin raised in that characteristically defiant pose.

"I'm sorry," I said. "I put it the wrong way. Maybe

I *am* being paranoid. But if I am, it's your doing. You still, for instance, haven't answered about your brother."

"We had a business relationship," she said coldly. "It's over now. The sooner you and I forget about it, the better."

"Funny. That's what he said."

"What did he say?"—unwinding the towel turban and shaking her hair free.

"He said better to let sleeping dogs lie."

"Well, that's the smartest thing he's said in a long time. Now will you please hand me my towel?"

Anchored in the floor near the tub was a heated metal rack with thick oversize towels adorned by Kitty's new monogram. I pulled one free from the rack but held on to it.

"If that's the case," I said, "then why did you tell him about the Trusteeship?"

"Why did I what?"

"You heard what I said, Kitty. Why did you tell him about the Trusteeship?"

I expected her to deny it the way he had. Or try to.

"For God's sake, will you give me the towel?" she said, reaching and shouting at once.

"Not till you answer the question!" I heard myself shout back.

"You bastard!" she said, incredulous and enraged. "You're talking to me as if you *owned* me. Here I am, exhausted, trying to relax, and you come charging in here, accusing me of God knows what and acting like you *own* me!"

"I *do* own you," I retorted. "A piece of you. What the hell else do you think marriage is about? I own a piece of you and you own a piece of me!"

She jutted her jaw toward me in angry attack.

"Well, if that's what you really think, mister, then you and I have just made one major mistake."

She reached awkwardly for the towel and missed.

"You still haven't answered my question, Kitty."

"*What* question?"

"Did you or did you not tell your brother about the Trusteeship?"

"Well, what if I did? Maybe I mentioned it to him. So what?"

"For one thing, it hasn't even happened yet."

"So what? It's going to. I didn't know it was such a deep dark secret anyway. What, I'd like to know, is so special and sacrosanct about your goddamn family?"

"And what," I said back, "is so special and sacrosanct about yours?"

She glowered at me, her wet body ramrod stiff. She started to say something back, then stopped, and I could see her jaw move from the gritting of her teeth.

"My towel, please," she said, chin lifted.

"Pick it up yourself," I said, dropping it on the floor, and, turning, stormed from the room.

Before that night, I don't think I'd had any real understanding of the role sex played in our life. Almost invariably, whenever we had reached the point of no return, with its attendant anger and recrimination, we had been able to get through it, exorcise it, by lovemaking. A reverse sort of sublimation, the analysts would probably have called it. Love in all its myriad forms—and I've refrained here from giving, as it were, our full catalogue—had always been our way out, our narcotic. I'd be tempted to say it was Kitty who'd taught me that, but I admit, judging from the comparatively pallid sex of my previous relationships, with their well-worn rituals of endearments and appropriate foreplay, that I'd at least been ready for it.

When I came back into the bedroom that night, Kitty was lying on our new bed, her head on her pillow, eyes open. She was wearing a nightgown for the occasion, a rarity for her, and looked straight ahead, as near as I could tell, at nothing. I went into the bathroom and took a shower in the large marble stall, and I remember hesitating, when I was finished, over whether to reappear wearing something myself or in my habitual nudity. I owned not a single set of pajamas. A terry cloth robe, the enormous white one Kitty had bought me? I opted for nudity.

She hadn't moved from her position. I got into bed on the far side and, turning toward her, apologized. I said maybe I was as strung out as she was. The only point I'd really wanted to make, I said, was that I'd married *her* that day, not her brother. Beyond that, I felt bad about what I'd said. Maybe it was true, that weddings really were for the guests? Anyway, I would take it back if I could—not the wedding but the bad words.

She listened, then turned sideways toward me, her eyes dark-rimmed with fatigue. She accepted my apology almost formally. She, too, was very sorry about what had happened. We should both try to forget it.

No kiss, however, no word of love. One of us may have said that he, or she, was too tired, we should get some sleep. Perhaps neither of us did.

Inevitably I dreamt the dream that night, my recurrent one, the one where I had to rescue Starkie. I awoke from it, sweating as usual and holding my breath to listen for the distant sounds of the frightened child. I got up and padded across the room in my bare feet and out into the upstairs hall.

I remember pouring myself a drink in the living room (yes, from the Laphroaig bottle), which I carried with me on my nude and random travel, but I've no recollec-

tion of what else I did or thought, only of the sense of
impending trouble that the dream always inspired in me.
When I got back upstairs, Kitty was still asleep, face
down, left arm flung over her head in some possibly
protective gesture. I lay down next to her, somehow
afraid to go back to sleep, and listened to the quiet reassuring hum of the central air conditioning.

17

Shortly after the wedding, I was finally inducted into the Stark-Thompson Family Council. The meeting, originally scheduled for April, had been twice postponed because of Corcoran Stark's indisposition. In between I'd met in New York with two of the members, one being the Chairman—a kind of pre-interview for the Trusteeship, they'd led me to believe. Although of course nothing would be decided without him, Corky, they'd said, was going to step down. Then Corky recovered, we were reconvened, and one fine day in late June, in the new Mercedes Kitty had given me for a wedding present, I drove up to the Stark estate, a Tudor mansion sitting on parklike acreage in Columbia County, not far from the Hudson.

The house, one could have said, that the Trusteeship had built.

I was one of three new members, two of us male, one female, and clearly the youngest. Crandall Thompson Fly Jr. was a prominent architect from New York in his late fifties who, like me, was taking over the seat his father had voluntarily relinquished. (Unlike mine, his was in attendance and in fact presided over the meeting as outgoing Chairman.) Mildred Thompson Walker, a jolly and fiftyish matron whose husband was a Philadelphia banker, had lost her father that winter, and, since the Council had resolved the previous year "to encourage vigorously, and insofar as possible, the future participation of women," her presence was specially noted in the minutes.

The other members were all male, and for the most part septua- and octogenarian. A couple, as I said, I'd recently met; all of them I could more or less place on the family tree. They belonged, in dress, manner, speech, and attitude, to what most people would have called the privileged class, old Wasp America, and now that their lives were largely over, they seemed to look on everything, including the business before them, with a uniform and smug disinterest.

This wasn't, needless to say, the sole, or even the main, reason for my sense of separateness. I had, after all, been raised and educated to be one of them, and with regard to their particular self-satisfied form of snobbery, I could pass. Nor was it the age factor, nor even my newness in their midst. But I felt it the minute I walked into that cavernous Tudor room with the thronelike chairs (actually my cousin Corky's dining room), and the longer the meeting progressed, the more I realized how outraged they would be if they knew the truth about me.

(A *felon*, did you say? One of *us*? With appropriate adjustments of hearing aids.)

Our first business was quickly, even perfunctorily, dispensed with. We three new members were introduced, welcomed, and each of us presented with a set of the bylaws, a voluminous document bound in maroon leather, which we were urged to read attentively at our

leisure. The minutes of the previous meeting, held in
January, were read and approved. Then the Chair recognized the Trustee, Corcoran Stark, who presented and
briefly summarized the combined balance sheet for the
previous year, which on motion was approved and in-
corporated into the minutes.

While Cousin Corky spoke, I scanned the balance
sheet. The assets were ranged in a neat listing with numbers beside them, the liabilities below. Certain of the
captions I didn't immediately understand, but when I
came to the last one under liabilities—Stark-Thompson
Funds Equity, it was called—I think I quite literally
stopped breathing. I looked up, somehow convinced that
one or more of my fellow members would be watching
for my reaction. But none was, and Corky's voice, dry
and frail, continued to drone on. Then I looked down
again, even traced the line across to the corresponding
dollars with my forefinger because I was sure I'd misread.

I hadn't.

If I don't give the number here, it is not, Kitty to the
contrary, because I feel bound by some kind of honor
code to keep the secrets of the clan secret. It is, rather,
because I don't think anyone would believe me. And
with good reason. In all the listings I'd ever seen of the
Richest People in America, there'd never been any mention of us. This, as I would discover, was because the
Funds actually consisted of separate and distinct trusts,
a considerable number of them, leap-frogging the generations and ingeniously designed to circumvent two an-
cient and hoary principles of common law: the one against
perpetuity, the other against unreasonable accumulation
of wealth. While the combined balance sheet I mentioned
was a document simply for the convenience of the Council, suffice it that the people sitting in that room, and all

those they represented, had to constitute collectively one of the ten wealthiest families in the country.

I admit, too, to a shiver, a kind of rippling inner thrill which I had only experienced before, once or twice, in gambling situations when the stakes had suddenly become much higher than I could afford. But those stakes, of course, had been but pennies to the numbers now before me. I thought of Wanda Russell, probably the richest person I knew. But the interest alone on the Funds, I calculated, would have surpassed all Wanda's assets combined.

I'd had no idea!

No wonder the Senator had come to me for his eighty thousand dollars!

Even Ted Goldmark and his paltry one hundred eighty million . . . But God Almighty, we had committed *murder* to protect that!

I literally had trouble breathing. What I was looking at made *all* of it—Goldmark and Kitty and Safari and Thorne—seem so petty, so penny-ante. (To which list, needless to say, I have to add Stark Thompson, P.C.!)

Strangest of all, though: of all of us seated around that table, was I the *only* one who noticed the number? I remember glancing surreptitiously at them, relatives all. They had the same papers before them, they were sitting on the same fortune . . .

But not a murmur, not so much as a cough.

Nothing, other than Corky Stark's voice.

Corky finished his report. Crandall Thompson Fly Sr. reminding the Council that, by tradition, it was the prerogative of each outgoing member and officer to name his or (with a slight inclination toward Mildred Walker) her successor, then opened the subject of the new officers. He himself put forth his candidate for the new Chairman, another Thompson elder, who was approved, unopposed, by voice vote. The current Secretary was reconfirmed in his office. Then, with a nod to Corky, the outgoing Chairman raised the question of the new Trustee.

Corky Stark was, like many of us in the family, a tall and spare man, his figure somewhat stooped by age but still maintaining a kind of brittle and bony spryness. He stood again now, in a loosely fitting gray and white seersucker suit (which seemed to be the approved dress in the Council), and only the frailty of his voice, now and then interrupted by a hacking cough, revealed that he'd been ill. He'd had a stroke—a mild one, he assured us, and he claimed that he'd beaten it fair and square. Doctors or no, he'd already resumed his daily morning swim, before breakfast, thank you, half an hour's worth, and they could keep their drugs and medicines.

"I've been doing this thankless job for almost thirty years now," he said, coming to the point. "Even though I've had some criticism and a lot of second-guessing lately, I think it safe to say that the people sitting on this Council thirty years ago, of whom Cranny and I are the only ones left, would never have dreamt in their wildest dreams that we'd be where we are today."

He went on to describe the growth of the Funds during his dominion, saying we all should be proud of it, that he himself damn well was, even though the most recent exercises had been on the disappointing side. Then:

"I know there's a lot of sentiment around this table that the time's come for me to step down."

He paused, as though waiting for demurrers. But there were none.

"Well, let me tell you this: I'd be the last one to disagree with you. I think it's high time we had some new blood, and at the proper time I'll be glad to hand over my responsibilities and be done with it. But I want to make damn sure we have an orderly transition, and that I'm satisfied with my successor, and that it's all done as it should be. And that's not something I'm ready to do today. Therefore I recommend that we table the subject until our September meeting. If anybody disagrees, then let's have it out now."

Several times while he spoke, Corky Stark glanced at me—without, however, any particular expression, positive or negative, that I could read. It struck me as odd that, if I was the candidate and he had by tradition some kind of veto power, we hadn't yet sat down together. Yes, he'd been ill. But it could also have been that there were factions within the Council that had yet to surface.

On the spot, these were nowhere in evidence, and Corky's recommendation was accepted without comment. But I had partial answers that same day, during the buffet lunch served on the terrace next to the outdoor pool.

From Crandall Thompson Fly Jr.: "Dad tells me Corky Stark's been making the same speech every year for as long as he can remember. He says that as far as Corky's concerned, we're going to have to carry him out feet first."

From Crandall Thompson Fly Sr.: "Corky's been making that same speech every year for about as long as I can remember, Tommy. But I don't want you to worry. We'll have to keep the pressure on him. He'll come around in time. It's just that nobody had the heart to push him today."

From Corcoran Stark: "I think it's time you and I got to know each other . . . It's Tommy, isn't it? . . . Yes. Well, I'm going to phone you, Tommy. I'd like you to come up here, if it's no great hardship. There are any number of things you need to know. For all I know, you may not even want the damn job once you've heard me out."

There was more, too, from my Cousin Corky.

When the luncheon was over—a rather bland and even skimpy buffet composed mostly of salads and fruit, though with a well-stocked bar complete with uniformed bartender—I bided my time, not wanting to be the first to leave but watchful for the first opportunity. Then I saw the Flys, Sr. and Jr., making their way through the group, shaking hands. Apparently they had shared a limousine up from the city. I gave them a head start, then circulated through the group behind them, pleading a business appointment and noticing how, as often happened, there was a sudden stirring throughout, as though suddenly it had become important not to be left behind.

But as we made our way back through the house and out the main entrance to the wide gravel driveway where my Mercedes looked suddenly humdrum in the collection (there was, I remember, an elderly but gleaming Bentley of stately and understated elegance), Corky took my arm and insistently held me behind the others.

"Well, young man," he said. "Like I say, you may not even want the damn job once you've heard me out. But I'm going to call you."

I made some noncommittal reply and, assuming I was now free, started to thank him for his hospitality.

"Never mind that," he said, pulling me back toward him. "I understand congratulations are in order, is that so?"

"Congratulations for what?" I answered.

"Well, you just got married, didn't you?"

"Yes, I did. Thank you very much."

"Not one of us, is she?"

The remark, needless to say, disconcerted me. I looked toward the others, the last of them now several yards in front of us on the gravel.

"Never mind them," Corky Stark said confidentially,

squeezing my arm. "The Jews are all right, no matter what anyone says."

Fortunately for me, for I'd have had no idea how to answer, he started to laugh, and then the laughter turned into a cough, and, relinquishing my arm, he pulled a handkerchief from his pocket and covered his mouth, meanwhile staying me with his free hand.

"Sorry about that," he said, recovering. "When you're my age, everything breaks down. Turns out I knew her first husband, did you know that?"

"Who?"

"Your wife's. Sprague? Gar Sprague? Good family. They say he was crazy about her. Drank too much, though. Poor bastard drove himself off a cliff."

I'd started to say something. I stopped short.

"He . . . what?"

"I said he drove himself off a cliff," Corky repeated.

"But I'd always heard he drank himself to death."

"And so he did," Corky said. "No contradiction there. He was drunk as a lord when he did it, poor bastard." Then, squeezing my arm before letting me go: "Let it be a lesson to you, eh, Tommy? Don't drink too much!"

Dazed by what I'd heard, I headed across the driveway. I think some of the cars had already gone. I was suddenly anxious to get out of there myself. Is it possible to feel claustrophobic in the open air?

I was at the Mercedes when I heard him calling behind me.

He was standing in front of his open front door, stooped, his hand raised in a half salute and grinning crookedly at me, shouting the while.

"Don't forget to read the bylaws!" was what I heard.

* * *

Yes, read the bylaws.

But something funny happened to me on my way south from Corky Stark's. I'd left there, as I said, in a daze, shocked by what he'd said so casually. It had to be true, and I knew that, but believing it was like the shattering of crystal, the explosion of atoms, the breakup of all my assumptions.

Yo, Tommy, who said the world had to be round?

Somewhere on that parkway south, though, I had to stop. It was a matter of necessity: I'd become giddy with fear. I remember pulling off onto the shoulder, stopping, turning off the ignition, getting out. Striving for deep breaths. There was little traffic, yet the new Mercedes itself had become a trap, a potential tomb.

For *there* was the truth of it, wasn't it? . . . *Crazy about her . . . Drank too much . . . Drove himself off a cliff.* It had suddenly, indelibly, become clear to me: Robert Thorne hadn't been her first; Gar Sprague, drunk or sober, had died in a car crash, too! The coincidence was simply too great. Sprague, like Thorne, had to have been an accident waiting for her to make happen.

(Did you have help then, too, Kitten? Someone to put Sprague's car into drive for you? And did you murder him beforehand too, throwing up—how decorous—after the deed? Or were these later refinements, for Thorne only?)

And who was there to say Sprague himself had been the first? Or that Robert Thorne would be the last?

And where precisely, dear Kitten, did I fit into your master plan?

And what to do? What should *I* do?

I can tell you what I did do.

I started to laugh.

Call it my Wasp sense of humor, if you will, gallows corner, what a Wasp will do when the fear wears off a little and he discovers, hyperventilating, that he is at least still breathing, and that the air is redolent with the fresh smells of late spring, and he asks himself finally: What, after all, is so new about what you just found out?

Only that the murderess I had married a couple of weeks before was more experienced at her secret craft than I'd thought.

But beyond that?

Only that I craved her still. Or even, so help me, craved her more. I remember leaning against my car, sucking on a long blade of grass, breathing deeply now, laughing aloud at the images that rose in my mind in spite of everything: smells of Kitty, teasing tastes of Kitty, curves and curls and whirls of Kitty rising, rearing finally against the prancing stallion that I had become.

I didn't drive into the office that afternoon. I went directly home instead, and it was there, that same afternoon, that I put the first elements of this account on paper.

Some hours later—it was near dusk, on one of the longest days of the year—Kitty's chauffeured car, a sedate Cadillac Seville, pulled slowly in front of our Georgian columns. By then I was standing some twenty, thirty paces away, in a pair of shorts, sneakers, a T-shirt. A drink in one hand, a hose in the other. I'd been watering some rosebushes. Somewhere I'd read that it was impossible to kill rosebushes by drowning, and I think I'd set out to test the theory.

Kitty was wearing a light-colored suit, linen, without lapels—the Chanel look—with a ruffled white blouse underneath. High heels. I remember the high heels on our gravel, and the wraparound full-tint sunglasses she always wore in summer.

"Tommy!" she said, startled. "For God's sake, what are you doing there?"

"Just what it looks like I'm doing," I replied. "I'm the perfect country gentleman."

I watched her turn, stooping to talk through the window to the driver, the movement causing her skirt to tighten around her hips, her ass. Probably she was telling him what time she wanted him in the morning. Then he backed the Cadillac around neatly in the driveway and drove off.

"Come on, Tommy," she called to me. "Stop what you're doing and come in the house."

"You take one more step, Kitty, and I'll have to douse you from head to foot. Come over here."

I remember testing the hose, holding one thumb across the nozzle and shooting an experimental jet across her port bow.

She dropped whatever she was carrying.

"For God's sake," she called, annoyed, "watch what you're doing. What's wrong, are you drunk?"

Was I drunk? Drunk on Kitty, at least.

"Nothing's wrong," I answered. "But I've got something to tell you. A certain number to whisper in your ear."

"Oh, the Funds!" she exclaimed. "I all but forgot! Did you get it?"

"We'll see," I said. "But come here now, Kitten."

I must have dropped the hose.

(I've no recollection of turning the water off, but the roses didn't drown.)

I watched her make her way toward me, heels unsteady in the grass, arms reaching out for balance, and the mere sight of her, her sunglasses now perched in her thick hair, followed by the heavy, engulfing smell of her as she took my hands and I pulled her to me, brought back the erection which had been how long—some six hours?—abuilding.

"Tommy!" she exclaimed, laughing and trying to push me away. "At least let's go inside. The help'll see us!"

We had, through Kitty's business, hired an Irish couple, who took care of everything from gardening to a generally acceptable cuisine.

"No they won't," I answered. "I gave them the night off."

"You what?"

"Just what I said. I even gave them the money to have dinner out. On us. I told them I wanted the evening alone with my wife."

"You—"

"Listen, Mrs. Thompson," I said, gripping her firmly, her eyes now caught between protest and curiosity, "once upon a time you told me you found money sexy. Now I've taken you at your word. I bring to you one of the great American fortunes, not yours to keep, alas, but yours to manipulate, play with, throw in the air and try to catch before it hits the ground. All those zeros. Do you want the number? Come here, let me give you the number."

I whispered it into her ear. She started to giggle and twist away.

"What . . . ? What did you say?"

"You heard me. Now I want to fuck your brains out."

"Tommy! For God's—"

In some kind of parabola, whether awkward or graceful I couldn't say, we tumbled into the grass, husband and wife, accomplice and murderess. Protest she might, and protest she did, but there was no one to hear her and no way for her to blunt my lust.

Then later, yes, I read the bylaws.

18

It's a unique set of documents, wouldn't you say?'' Corcoran Stark asked.

This was at breakfast, his choice, in fact his insistence. We sat at a long glass and wrought iron table beside his outdoor pool, shaded by two tall umbrellas and served from an adjacent table by a young black manservant in white ducks and sneakers. Although the sun had begun its lazy summer climb, the air was still cool from the night, but Cousin Corky, his body creased and creviced from age, sat only in his bathing trunks and sandals. He'd been up even before me, he announced, had had his regular morning swim, which he did the year round (though indoors come October), had had his coffee, had read all the papers, had even had time for a couple of phone calls.

Although I agreed out loud with his observation, I had no way of telling if ''unique'' was accurate. Maybe there had been other brothers, or families, in the nineteenth century who had decided to make their own reach for immortality through such a legal instrument, or series of instruments. But curious, certainly, if not unique. Two brothers from Pennsylvania who had apparently made some money in the canal business (something called the Thompson Tow Company in New Hope, Pennsylvania) had wanted to set aside a (now indeterminate) sum for the benefit not of their grandchildren but their "grandchildren's grandchildren and the further generations," only to discover that such a scheme ran counter to the law.

As we all learned in law school, the only legally permissible perpetual trust is one established for charity. Otherwise, there prevails a so-called rule against perpetuities. Under the old English common law (which, after a series of statutory changes in the nineteenth century, has once again, quite recently, become American law), no form of trust could endure longer than a reasonable number of "lives in being" plus twenty-one years. What "lives in being" meant practically was that a man, if he wished to, could establish a trust that would survive the death of his wife, his children, and his already-born grandchildren by twenty-one years, at which time the trust would have to be distributed to the surviving beneficiaries. In fact, at the time of the original Thompson brothers, American law had substantially reduced the duration of lives-in-being plus twenty-one years by the "two-lives rule," meaning that no trust could, for example, survive a man's wife and one of his children.

What the brothers had done instead was to establish not one but a series of trusts in the names of their generation (Stark, it appeared, was the married name of the brothers' sister), also, in due course, in the names of their children, so setting into motion a complicated series of leapfrogging and proliferating legacies which were accompanied by a most curious document—an "open letter" of instructions to their heirs and descendants. It was there that the phrase "grandchildren's grandchildren and the further generations" was to be found. The trusts, the brothers ordained, were to be reconstituted upon their expiration, in accordance with the prevailing laws of the day, and the Funds, in principal and interest, reinvested at the prudent and best discretion of the succeeding generations. Control of the Funds was vested by the letter in the oldest males of the family's branches, generation unto generation. In time, changed and amended through the years, this "open letter" had evolved into what we called the bylaws, and early in the twentieth century, the idea of the Council, an outgrowth of the "oldest males" of the letter, had been codified along with the role of the single Trustee as manager of the Funds.

The whole edifice was, as far as I could tell, perfectly legal. The assets of all the trusts had simply been commingled for investment purposes, through the administration of a single trustee. What surprised me was not that it hadn't been challenged in the courts, but that no one, in the succeeding generations, had tried to tear it down. For whose benefit was it? Hadn't anybody ever asked that question to which there was but one answer? To no one's benefit. The era of the "grandchildren's grandchildren" had in fact already arrived—I myself was one of them, I'd calculated—yet the Funds went on, accumulating and multiplying, and one of the first questions I had for Corcoran Stark that morning was why nobody had even challenged its very existence.

"The answer is that they have," he replied. "Many years ago there were even defections—not many—beneficiaries of this or that trust who refused to go along with reconstitution. Of course, they and their branch were immediately ostracized—we have a mechanism for that, perfectly legal. But the truth is that no one individual could cause much harm to the whole."

"But a group certainly could," I said. "And a generation could create havoc."

"Yes," he said. "We almost had that happen, too."

The last time it had come up seriously, Corky said, was before the war (by which he meant World War II). Apparently certain branches of the family had barely managed to scrape through the Depression, and it was these who'd turned to the Council, first for relief, then with the aim of toppling the Funds entirely.

"Of course, the Council fought them, but it set off quite a crisis in the ranks. It was at that time that somebody on the Council invented the loan system. Also the Council members' stipend was introduced and a special dividend declared. This bought the rebels off temporarily, and then the war came along, for better or worse, and the whole thing blew over.

"Probably there have been naysayers since the very beginning," he went on, "but you have to remember that for a very long time the Funds didn't amount to all that much. Look back at the records of the first fifty years—longer, say, the first eighty—and you'll see what I mean. The clan grew a lot faster than the Funds at first. It's only since the war that we've really taken off."

"Thanks in large part to you," I said.

"A graceful compliment," he answered with a nod at my flattery.

"Forgive me please for belaboring the point," I said, "but I still don't really understand. If the Funds was broken up today, we would all be millionaires many times over. We, the grandchildren's grandchildren. Yet we voluntarily let it go on. Is it out of altruism? The goodness of our hearts? Or the family's powers of persuasion?"

He smiled at me and shrugged.

"Some of us already are millionaires," he said matter-of-factly. "And some not, it's true. But the fact is, we've been advised we couldn't go out of business even if we wanted to. Not without inviting one lawsuit after another, which would tie up the Funds till *your* grandchildren's grandchildren.''

"Why would there have to be lawsuits," I said, "if it were done equitably?''

"Equitably," he repeated with a creased smile. "Now there's the key word. Look, young man, maybe you're smarter than the people we've had in to look at it, but there are a few things you ought to take into consideration. The Council, big as it is, still doesn't represent all the branches of the family. Far from it. We're not a democratic body. We rule with a certain secrecy, always have. Second, do you realize how many of us there must be by now? Starks and Thompsons? First cousins, second cousins, third, fourth, fifth? We've made efforts to keep track, but it's hopeless. And then there's the question, Who's entitled and who isn't? Should there be full shares, half shares, quarter shares? Well, somebody will say, the beneficiaries named in the trusts, that's perfectly clear. But is it so clear? Of course not. The beneficiaries are a vehicle, in the founders' intent, and with a few exceptions that's the way it's always worked.

"But suppose we could get past all that. I'm not saying we can, but suppose we could. Suppose the Council sent a letter to every Stark and Thompson it could find, saying, We're tired of being responsible for all this money, we're going to break it up over time and distribute it as fairly as we can. We estimate your eventual share to be x dollars.

"And suppose—a big suppose—but suppose nobody squawked? Would you still be home free? Hell, no. Because the minute the word got around—and it certainly would get around—somebody you've never heard of would show up from Texas and somehow prove he's a bona fide Thompson. Or say he could prove it, with a smart lawyer on a contingency fee. You're a lawyer yourself. Would you go to court over it, or settle? Probably you'd settle, or try to, but the minute you settled, up would pop another one from Oregon, another from Timbuktu, another from Outer Mongolia, and by the time you were done trying to sort out the Thompsons from the Thompsons—though who's to say you'd ever be done—it'd be the lawyers who'd walk away with the lion's share.''

According to Corky, then, a form of perpetual trust had, in some very practical sense, come into being. He said every new generation on the Council had faced the issue, tried to tackle it, and in the end had given up. And the longer it went unresolved, the more the dollars grew and grew.

"Of course, we've tried to get around it every which way," Corky said. "The stipend, for one. We've upped it steadily. We've declared dividends, too. In a real sense, the Funds finances how we all live. Your house, for instance. And the Trustee does well, too . . . very well in a good year. Also, we have our philanthropic endowments. Even so, I'm afraid there's no way we could come close to spending it all, even if we wanted to.''

I already knew the current Council members' stipend. It would pay me more annually than I had ever taken home in my days at the firm, this for four meetings a year plus some committee work. I still had no idea how much the Trustee made. I assumed this would be his next topic.

"If I read you right," he said, "you're thinking, one, When does this old fart stop talking? Two, When do I take over? Three, How much am I going to make at it? Is that right?''

We both laughed, Corky's eyes dancing under his

heavy lids until he started to cough, hacking sounds and shoulders shaking. He apologized with a wave, at the same time waving off my offer to help, and picking up a table napkin, coughed into it and wiped his mouth.

"Jesus Christ," he said when he'd recovered. "I'll give you one free piece of advice, young man. Don't grow old. Now where was I? Oh, yes. Well, I wouldn't blame you for a minute if that's what you're thinking. Don't forget, I was in your shoes once. How old are you now?"

"Forty-two," I said.

"I became a member at almost your age, a little older, but it took me another ten years to become Trustee. Don't worry, you're not going to have to wait that long! But I can't help asking myself, What's the rush? I know, I know, suddenly everybody's in a hurry. Suddenly Corky's too old, he's senile, he's costing us money, and so on. And I *agree* with them! Not that I'm senile, but I'm eighty-three, my health isn't a hundred percent. I could live another ten years, or ten days, who knows? Plus the markets are booming and we haven't kept pace, that's the crux of it, isn't it? And all my fault? Well, it's a terrific responsibility, let me tell you. The Trustee has a very wide latitude with the money—too wide, I've always said, but nobody else wants to be bothered. And there's something else, too. I have no children, I lost my wife to cancer almost twenty years ago—this is the only work I have left. Maybe I should give it up, but maybe I shouldn't. Hell, why should I? Last year—an off year, mind you—it earned me personally almost three million dollars. Did you earn three million dollars last year? Maybe you did, and more power to you, but why should I be in a rush to give up an income of three million dollars a year?"

His tone, as I've tried to convey, was a peculiar mix

of belligerence, as though I was the enemy, and whee-dling, as though he was looking to me for some kind of approval. His real argument, it seemed to me, was with the Council. They'd appointed me his heir apparent, so to speak, and clearly he wanted no part of an heir apparent.

Under other circumstances, I might simply have gotten up and left, but there was too much at stake. Somehow, without quite having realized it beforehand, I'd already committed myself.

"Aren't you the least bit curious as to how I do it?" Corky said, narrowing his eyes. "What's the matter, Tommy? Cat got your tongue?"

"Look," I said, trying to keep calm. "I find myself in a very awkward situation. Maybe there's been some kind of misunderstanding. I thought the job had been offered to me, not that—"

"Oh it is, it is!" he interrupted, waving me off. "It's going to be all yours, Tommy! It's just a question of the timing, that's all, and some details we have to clear up. I'm just griping out loud, that's all. For Christ's sake, that's what old people do, they gripe all the time, didn't you know that? Can't you put up with a little griping in exchange for three million a year?"

He started jotting numbers quickly, if shakily, on a legal-size pad, talking as he wrote. Corcoran Stark was an accountant by background and the founder, years before, of a firm that, after several mergers, had emerged as part of one of the accounting Big Eight. He'd retired young, already a rich man. The system of compensation he described, which would pass on to the new Trustee, resembled the one I'd used with my own clients in that it provided for an escalating percentage of profits. Smaller percentages, yes, but of a vastly bigger pie. According to Corky, the system dated back to just after the war, which coincided with the period when the Funds had really taken off.

"Nothing like the old greed factor, is there? To motivate somebody? The smartest thing the Council ever did. For my sake, sure, and I made a lot more than three million in my heyday. But so did everybody else, at least on paper!"

He excused himself then, saying he stiffened up if he sat too long in one place, and when he stood I could hear his joints crack like knuckles. He kept on talking as, steadying himself on the backs of chairs, he made his way out from under the umbrellas into the bright sun and, stooping over on his spindly legs, gazed down into the pool. Something about how he'd like another swim, though he wasn't supposed to overdo it. Maybe he'd wait till afternoon. Then something more pointed, about how he knew I was impatient, and why was it, did I suppose, that old people, who had no time left at all, had all the patience in the world, while young people, who had none of the patience, had all the time?

And then, coming back to the table and, with a sigh, easing his body into his chair, he hit me, as it were, right between the eyes. Or, more accurately, blindsided me, for I'd had no idea what was coming.

"Well," he said, "let's get to a small matter we've got to clear up. How carefully did you read the bylaws?"

"I'm not sure I could recite them by heart," I answered, "but pretty carefully."

"The provisions about the loans?" he asked.

"Yes, of course."

"And what do they say, in substance?"

"In substance? That upon suitable application, the Trustee can make loans to family members, subject to approval by the Council, if I remember correctly."

"That's right," Corky said. "And what happens to the loans?"

"I don't get what you mean: What happens to them?"

"Well, if they're not paid back. In default. You have a loan, for instance, don't you? On that house of yours?" Yes, I thought in irritation, and I've been paying it off for as long as I can remember. "What happens to it if you die?"

"Well," I said, not recalling anything specific, "I imagine it would become an obligation of my estate, wouldn't it?"

"Wrong!" he said, clearly pleased to have caught me. "You have a son, don't you?"

"Yes, that's right."

"Then it would become his. His obligation."

"But that's illegal!" I exclaimed. "You don't *inherit* debts like that. You wouldn't stand a chance of collecting in a court of law."

"I doubt it would ever go that far," he answered mildly. "Not if he wanted your seat on the Council."

Irritated as I was, I still, however obtusely, failed to see what he was driving at.

On the table near him was one of those accordion-type gray file folders, the kind you rarely see anymore, which are tied with a ribbon. I'd noticed it earlier, had assumed it contained details of his operations and that in due course, after he'd put me through his hoops a few more times, we would get to it. Now he patted it absentmindedly, saying meanwhile:

"This is the Senator's loan file, Tommy. Now answer me honestly: Do you know anything about it?"

"No," I said, feeling myself stiffen. "I don't know what you're talking about."

He stared at me a moment, eyes lidded, as though satisfying himself that I was telling the truth. Then:

"I guess I'm not surprised after all. He's an old friend, Tommy, a man of great qualities and certainly the most illustrious member of the clan alive today. But when it comes to finances? Finances and women? Zero. Absolutely zero."

"How much is involved?" I heard myself say.

By way of answer, he untied the ribbon, reached into the folder, extracted a summary sheet, and handed it to me.

I couldn't believe what I saw. In principal and interest, my father's indebtedness to the Funds came to just under five million dollars.

"My God," I think I said. "How did this happen?"

"It happened over a long period of time," Corky replied. "And because, where the Senator was concerned, I was too soft a touch."

I could think of nothing to say.

"For the last few years," Corky went on, "we've been withholding his stipend, but that doesn't even match the outstanding interest payments." It did explain, though, I realized with mounting bitterness, why the Senator had been so willing to hand me down his seat on the Council. "You know, not so long ago—maybe it was last year— he came to me. It was very embarrassing for him, for me as well. He said, 'Corky, my old friend, all I need to tide me over is sixty thou. That's all, sixty thousand dollars. What possible difference will sixty thousand dollars make to you?' And he was right, you know? It wouldn't have made the slightest difference to the trust. But I'd been to the well with him too many times, Tommy. I had to turn him down."

Yes, I thought, and the sixty had become eighty by the time he talked to me. But still too much of a pittance, he'd said, for him to bother the Council about.

"But what does all this have to do with me?" I asked once Corky had finished.

"I'm afraid it's become your obligation."

"Why is that? He's still alive and kicking. As far as I know, he hasn't declared bankruptcy."

"That may be, but he's mortgaged to the hilt. There's no way he's going to pay us back."

"So because *you* were too soft a touch, you're telling me *I'm* stuck?"

He took the accusation with apparent aplomb.

"That's about it," he replied. "But I don't see why you're getting so worked up about it. Once you're Trustee, you'll make it back within a couple of years. Sooner, if you're smart about it."

"Does the Council know about this?"

"Yes, of course. It was my duty to so inform them before the Senator stepped down and you were named a member."

"And what did they say?"

"Everybody was embarrassed about it, but we all assumed you would make the Senator whole. We understand you've been doing very well on your own—"

"But nobody saw fit to talk to me about it beforehand?"

"We assumed the Senator had."

"Well, he didn't."

Maybe it was a tactical mistake to show such filial . . . what? Disloyalty? . . . But I couldn't help myself. I was choked and enraged inside. At my father certainly, that *most illustrious* member of the clan, and the blithe and lying insouciance with which he'd dealt with me. But angry, too, at Corky and the rest of them, who now, in a totally unforeseen way, seemed to hold my fate in their hands. It was all very well for them to understand how well I'd been doing, but I knew the numbers, knew how much I'd drawn against my eventual profit share on my accounts, knew that I couldn't put my hands on anything like five million dollars.

"Let me see if I understand this," I said. "According to the bylaws, the indebtedness of the father becomes, upon his death, the obligation of the son. The last I heard, my father was very much alive. Yet you still expect me to make good?"

"That's correct."

"And supposing I don't?"

"Well, I'd say your future participation in the Council would be jeopardized. I for one would take a dim view of it, and I doubt I'd be alone."

"And the Trusteeship?"

"Well, that of course would be out of the question."

"Then let's turn the question around. Supposing I do make good, five million dollars give or take. Then what?"

"Then everything proceeds as before," he answered.

"And the Trusteeship?"

"All in due course," he said. "I've already indicated to you that it's going to be yours. It's just a question of timing."

"But no guarantee on your part?"

"No more than what I've just said."

"In other words, I'm supposed to write out a check for five million dollars and then take everything on faith?"

"Oh, I didn't say it had to be all in cash," he said. "I could accept a goodly portion in cash—say, half—and the rest in a promissory note. That would satisfy me."

Yes, and with interest on the note, I was sure.

"And the Council approves this?"

"It's not a Council matter," he said. "Not yet, in any

case. It's up to you and me to work out, between our-selves.''

I wondered about that. I wondered how much the Council knew, and whether they knew that Corky was stonewalling me on the succession.

If I'd antagonized him meanwhile, he didn't show it. His tone was benign, matter-of-fact, almost as though he didn't care one way or the other. He stood up then, abruptly ending the meeting, but saying in a conciliatory manner that he hadn't intended our conversation to dwell on this one issue. It was only a detail, he said, something we had to clean up, to be sure, but not right then and there.

"In any case," he said, "it's time for my nap. You're welcome to stay if you want to. Make yourself at home. Have a swim, stay for lunch, we could talk some more this afternoon. There's a great deal for us to talk about. But meanwhile, if you'd be so kind, would you help an old man to his bedroom?"

I said I couldn't stay, but with his arm around my shoulder, mine around his waist, I accompanied him into the house. His body seemed surprisingly light to me, brittle-boned. The ploy—that he needed help to get to his bedroom—struck me as another move on his part, not for approval but for sympathy. Sympathy wasn't my strong suit right then, but I walked him through the cool interiors downstairs and up to his room, a darkened place of massive furniture, with curtains and drapes pulled against the sunlight and an aromatic, vaguely musty odor.

"I'm all in," he said quietly. "I get up with the birds. Sometimes I wake them up."

Then, before dismissing me:

"A word of advice, Tommy. Be patient with us old codgers. And don't be too hard on the Senator. I wish we all had his qualities."

* * *

I couldn't find my father at first. Then, when I did (at the summer home in Rhode Island of a former U.S. Secretary of State), he was off on some sailing trip. Finally, after repeated calls from me, he called back. If it was so urgent, he said, why didn't I come up there? Otherwise, the best he could do was see me the latter part of August. He wouldn't be in New York before then.

I settled for the latter part of August, in my office.

I won't describe the interview in all its details. This is not because of any embarrassment on my part or, for that matter, on his. In fact, he seemed to think I'd summoned him because he'd missed the last payment on the eighty-thousand-dollar loan, which he promised to forward after the first of the month, when he would have a positive cash flow. (He never did.) But the rancor I'd felt toward him upon learning the truth from Corky Stark had given way in the interim to more practical considerations, such as how to keep him from poisoning the atmosphere with Corky or other members of the Council.

I asked him simply to verify what Corky had told me.

Yes, he was in debt to the Funds.

The amount—almost five million dollars—sounded on the high side to him, but he hadn't looked recently and he trusted Corky when it came to arithmetic.

Yes, he was aware that the indebtedness might devolve on me, even though he was still alive. Why hadn't he told me about it, then? Well, probably he should have. It must have slipped his mind. He'd been more focused on the eighty-thousand-dollar loan when we'd last met, because he'd absolutely had to have it. All in all, though, he thought he'd done me a favor, even with the debt question, by stepping down from the Council before he had to.

I let that pass, also that he'd lied to me about not

having applied to Corky first before he'd hit me up. I asked him instead to review his finances for me. His problem, he said, was that he was cash poor. Well, he'd always been cash poor. He'd had too many dependents, myself included. Some poor investments, in addition, that hadn't panned out because he hadn't had the time to devote to them. He'd probably have done better to give all his money to somebody like Corky and pay him to deal with it. But he'd always managed to scrape through, and he would again.

"How?" I asked him. From what I could gather, he was already functionally bankrupt.

Well, he didn't know. He said he'd been counting on his share of the firm's profits (having forgotten apparently that he'd already told me his share had been greatly reduced), but from what he'd heard the firm's profits this year were going to end up in one mammoth lawsuit, partner against partner, and maybe even in breakup and bankruptcy. Mac Coombs was tearing his hair out. Had I heard? Yes, something of the sort. Well, he said, he was glad to be out of it. He'd be damned if he was going to ruin his golden years worrying about things like that.

He asked me, in turn, if I was going to pay up to the Funds. He imagined Corky would make me pay up—Corky was something of a skinflint—before he handed over the combination to the safe.

I told him the question was under discussion.

Did I need him to do anything? Intercede in any way? No, I thought not.

"Well," he said, smiling his old charmer's smile, "if it's of any concern to you what your father thinks, I'd be most grateful if you did pay up. It'd be nice for me to go out with a clean slate."

I assumed he meant go out of life, or at least out of the Council. But the way he said it, it was with the same insouciance, as though he was asking me to pick up the check before we left the restaurant.

That was the last time I saw him before Corky Stark's funeral. Which, in fact, was the last time I saw him.

19

It would have been hard to realize, that glorious hot summer, when Kitty took to entertaining at home and the Dow reached an all-time high every day, but we had already entered a season of suspicion, of investigation and accusation, of things coming unstuck. Everyone you talked to, it seemed, was making money in the market. Even my blue-haired ladies, under my expert guidance, were making money—meaning simply that, by following the conventional wisdom, which was the only tool I had working for me, and concentrating on the blue chips, the 30 Industrials, the *Fortune* 500s, I was keeping pace for them . . . and myself.

I needed to. My children were both in camp that summer and going to private schools in the fall. The bills on our new establishment (what else to call it?) were breathtaking, even though Kitty wrote off a good portion of her entertaining against Katherine Goldmark Enterprises. We had sold my apartment when we moved but had kept hers on Central Park South, which, even though empty most of the time, cost money. There were the cars, and the help, and the taxes, and a further beefing up of staff at Stark Thompson, P. C., for if, sooner or later, I was going to take on the Trusteeship and still hold the business at hand, it was time to gear up.

Kitty's business, meanwhile, was flying, to a point where she herself rarely attended the parties she gave and instead concentrated on new acquisitions and contacts. Having made a success of the failing Connecticut enterprise she'd taken over, she had branched further out and now—or so it seemed to me—pretty much owned the up-market party business from Princeton, New Jersey, all the way to Montauk in the east and, say, the Danbury–New Haven line in the north. This kept her on the road much of the time, or on the phone when she wasn't on the road, but almost every weekend that summer was open house at our place. Our home was a showcase, Kitty maintained, for what she could do. If people—the right people—were impressed by how she entertained at home, where would they turn the next time they wanted to give a party?

In this calculation she was undoubtedly right, and I even had my own role to play. Marrying me, Kitty said, had broken down the last barrier to her business, and to judge from the mixed crowd of guests who showed up for her "entertainments" that summer, from the Fourth of July fireworks and clambake on, I'd say she was right about that, too. One Sunday there was a tennis match on our court between two nationally ranked women pros, another a performance by a touring group of Chinese acrobats on our front lawn. And always music, always the booze flowing, always an exceptional cuisine, and she began to be written about in the society and gossip columns as well as the food pages. Not only did Kitty's friends show up—the Buddy Spodes, say, from Scarsdale—but people I knew too, like the Thatchers from

New Canaan, or the Buck Charleses (recently reunited on a trial basis) from Darien, people, Kitty guessed, who'd never had a Jew walk through their front doors. Jews exchanged small talk with Wasps, new money with old, Ellis Island with the *Mayflower*. The barriers broken, the old distinctions blurred—except, perhaps, to an increasingly rare observer such as myself, who still caught the telltale turn of phrase, the gesture, the giveaway remark.

How then, in this near euphoric climate, could I talk of the sense of things coming unstuck? I could as well have been an astrologer, discovering a nefarious trining in the futures of certain signs, or a seismologist sensing the coming quakes in the too-quiet fault belts of the California coast. But no, with the benefit of hindsight, there were signs closer to home.

I ran into old Mac Coombs that summer—in fact, at one of Kitty's Sunday parties—who confirmed what my father mentioned, i.e., that the firm was coming apart at the seams. The way Mac explained it, they were topheavy with partners, and in the rush to acquire and expand had made certain commitments to new partners, such as minimum guarantees, which now, it seemed, couldn't be met without stripping the older partners' incomes to the bone, if then. As a result, some of the older partners were in a state of near revolt and threatening lawsuits, and Mac predicted, with an air of gloomy resignation, that the only answer to the mess might be bankruptcy and dissolution.

Then, too, there was the announced investigation of Braxton's. If, by the time I'm talking about, Wall Street was well accustomed to scandal—in the wake, that is, of Ivan Boesky, Dennis Levine, and the resultant shakeups in firms old and new—the fact that a Braxton's should now come under suspicion, with rumors of diverted funds, insider trading, market-rigging, and the like, threatened the very firmament of high finance. Braxton's under fire was like half the Harvard faculty suddenly being indicted for drug smuggling. It conjured forth images of, say, J. P. Morgan being led forth in manacles and thrust into a cell with Al Capone. It was, in other words, unthinkable, and I always felt that, in and of itself, was one of the reasons the investigation increasingly centered on Ted Goldmark—an anomaly in an institution of otherwise simon-pure pedigree—and how it was that he became both the target and the principal spokesman in the firm's defense.

Closer to home, as I said.

Closer still, and indeed so close that it froze me to my chair, was a call I had at the office from a certain Suffolk County detective, Hammerson by name. He wanted to come interview me concerning the death of one Robert Thorne.

But what could he possibly have on me? What could link me to Thorne? The only thing I could think of was Katherine Goldmark Enterprises, but Kitty had already been questioned about her affair with Thorne and the payments Thorne had made to her company. And if it was that, if they'd discovered some discrepancy, why would they want to talk to me and not her?

There was no way, obviously, that I could push Detective Hammerson for answers over the phone. And Kitty, that night at home, was little help.

"How should *I* know what they want to talk to you about?"

"But there's nothing, absolutely nothing, to link me to Thorne. I only met him once. I hardly knew him."

"What do you think I've been trying to tell you, Tommy?"

"Except maybe Katherine Goldmark Enterprises?"

"Nonsense. You don't know anything about Katherine Goldmark Enterprises. And they already talked to me about that."

"Then it has to be Safari."

"It can't be. If it was Safari, you wouldn't be seeing a detective from Suffolk County. You'd have the heavyweights on your doorstep. But there's no way—how many times do I have to tell you?—that they can link you to him on Safari."

"Then what do they want to talk to me about?"

It took only twice around the circle with this conversation for Kitty to become exasperated. She was doing her nails, I remember. Wrapped in a towel, she was perched on a white wicker stool in our master bathroom, bent over one hand with one of those miniature paintbrushes in the other. From time to time she dipped the little brush into a little vermilion bottle that sat on a companion wicker stool. Priorities, after all, are priorities. Yes, it might have been that we'd committed murder together and that an investigator was coming to talk to me about it the next day. But a woman's nails are a woman's nails.

The next time I asked her the same question ("What do they want to talk to me about?"), she simply glared at me over her shoulder, her pupils small and glittering, as though she wanted to clench her fists but couldn't because the nails were wet, and said, teeth clenched instead:

"For Christ's sake, Tommy. Why don't you just see him, and play dumb, and find out?"

Which, no thanks to Kitty, was largely what I did.

Detective Robert Hammerson, so identified by the credentials he passed over to me the next afternoon, was a small man, middle-aged and furtive, with a penchant for ducking his head, and I couldn't escape the notion that somehow he had tunneled his way into the city, like some mole or field mouse, and that surfacing so high above the street, in my office, made him feel distinctly out of his element. He was also one of those people who prefer to get others to talk first, and I accommodated him by expressing my relative surprise that the police were still investigating Thorne's death. I knew of it, of course, from the media coverage. But finally it had been an automobile accident, hadn't it? And the body burned almost beyond recognition?

Yes and no, Hammerson said. There was some evidence that suggested otherwise. For one thing, Thorne had been an experienced driver, and they could tell he hadn't been under the influence. For another, their reconstruction of the event indicated that Thorne's car had been moving forward at very low speed when it went off the cliff, and there was some question among the experts as to whether the fire had been accidentally set off. While they couldn't rule out accidental death, therefore, they also hadn't been able to rule out suicide either, or, finally, homicide.

"So the file—that's what you call it, isn't it?—is still open?" I asked him.

"Yes, it is. I'm not saying we'll ever close it, either, Mr. Thompson," he said a little sheepishly. "The case isn't our A-one priority anymore. No one seems to much care why Thorne died. But we're taking the investigation in a new direction. We're taking another look at whoever stood to gain most from his death."

I said nothing.

"The old greed factor," he added with a ducking half smile.

"And that brings you to *me*?" I said. "I'm afraid I don't get it."

"Just legwork," he answered. "Running down leads." Then: "You knew Thorne yourself, didn't you?"

"I'd say I knew *of* him more than I knew him. I think I only met him once."

"I guess that's the time I'm here to talk to you about," Hammerson said.

"Really?"

"That's right." He consulted the spiral notebook he'd taken out when he first sat down. "It was at a party, wasn't it? Given by a Wanda Russell?"

"Yes," I said. "Mrs. Russell happens to be a client of mine."

"Well, I'd like to take you into our confidence, Mr. Thompson," Hammerson said. "The person we're looking at happens to be Thorne's ex-wife, a certain Martine Brady. Do you know her?"

"Yes, I do," I said. In my sudden relief, I even started to say I'd seen her the weekend before, at my house, for Martine had shown up at one of Kitty's parties. Instead I added, "Not very well, but I do."

"And they had a fight at this party, didn't they? Thorne and the Brady woman? A pretty public fight, too?"

"Yes, they did. And I was a witness. Come to think of it, is that why you're here?"

"You've got it," he said. "Brady's given us her version. In fact, she herself was the one who told us you'd been a witness. If you don't mind, I'd like you to tell me what happened."

Thanks a bunch, Martine, I thought, for warning me ahead of time.

Nevertheless, I gave Hammerson my recollection of it: that Martine had needled Thorne to the point where he'd slapped her, to which she'd reacted angrily. Also the names of others I remembered who'd seen it. Hammerson seemed generally satisfied with my account. Then, folding over his notebook:

"A pretty unsavory character this Thorne, would you say?"

"I'm afraid I can't help you much there," I answered.

"They say he was involved in some pretty shady stock deals, but with him dead nobody's been able to get to the bottom of them. You wouldn't know anything about that, would you?"

"I'm afraid not."

"No, I didn't think you would. Anyway, thanks for your time, Mr. Thompson."

I stood up with him.

"But this doesn't make Martine Brady a serious suspect, does it?" I asked him.

"No, it doesn't. In fact you've pretty much corroborated what everybody else has told us, her included. But like I say, it's the greed factor. She's the one who gains the most. So we're just trying to tie everything up."

Once he was gone, I confess that only the second call I made was to Kitty, who wasn't available in any case. The first, by way of celebration, was to a number I had to look up in the phone book.

"Why didn't you ever tell me you were a suspected murderess?" I said when she picked up.

To which Martine, once she'd done a double take and identified my voice, burst into delighted and raucous laughter.

No matter how badly I wanted the Trusteeship, I thought I'd be crazy to commit myself to paying back my father's debt without an equally firm commitment from Corky on his stepping down. Kitty agreed. As she put it, longevity ran in my family. Who was to say Corky wouldn't fulfill his threat to live another decade and that the Council, barring an absolute catastrophe in his handling of the Funds, wouldn't continue to back off from ousting him against his will?

As to the other side of it, that is, that Corky really did make what he claimed he made (and more, as I discovered), that I could do better than he had from an investment standpoint, and that—incredible though this still seemed to me—he had virtually carte blanche in what he did with the Funds' assets, all these things I verified in two subsequent meetings with him and numerous phone conversations. Very forthcoming with information and records, sure that when the time came the Council would give me whatever I wanted, he seemed, in every respect save the one, to have already accepted me as his heir apparent. And even in that respect, I suppose. For how many fathers, of their own free will, abdicate in favor of their sons until they are, as Corky would have said, damn good and ready?

Meanwhile, at Kitty's urging, I set out on a conscious campaign to woo my fellow Council members and to win them over before our next meeting, which was scheduled for late September. The summer found them scattered all over the eastern seaboard, from Bar Harbor to the Adirondacks, where the Flys, Sr. and Jr., owned adjoining properties (both adorned, if that is the word, by ultramodern, fortresslike homes designed by Cranny Jr.), to Bala Cynwyd, Pa., where I found Mildred Walker in a more classic, Georgian residence. Two were unavailable until September—one in Europe, one (an intrepid Thompson in his late seventies) on a fishing trip in western Canada—but well before the meeting I had completed my rounds.

My visit to the Flys exemplified the reception I got: warm, cordial, but from the point of view of what I was after, absolutely maddening.

When I told them what I was doing, and why I was there, they both voiced unqualified support—this on a stone terrace off Cranny Jr.'s second floor, under a warming sun and with a spectacular view of the Adirondack lake shimmering below. It was high time Corcoran Stark stepped down, they agreed, and clearly I was the best candidate to replace him.

"In fact," Cranny Jr. said enthusiastically, "I can't wait for you to get started, Tommy. From what I know of it, the Funds is like a drifting iceberg—huge, yes, but melting away little by little. If we don't take charge of it soon, the process can only accelerate."

"I agree with you," I said, although I found his metaphor a little off. (How does one "take charge" of an iceberg?) "And as far as I know, everybody agrees with you . . . except Corky."

I then related to them what Corky had said to me, and the sense I had that he wasn't about to resign unless he was pushed, in fact pushed hard.

"Oh, that's just Corky," Cranny Sr. put in. "He's something of a curmudgeon, isn't he? At least that's what he wants us all to think." Cranny Sr. laughed at this, with a phlegmy sound which stopped only when he cleared his throat. "But don't worry about it, Tommy. He'll come around."

"I'm not so sure of that. At least on the timetable everyone seems to want."

"Well, I am," Cranny Sr. said testily, "and I've known him a lot longer than you two."

"When will that be, though?" I persisted. "When will he come around?"

"Well, I'd say your next Council meeting would be the proper time. And that's just a few weeks off, isn't it?"

"You mean, if Corky comes to the next meeting still unwilling to step down, the Council will act?"

"I think that's for you Young Turks to decide," Cranny Sr. said, laughing again. "I'm no longer a member."

"Don't worry," his son concluded, "I'm with you all the way, Tommy. And I know I'm not alone."

And that was about as far as I could move them, any of them, which led me to conclude that if the Council was going to act on Corky, I was the one who would have to instigate it. For I found no volunteers in my travels.

On the subject of the Senator's indebtedness, I did better. Cranny Fly Sr., like most of the older members, knew about it vaguely. Cranny Jr. didn't. Both were surprised by the actual number; both shook their heads over my father's profligacy. Since I had now taken his place on the Council, Cranny Sr. felt that the debt ought certainly to be repaid, but he thought the Council should be flexible as to the schedule. He expected they would be. I told him Corky hadn't been.

"I think you worry too much about Corky," Cranny Sr. said with irritation. "What I'm telling you, even though I shouldn't be, is that as far as the payback is concerned, you can pretty much name your own timetable."

I decided, with the Flys as with the others, to keep to myself my discovery that Corky had been cheating us. I was sure no one had ever noticed—I myself had only happened on it by accident—but there were instances, usually involving the selling of certain assets and the shifting of the proceeds, when very considerable sums flowed through Corky's hands, en route, as it were, from one account to another. Cash in and cash out always matched, and that was the problem. There should have been interest on the float—sometimes only a day's worth, sometimes a week's or longer, but sometimes too with millions of dollars in play. But I could find no record of it in Corky's accountings, and the longer I looked for it, the more I became convinced that he had simply pocketed it.

I wasn't at all sure, though, that the others would look on this as cheating. Furthermore, assuming they approved my continuing to operate just as Corky had, I didn't want to rule out the possibility of doing the same thing myself.

Along the way, I kept Kitty informed. Or tried to. We were both on the road so much in those weeks. The rare nights we spent at home, and the rarer days, seemed like a respite, the eye of the storm, Kitty said, when the last thing she wanted to do was talk business. I knew, too, that she was preoccupied by Katherine Goldmark Enterprises, by its very success and the success of her summer's campaign. That September she began negotiating the licensing of a line of gourmet foods and products bearing the Kitty Goldmark label, and she'd been approached by two rival chains in the up-market kitchenware and gadget business to act as their national spokesperson. Some nights she stayed in the city; when she was home she seemed to spend half the time on the phone. Preoccupied, distracted, she was even, I discovered, insomniac, and she'd taken to keeping a bottle of Valium by her bedside. She looked tired, too, with the ever-present sunglasses off. But whenever I counseled her to slow down, she'd snap back that there was no way for her to stop now.

So, in any case, did I explain away her indifference to what I was up to. In a way, she even disparaged it. She knew I would succeed, anyway; the people I was dealing with were idiots to begin with, and half of them were probably senile. Manipulating them was like shooting fish in a barrel, wasn't it? So what was I worried about?

"I'm worried about Corky Stark," I would say.

"He's the crooked one, isn't he?" she'd reply, for I'd described Corky's float to her. "Well, don't worry about him. You'll know how to deal with him when the time comes."

The only point on which she expressed an opinion was the cash. She thought I was crazy to go to Corky, or the Council, or whoever, with anything on my father's debt.

"Didn't you say they'd told you you could be flexible about it? That you could decide your own schedule?"

She had, it seemed, been listening after all.

"That's right."

"Well, there you are. Why don't you take them at their word?"

"Because I think it'd be a mistake, psychologically."

"Well, I don't. I think you'd be a fool for doing it. But suit yourself, it's your money."

"No, it isn't," I said back, reminding her that anything I pulled out of the firm was half hers.

"Oh, for God's sake. Do you want my *permission*?"

I didn't answer, and seeing my incomprehension, she added, "Look, Tommy. Just do it. Just do what you have to do."

And leave me alone, I added mentally for her.

In the spirit, if not the letter, of confession, let me not stack the deck too heavily. If I failed to understand what was going on in Kitty, part of it had to do, I'm sure, with the fact that I myself wasn't looking. Martine Brady said as much, though in a different context.

"And why shouldn't you be doing what you're doing?" she said (arms akimbo, in that strutty, leggy way she had). "How do you know Kitty's not doing the same thing? Wives do, you know. How can you be sure she's not playing around on the side? Didn't she keep her old apartment? You say she's too tired, works too hard, but how do you know she's not using her business as a beard?''

In the same confessional spirit, yes, I had a dalliance with Martine that season. *Dalliance* was apt, for I knew nothing would come of it, which is why I think it happened at all. We had run into each other at Kitty's party. Then, on a whim, I'd called her after the detective's visit, and one whim, so to speak, had led to another. Martine, at least at that stage, was anti-marriage. All she wanted out of life was money and fun, not necessarily in that order. Thanks to Thorne's death—and no, she assured me, she hadn't been involved, not that she hadn't thought it was a good idea—she had the money. At the moment, I represented the fun.

Another apt word. Sex with Martine *was* fun. After almost two years of a kind of mutual ravaging, culminating in total physical exhaustion, I had forgotten that sex could also be amusing, adroit, and—above all—relaxing. Being with a woman who made no demands on me, as I made none on her, was perhaps just the respite I needed. It was what it was. It meant nothing. It wouldn't last.

And as for Kitty? No, Martine was wrong, had to be. I knew what turned my Kitten on. Money. Money, or its pursuit, was what was sexy. And the closest I came that season to understanding what was really going on for her was the fleeting thought that maybe, just maybe, my money wasn't as sexy as hers.

20

Corcoran Stark died at the end of September in his eighty-fourth year, the result of drowning. It happened in the early morning hours, in his own swimming pool—the outdoor one where the water, though heated, was yet icy to the touch—and during the brief ensuing investigation, his personal physician confirmed that he had repeatedly warned the patient against overdoing. To no avail, it appeared, Corky being Corky.

Actually, I'm obliged to say, the event was a virtual consequence of the Stark-Thompson Council's quarterly meeting, which preceded it by a little less than a week.

We met once more in Corky Stark's dining room. The participants in the throne chairs were the same as before, except for Crandall Thompson Fly Sr., who had resigned. The weather was cooler. Fall comes early up along the Hudson.

The new Chairman, Arthur Hallandale ("Hall") Thompson of Saddle River, New Jersey, and Palm Beach, Florida, opened the meeting with a brief speech of welcome. The minutes from the previous meeting were read and approved. The Trustee then presented preliminary figures for the first six months of the current year's exercise, which were also approved, and the Chair opened the floor to new business.

Silence.

I had the impression, in those few seconds of absolute and awkward quiet, that nobody dared so much as look at anyone else. Heads down, eyes fixed before them, they waited like so many children in some strict patriarchy, staring at their empty plates.

Then I stood up and asked for permission to address the Council.

Permission granted. My fellow members shifted in their chairs and lifted their eyes toward me.

I paid due homage to Corky Stark, his lengthy service to the Funds, the tremendous growth in its assets during his tenure. I was honored, I said, to have been chosen to succeed him by, unless I was mistaken, all of them, Corky included, and I was personally grateful to him for his generosity and his time in reviewing his activities with me. Certainly, as long as he himself would permit it, I would want to turn to him for guidance in the management of our assets.

Et cetera. Et cetera.

"However," I said, "I find myself put in a most awkward, indeed untenable, kind of limbo. While all of you, Corky included, have expressed full confidence in me in the many conversations we've had, the truth is that you, Corky, have exhibited little inclination to step down. Believe me, I respect your right to so decide, as I respect the tradition of the Council that you should do so of your own free will and choice. But under the circumstances, and assuming you and the Council wish and choose to preserve the status quo, then I wish to withdraw my name from candidacy as of today and to go about my own business.''

I noticed that Corky Stark had kept his eyes straight in front of him and his head down while I spoke. The others, too, one by one, had begun to avert their gaze— a bad sign, I thought, and I had to fight the irritation it inspired.

"Finally," I said, "there is one other matter I must mention. It would not normally be a Council matter, I'm told, but each of you is aware of it, and it is important to me that it be resolved in a mutually acceptable and honorable way. I'm referring to my father's indebtedness to the Funds. As a sign of my own good faith, and even though our bylaws in no way oblige me to do so, I have brought with me a check for one million dollars, with promissory notes to cover the balance due over a five-year period, all payable to the Trustee. I am ready to hand these over to the Trustee at the end of this meeting. All I ask in exchange is that the question of the Trusteeship be resolved today.''

Needless to say, I'd wrestled over this last. The family scarcely needed the money, and the sense of my private discussions was that all of them except Corky looked on it strictly as a side issue. On the other hand, they clearly needed to be pushed—I'd calculated that the chances were strong that if I could force an either-or decision at the meeting, they would decide in my favor—and I wanted to remove as much ammunition as possible in the event that Corky dug in. It could backfire; I knew they wouldn't like being forced to the wall. But that was a risk I'd decided to run.

As soon as I sat down, Corky rose.

His speech was short and delivered with his head down.

"I am ready to resign the minute this Council instructs

me to," he said. "Otherwise, I will continue to fulfill my duties as long as I am able."

And that was that.

I took what he said as an important step forward. In effect, he was no longer refusing to resign under any circumstances. He was simply asking to be pushed.

But whether my fellow members got the same message I couldn't immediately tell. After considerable coughing, throat-clearing, chair-scraping, and other manifestations of communal uncertainty, the Chair determined that, given the awkwardness of the situation—unprecedented in his experience on the Council—he would invite Corky and me to leave the room, allowing the rest of them to debate the issue freely. Did this require a formal motion? he asked the Secretary. The Secretary thought not. Did either Corky or I object? Neither of us did. Did anyone else? No.

Where Corky went, I've no idea. It was his house. As for me, I paced the grounds outside, alternating between expectation and frustration. I had put my very fate in the hands of a group of people I scorned. I scorned them not because they were rich but because they were self-satisfied, self-righteous, and incapable of making the least decision. (Did it require a formal motion what we should eat for lunch? No, probably not, but then on the other hand, what do you think? And need we all eat the same dish? Yes, probably we should. But then on the other hand . . .) The worst kind of social elite, in sum, but right then, even as I inveighed against them, they were deciding whether or not I should have three million a year, base income, and with—whether they knew it or not— an open license to steal!

I wanted that three-million base. Yes, I wanted that. And in some almost palpable way, I thought it was my due.

They debated, or talked, or sat, or stood, or all of the above, for a long time. Luncheon was even delayed beyond the usual time—a fact duly noted by the Chairman when we reconvened. But finally, near one o'clock, I saw Cranny Jr., their emissary to me, calling from the house, and I headed back to that heavy, forbidding room, asking him how we were doing as we went.

No comment from Cranny Jr. Lips sealed.

I took that as a bad sign.

"Gentlemen and lady," the Chairman said, "my apologies to one and all for the inordinate length of this meeting. I promise we won't do it again. But we have decided in the end not to decide. It is the consensus of this Council that the Trusteeship question be tabled until our next meeting in January. If there's no further business, I will gladly entertain a motion that we adjourn for lunch."

Motion made, seconded, passed.

I learned then, from Cranny Jr., that there had been no way to budge some four or five of the old guard. Sympathetic as they might be to the needs of the Council, they'd remained intransigent when it came to firing Corky. They'd voted three times. The closest I'd come was 12 to 4. They'd even voted twice on the unanimity issue, i.e., whether it should apply. The vote there had come out even, 8 to 8.

"I shouldn't be telling you this much," Cranny Jr. said, "but it's really the old guard against the new. I think my father, and yours, started a trend. They may even all be gone by January, or early next year. We have to bring the Funds into the twentieth century before it's over."

"What about my father's debt?" I said.

"Oh, that? We didn't even discuss that."

Cranny Jr. counseled patience—like Corky himself, I

realized—and I forced myself to take his advice at least for the duration of the luncheon.

(No hard feelings, Tommy, old man? No, of course not, no hard feelings.)

I won't pretend either that the idea waited for that day to occur to me. But that was where it took root and flowered suddenly, on Corky's terrace, while I beheld my no-hard-feelings colleagues who had just deprived me of three million a year.

Because what difference would it make to them? To any of them? After the fact, would the truth even occur to them?

Besides, they were moribunds themselves, weren't they? With their canes and hearing aids and failing glands, and all the ailments and illnesses which took up most of their attention when they weren't simply eating and awaiting death? When you looked at the question that way, head on, didn't their continued presence in the world only hold the world back? At the world's expense?

And what of Corky Stark himself, the Great Accountant, Beloved Trustee, with his three million a year and his penny-ante cheating, who needed to be helped up the stairs to his room? What right did he have to keep me from what was rightfully mine? Did the spite of an old man constitute a right?

I hadn't talked to him that day, hadn't so much as met his eyes during the meeting or the luncheon, and he'd left the terrace before I did. But when I went out the front door to my car, there he was, waiting for me.

No hand extended, just standing, stooped, eyes heavy-lidded.

"You thought you could end-run me, didn't you," he said, his voice making a statement out of the question.

"I did what I thought was best for all concerned." I answered noncommittally.

"Best for all concerned?" he said, coughing. "There's a good one." Then his face went all wizened, like a nasty and vindictive child's. "Best for you, you mean. Best for Tommy. Well, let me tell you something, sonny. As long as I live, you'll never get your hands on the money, not after your grandstand play today. I advised you to be patient. You didn't listen. Well, now I'm going to teach you what patience is really all about."

I think that was all he said, and I think I gave no reply. I remember getting into my car and starting the engine, but beyond that, the roaring in my ears must have been too loud for me to hear.

The deed itself was too banal to warrant description—except, perhaps, for one moment of it.

I got up in the middle of the night and dressed in gray hooded sweats over my bathing suit. Sweat socks and Reeboks. The only other equipment I needed was a towel. I drove north and, before dawn, parked a mile or so past Corky's house. I made my way back in near darkness. The early morning air was cold on the exposed parts of my skin, but I was sure (not that it mattered) that it would have taken a snowstorm for Corky to have moved to his indoor pool before the first of October.

And I was right.

Silently I skirted the pool area on the side away from the house, keeping in shadow, until I spotted him doing the crawl up the pool toward the deep end, virtually without a sound and at a rhythm so slow the surface of the water barely stirred. From where I stood, I could see lights on the ground floor of the house. The kitchen, I thought, probably some of the staff. But otherwise nothing.

I stood stock-still, senses sharp in the dim light. I could hear a humming, whirring sound—the pool filter, I thought, and its heating system—and then, more faintly, a lap-lap from the water itself.

I stripped to my bathing suit in the cold air and, advancing to the edge of the pool, slipped into the shallow water. It was considerably warmer than the air. I waited for him to pass me one time—even though he was breathing on the side away from me, I believe his eyes were closed—and then, as he came out of his turn, his head still underwater, I seized him by the shoulders to either side of his neck and forced him under. He struggled briefly, feebly. I'm not sure he even knew what was happening to him. Maybe he mistook it for a dream. I held him under for a very long count, long after he seemed to have stopped bubbling, then released his body and climbed out of the pool.

And then it came, without warning. Suddenly, having taken off my bathing suit and standing next to the pile of clothes, towel on top, I found myself unable to move. I had begun to shake from the cold, and though the longer I stood there, the sooner someone might come looking for him, I was shaking so violently, from the inside out, incapable of doing anything else, telling myself I had to stop because I thought I'd heard something and my own teeth were chattering.

The practical explanation might be that the abrupt transition from the heated water of the pool to the cold air had taken my system by surprise. Were I a religious man, I . . .

But I am not a religious man. Nevertheless, and appearances to the contrary, I do not commit murder every day.

As suddenly, the spell passed. I could and did force myself to dry my body and dress again. Had I actually noticed something? Some change in the ambience—an animal perhaps, or the silhouetted shadow of one of his staff crossing a kitchen window? I think not.

I knelt, still shivering a little, to tie the laces of my Reeboks, my eyes on the lit windows across the pool. Then I wrapped the bathing suit in the towel and made my way silently back through shadows to my car.

I never looked back. I heard nothing, saw no one, and I was home in time to bring Kitten her breakfast on a tray.

"Good morning, Kitten" was what I said. "You're looking at the new Trustee of Stark-Thompson."

"What are you talking about? I thought you said your cousin would have to die before that happened."

"That's what I said."

"Well? Is he dead? How did you find out so early?"

I looked down at her. Sleepy-eyed, she was lying against her propped pillow, the covers pulled up, her dark hair a little frizzy.

"Because I saw to it myself," I told her.

"You . . . ? You *what*?"

"That's right, Kitten. I just joined your club."

She sat up abruptly, clutching the covers to her breasts.

"You *what*?" she repeated, her eyes now wide. "Joined what?"

"I only carried out orders, remember? You yourself told me to deal with it. So? So, I've just dealt with it."

"You . . . ?" she started to say. "Oh, my God! Look, Tommy . . ." She dropped the covers, leaving herself bare-breasted because her hands were gesturing. "Look, darling, I just can't deal with this. Not now. Not on top of everything else."

Her voice was suddenly harsh and a little frantic.

"What everything else?" I asked.

"Never mind." Then, her voice softening as she

seemed to focus back on me: "Oh my God, Tommy. Why at least didn't you tell me about it?"

"It hardly seemed necessary," I answered, feeling some stirring of pleasure at the fact.

She covered her mouth with one hand, as though the reality of it was just dawning on her.

"You'd better sit down," she said. "Please." She moved over under the covers. "You'd better tell me about it."

I sat on the edge of the bed and described what I'd done. She played devil's advocate, questioning certain details: the possibility of evidence (I saw none), and how did I know Corky was dead (because I had looked into the question of how long even expert swimmers could hold their breath), and how could I be sure there'd be no autopsy? I saw no reason why there would be. He was eighty-three, with a bad heart, had even been advised against overexercising. But even if there were an autopsy, what could it prove? That he died of drowning instead of heart failure? There would, I was sure, be no sign whatsoever of a struggle.

She shook her head when I was done. Her eyes closed, and she rubbed at one of them. Then a trace of a shudder.

Goodness, I thought, why such horror at someone else's crime? I remembered her telling me she had thrown up after she killed Thorne. And then I remembered something else as well—as unseemly then, at five A.M., as it would be now.

Yet since when had unseemliness ever held us back?

"When will it become official?" Kitty said. "The Trustee business?"

"There you go," I said lightly. "That's more like my Kitten."

"But when?"

"I don't know. It can't be left vacant for very long.

Probably they'll call a special meeting of the Council—"

"But when?" —with some urgency.

I savored the change in her, from the shock of murder, the appropriate horror and dutiful dismay, to the practical consequences. Her eyes widened and took on a glaze, stimulated, I surmised, by thoughts of dollars.

Whereas for me:

"Let's worry about that later," I said. "Right now, if you absolutely insist, I'll let you have one sip of coffee. But just a sip. Then I have other things in mind for you."

"What on earth . . . ?" she said, not reading my intent until I pulled the covers away from her hands. The sight of her bare flesh, her full and luxurious body, intoxicated me beyond belief. "Tommy, for God's sake! I don't *believe* you!"

"Don't," I said with an urgency of my own. "Don't believe me. Believe this instead." At which, taking her hand, I circled it around my sudden erection.

"My God, Tommy, I . . ."

"Remember? You did it to me, remember? After Thorne? Now I want you the same way."

I will say this for my wife: taken aback she may have been (and I believed she was), but she could ready herself for sex in an instant. And so, that morning. Soon she was talking away—to me, to us:

"You did it for me, didn't you? Tell me you did it for me, even if it isn't true. Did you? Did you?"

"Yes," I replied, breathing hard, "for you."

"Oh, my Tom, my darling man, my . . ."

I held her there, though. I wanted the words. Yes, the clawing, yes, the arching, drawing me deeper inside her, but the words more than anything, the desperate words. Because I saw another mirror image of that other night, or morning, after Thorne, and yes, I wanted her afraid of me for the first time, as I had been then, and I wanted her babbling to cover her fear. And yes, she babbled as she came, arching and flattening, and I spurted into her, riding our waves.

I loved her, just then, in a new way, loved her as she lay back, alabaster skin and dark dripping muff against the pale sheets, eyes exhausted, loved her in the way of the master, he who, having long been seduced, turns seducer, he who, having been worked, manipulated, coerced, and otherwise cajoled, now emerges, full-blown, heart pounding, the consequence.

How hilarious it now seems to talk of it this way!

Yet Kitty saw it, too.

"A monster," she murmured, eyes half closed. "I think I've created a remorseless monster."

She reached for me again.

Only later did we talk about the money, my access to it, the when and the how of it.

21

Corcoran Stark had asked to be buried in the small Connecticut town to which the founders had for some reason repaired after having made their money in Pennsylvania. Over half its graveyard, behind the white-steepled church, was inhabited by my ancestors, and although many years had passed since any Stark or Thompson had actually lived in the community, that was where we, his mourners, went, on one of those wet, dark days in early October, under umbrellas, with a chill drizzle dripping intermittently and a steady mist in the air.

The turnout was surprisingly small for a man of eighty-three whose passing had earned a headline on the obituary page. But Corky Stark's wife had predeceased him, they'd had no children, and while a few other relatives showed up, much the largest contingent was from the Council, some eight of us, plus my father, plus Cranny Fly Sr. Corky's own minister officiated, and Hall Thompson, our Chairman, made a brief speech.

I had talked to Hall Thompson several times by phone in the immediately preceding days. In fact it was he who'd

called to inform me of Corky's death. At Kitty's prod-
ding, and though, as I'd told him, I hated to bring up
matters of business in the midst of our loss, I'd pushed
him on the Trusteeship. His suggestion was that I become
Acting Trustee, pending our January meeting. I pointed
out to him, though, that in the absence of certain formal
acts required of the Council—empowerments, authori-
zations, and the like—I would be effectively hamstrung
if we waited until January, and the markets were too
volatile for us to leave our assets dormant for three
months. Of course what was on my mind, and Kitty's,
was that if I pushed now, in the vacuum created by
Corky's sudden death, I could get anything I wanted out
of them.

Hall Thompson agreed with everything I said, and to
his question of how to accomplish it, I suggested we meet
immediately after the funeral, those of us who attended,
and that he poll the absentees by phone to obtain their
consent to whatever we decided.

We went then, in the rain, in a short cortege of limousines and expensive cars, to the dining room of a local
motel a few miles from the town. We were, as I recall,
the only people there. I had prepared all the documents
myself, the delegations of authority, the rights to buy
and sell and handle monies in the Funds' behalf, all
subject to the Council's (later) approval, plus my own
compensation plan, and in the margin, as it were, of a
spate of reminiscences about Corky and the drinking of
toasts to his memory, I presented them, reviewed them,
explained them. I circulated copies for all. No one, however, posed a question or raised an objection. Motions
were made, seconded, passed by voice vote, and Hall
Thompson signed on the dotted lines.

The atmosphere was strangely and, for a funeral, atyp-
ically convivial—due, it appeared, to the presence of my

father and his hail-fellow-well-met style. You'd never have guessed, from my father's anecdotes about him, that Corky Stark was the dour and curmudgeonly old man we had all known. The Senator even managed to make a distinctly elderly assembly feel good about the "lottery" of life and death. He'd learned during the war, he said, that survival in combat was a lottery. So, he realized in his old age, was life. Today we put Corky in the ground, the latest loser. Who would be next? In a way, he said, it didn't matter, because in the lottery of life, where everybody lost, what really did count was "how you played the game." At which he lifted his glass not to Corky Stark but to all us survivors.

I'd have thought, as noted, that remarks of this sort would have depressed the group. Not so, however, and in the midst of their high-spirited camaraderie, my own tawdry business passed through unnoticed.

In other words, the Senator won the popularity contest that day at the Connecticut motel, while I walked off with the money. And all he said to me was (his arm around my shoulder, within sight but not earshot of the others): "Do you see, Starkie? I can't be all bad. Look at what I've done for you."

Yes.

In any case, I had pulled it off. This realization made me euphoric, and all the way home in the windblown drizzle I anticipated holding the mood, with the help of a few glasses of good Scotch malt, until Kitty returned. As it happened, though, she was already there. I found her in the solarium, the large glassed-in room, furnished in nineteenth-century wicker and chintz, which had become where we spent most of our time.

"What are you doing here?" I said, bending to kiss her. She was stretched out on a couch, pillows in large floral designs behind her head, thumbing through some magazines.

"I thought you might need me, poor darling," she said, tossing the magazines aside and kissing me back. "Besides, I'm a little played out. How did it go?"

"It's done," I said. "Corky Stark is in the ground, and I'm the new Trustee."

"You're kidding!"

"Would I kid about something like that?"

She smiled at me with her eyes.

"You really pulled it off?"

"I really pulled it off."

She stood in her stocking feet, eyes wide, arms around my neck.

"Well, Stark Thompson, I think we'd better drink to that! What will you have? Champagne, this once?"

I laughed at that. Neither of us particularly liked champagne, but to a traditionalist, and in her tastes that's what Kitty was, the great occasions—such as, I suppose, a gathering of successful murderers—called for champagne.

So champagne it was, an excellent Dom Perignon, brought by Kitty in an ice bucket with a towel wrapped around the bottle's neck, and accompanied, on a black lacquered tray, by a mound of black caviar, in crystal, on an ice nest, surrounded by lemon wedges, chopped onions, and little squares of toast. (And why should I spoil the moment by pointing out that it couldn't all have been prepared spontaneously?)

We toasted each other in silence.

"When do you get access?" she asked, eyeing me across the top of her flute.

"Access? I already have access."

"No, I mean, full access to the money."

"That's what I said," I answered, grinning at her.

"Full access to the money. I already have it. Does Katherine Goldmark Enterprises need capital for expansion? How much do you want? Ten million? Fifty million?"

I laughed at her evident incredulity, and she laughed too, her high-pitched giggle. Somehow, she said, she hadn't really believed it. There would be further delays; something would have gone wrong.

I reminded her that I'd drawn up the papers myself. Arthur Hallandale Thompson had signed them, with a blanket waiver from the absentees.

"So you have full powers?"

"Yes, as of this minute. In fact, as of a couple of hours ago. And I haven't so much as spent a nickel yet."

"And what about the million?"

"What million?"

"The million you were going to pay them back. The Senator's loan."

"Nobody so much as brought it up," I said. "The trouble is, now that you mention it, I've got no one to give it to, do I? Except, of course, to myself? The Trustee pays the Trustee?"

"Well, don't be in any rush," Kitty said. "We may need the money."

"What on earth for?"

Even before she put the champagne flute down, though, I saw the change in her. Ah, yes, Kitten had something on her mind. The mirth left her countenance, replaced by a calculating look. I was sitting now on the couch where I'd found her, my legs crossed, and she standing, only her eyes in motion.

"Look, Tommy," she said, and inhaled, exhaled. "There's something I have to talk to you about. I may as well be up front about it and say I don't think you're going to like it, not one bit. But I've got no choice."

I smiled at the thought that I hadn't heard a woman

talk like that in years. Not since college, in fact, when I'd been hit up for money for an abortion.

"Your word is my command, Kitten," I said fliply. Then, when she didn't react: "Well? Out with it, my dear! What in God's name is it?"

"My brother," she answered. Suddenly that sharp, chiseled look, eyes small, lips taut.

"What's wrong with your brother? He's not going to jail, is he?"

"He might be. Unless he can come up with a great deal of money in a short time."

"Ahhh," I said, it being my turn to stiffen. I uncrossed, recrossed my legs. "So the eminent Mr. Goldmark comes with outstretched hand?"

"It's not funny, Tommy. It's real."

"I didn't mean it to be funny."

"I can't explain it all—it's too complicated—but hear me out, please."

She sat down next to me, facing me sideways on the couch, her arm along the back of it, and filled in the seamy story for me, the parts, that is, that I didn't already know.

The firm of Braxton's, the benighted Braxton's, crème de la crème of the Wall Street houses, was, as I've said, under investigation. Apparently it was open season. Everybody was in the act, from the U.S. Attorney to the SEC to the various stock exchanges to, in point of fact, Braxton's itself. Braxton's, in other words, wasn't going to let anyone out-Braxton Braxton's, and in the time-honored tactic of the accused turned accuser, the firm was conducting its own internal audit, ahead of the outsiders and under the leadership of . . . guess who? The Senior Managing Director, Mr. Theodore Goldmark.

What was more, according to Kitty, or so at least her brother had told her, Braxton's stood every chance of beating any charges. The entire firm, she said, had rallied behind Teddy. Even the old guard among the partners. Even old Charlie Braxton, whom they'd pulled from retirement to give a fiery press conference against "the witch hunters out there who are hell-bent on destroying our company and our industry." Maybe on some minor points at issue Braxton's had acted inappropriately (though never illegally), but on the major issues—principally insider trading and attempts to rig the market on certain securities—Ted Goldmark said they'd win.

There was a rub, though.

What none of the investigators, outside or inside, had yet discovered—although the insiders were allegedly close—was that Ted Goldmark was personally on the hook himself. From Kitty's description, it involved what would legally be called the misappropriation of funds, or diversion of funds. Practically it meant that for some time, through a series of adroit jugglings involving the firm's accounts, Goldmark had been using other people's money for his own purposes. Apparently my old friend Henry Angeletti was also in the thick of it—had there perhaps been another reason Goldmark had hired him and his weird computer brain away from Thatcher?—and though Goldmark (or Goldmark and Angeletti) knew how to cover the traces so that nobody could find out what had happened, he had to come up with a very considerable amount of cash in order to do it. Short-term cash, that is, until the internal audit was complete. But he had no more than a week at the outside to do it.

And if he didn't?

Then not only he himself but all of Braxton's was going to blow sky-high.

"You mean he'll take them all down with him?" I said.

"He says he'd have no choice, once he's put under oath."

"Sounds to me like he's got a pretty strong basis for hitting up the partners. Why doesn't he go to them direct, say, 'Sorry, boys, but either we all swim together or we all sink together'?"

"Because he says they'd crucify him."

It would be a close call, I thought, but possibly he was right. The ultimate revenge of the Charlie Braxtons? Yes, I could imagine that.

"Wait a minute, though," I said to Kitty. "Before you go any further, there's something I don't understand. I always thought your brother was a rich man. Even a very rich man."

"I think he was," she answered. "But he got carried away."

"A hundred and eighty million dollars carried away?"

"I don't know what you mean."

"One hundred eighty million dollars, remember? At least his share of it? That, according to Henry Angeletti, was the total profit on the insider trading. And Henry, by his own admission, didn't have everything."

"But not all of that was Teddy's."

"Even so."

"No. Look at our part of it. Only half the profits, at the top, were yours, and you split that with me."

"That's right. And how much did you pay him?"

"Half," she said.

"*Half*!" I exclaimed. "Jesus Christ! You were being pretty damned generous, weren't you? With our money?"

"Oh, come on, Tommy. We wouldn't have made anything if it hadn't been for him."

"Maybe so," I said, "but who ran the risk? And who put up the capital?"

She didn't answer.

"Even so," I said, "half of your half would be twelve and a half percent of the total, wouldn't it? Assume that was what he averaged, twelve and a half percent of a hundred and eighty million is still over twenty million dollars."

"He didn't collect everything," she said. "Not on Safari, anyway. Not from Thorne."

"How come? Didn't he have an agreement?"

"Yes, but not in writing. Nothing was ever in writing."

"So Thorne took it to the grave with him?"

"I don't know where he took it," she said, "but Teddy never saw a lot of it."

I still found it hard to believe that Goldmark was broke, and I said so. He held one of the top jobs in a field where the top jobs are known to pull down eight figures annually. Besides, an operator like him would have seeded a lot more outlets for his information than just his sister, me, and Robert Thorne, and I'd have bet he'd found some way, in spite of everything, to invest on his own account.

"What can I tell you?" Kitty said tensely. "He says he can't cover himself. Why would he say that if it wasn't true?"

I think by this time I was standing, staring down at her on the wicker couch.

"So he comes to his sister?" I said. "Because he knows the guy she's married to has just gotten access to more money than God?"

She didn't answer.

"Well, if it's that important to you," I said, "and I gather it is, why don't you lend him the money yourself?"

"I can't," she said. Then, instead of leaving it at that, she started to say something else. "I've already—" But she caught herself and glanced away, as though momentarily confused. "Anyway," she said, catching herself again, "he needs more than I could ever raise."

"Wait a minute," I said. "You've already what?"

"Never mind."

I'd never—not once—heard Kitty say something inadvertent when it came to money.

"Don't tell me 'never mind.' What did you start to say? You don't mean to tell me you've lent him money yourself?"

She hesitated, still looking away.

"Well? *Did* you?"

She nodded.

"How much?"

"That's none of your business."

"Oh yes it is," I retorted. "If you're about to ask me to do something I may or may not want to do, it certainly *is* my business!"

Her head swiveled abruptly, and she stared up at me, eyes large, as though I'd just slapped her. Or was it in surprise that, in the midst of confrontation, I hadn't already folded my tent? Or in some belated recognition that the Stark-Thompson money was mine to deal with, and not necessarily hers?

She bit at her lower lip, and then she admitted the truth. Over a period of a month, more, she had taken her company's credit line, already stretched through its acquisitions, out to its limit. For her brother. For him of whom she'd said, not all that long ago, *My brother's a son of a bitch. What else is new?*

At least, I thought, it explained one thing: why, other than sheer greed, Kitty had been almost frantically trying to expand her business. Also why, when it had appeared that I might have to come up with two and a half million in cash for Corky Stark, she had pushed me not to offer anything.

Why? Because the money, it seemed, was already gone.

Still, I found it hard to believe. Of all Kitty's qualities, one that stood out strongly was her sound business sense. I'd seen it at the beginning, in our days with the Sprague estate, how she'd worried me over every last detail and penny. She ran her business the same way, forcing it to profitability, sharp eyed for opportunities. Yet here she was, throwing money into what sounded like a widening hole. For, whatever she'd given Goldmark already, it clearly hadn't been enough.

I pointed all this out to her, dotting, so to speak, the i's and crossing the t's. And for once in her life, at least in our life, she took it. Neck arched, head down. It turned out that the new number Goldmark had quoted her— what he claimed he now needed—boggled even Kitty's imagination, even though, according to Kitty, he had figured out a way to do it that involved no cash. All he wanted was that I, as Trustee of Stark-Thompson, authorize the shifting of funds within Braxton's from my accounts to an account number he would give me, and then he and Angeletti would take care of the rest. It would be short term, he'd told Kitty, a few weeks probably, the end of the year at the outside, and he'd pay a handsome premium for it.

By this time, I remember, the drink in my hand was Laphroaig.

"But how do we know that'll be the end of it?" I asked Kitty. "How can we be sure it won't keep escalating and that he won't need a still bigger number?"

"We don't," she answered.

"Then why, Kitty? For Christ's sake, *why*?"

"Because he's my brother," she said. "Because when

push comes to shove, I'm the one who feels responsible for him. That's just the way it is.''

Just the way it is.

Such fine and sororal sentiments weren't, of course, the whole story, but they were, in a weird way, genuine enough. I remember gazing down at her in that wickered room, the woman I loved, her eyes wet, her mascara smudged, and thinking that, yes, she meant it, also that I didn't understand and probably never would understand, and going inside from anger to incomprehension and back to anger again.

"So you want me to do it?" I said. "In spite of everything?"

She didn't answer at first.

"Well, I'll tell you one thing, Kitty. Whatever I do or don't do, I think the borrower had damn well better come apply in person, and not through the intermediary of his sister.''

"That's what he said you'd say," she said faintly.

"Oh? Did he?"

"He said you'd be a tough nut. He said you were too smart to entertain a proposition like this without hearing about it firsthand. He's at your disposal. Only he needs to move quickly.''

"And where am I supposed to reach him?"

"He asked that you call his office, anytime, day or night. They'll know where to patch you into him.''

"Well, then, let me ask the question again. Is this what you want me to do?"

"Yes," she said, her eyes averted.

"I'm sorry, Kitty, but that's not good enough. I want you to look me in the eye when you say it.''

It would take some literary genius to describe her expression at that moment when her head lifted and she brought her eyes up to meet mine, someone who could capture in a single flow of words the rigidity of her body, the defiant jut of her jaw, the slight trembling in her right lid signifying—what? Tension? Fatigue? And above all the steady boring of her black pupils into mine in overt and unmistakable animosity. But why the sudden animosity? Was it because, for once, she had lost control of a situation? Or had it always been there from the beginning, part and parcel of her erotic challenge, which I had chosen to ignore?

But as for me, a mere attorney and one inexperienced, besides, in courtroom theatrics, I can only say that, facing the naked hostility of her gaze, I'd have gladly withdrawn the question, had there only been someone to order it struck from the record.

But there was no one. Only Kitty and I.

"Yes," she repeated, and then the look was gone, and the clocks could tick again and life go on.

"There's something else you'd better keep in mind when you talk to him, Tommy," she said. "Don't forget, he could bring us down, too, if he wanted to."

"Meaning?"

"Meaning Safari and all the rest."

"That sounds like blackmail again to me," I said. "Is that what he told you?"

"Not in so many words, but he alluded to it. Said that if he's ever put under oath, in his own defense, against charges of insider trading—"

"But it's diversion of funds he's up against now."

"He said one thing could lead to another."

"So instead of blackmailing Braxton's because he thinks they'd crucify him, he does it to us? Your dear brother?"

No answer.

"Well," I said, "what do you think? Would he bring us down with him? In extremis?"

Her eyes gazed up into mine again, unflinching.

"Yes," she said.

22

She's a real ballbuster, that sister of mine," Ted Goldmark said to me in the back seat of his limousine the next morning. "I never would have had the nerve to ask you myself, Tommy. I mean, why the hell should you? You've just been named Trustee—that's one humongous responsibility. You'd want to get your feet wet first or, knowing you, prove yourself. Why the hell should you run any risks? Not that there are any, but you try telling Kitty it's going to rain when there's thunder and . . ."

I'd heard him on this kind of gambit before, though.

"That's not the way she told it to me," I said. "She said you kept after her to talk to me. She—"

"Did she? Really? Well, look, Tommy, I'm very grateful to you for even giving me a hearing. Genuinely grateful. I— Excuse me a minute, will you? This'll only take a sec—"

A red light was blinking on the console between us: the telephone. Goldmark picked up the receiver and started talking first:

"I said I don't want to be interrupted, not for— Who?

He *what*? At seven-thirty in the morning? Well, you tell him to go fuck himself. No, tell him if he comes with a subpoena, he'll get all the cooperation he— What? Well, let him. Put him outside in Reception, give him all the magazines he wants. But tell him he can sit there till hell freezes over and nobody'll talk to him, not me or anybody else. Not until he produces a subpoena. You got it?''

He hung up with a bang, saying, ''Damn. They're all over me like a tent, Tommy. I'm sorry. You've no idea. Now, where were we?''

Where we were was on the parkway headed into the city in the middle of rush hour. The time and place had been his idea, not mine. He hadn't wanted to use his office—it was a zoo these days—and he didn't want to come to mine, not even if he could break away, which he probably couldn't, because he was convinced he was being followed. Paranoia? Paranoia with reason, he'd said. I had no idea. So? He lived farther up the line than I did, why didn't he pick me up and we'd drive in together. We could talk in peace and quiet, and nobody to listen.

The peace and quiet were relative. We were interrupted frequently by the phone, and I half listened while he barked instructions to, I gathered, underlings at Braxton's, mostly having to do with the investigations. I use the word *bark* advisedly, for he had a staccato style on the phone, firing out short sentences, or half sentences, as though his mind was working twice as fast as his tongue. I wondered fleetingly if it was all staged for my benefit—the self-important businessman at work, with shirt sleeves rolled up, metaphorically, that is, for Goldmark wore elegant navy serge over a white-on-white shirt and regimental tie—but I decided it wasn't. The limousine was clearly his rolling office, complete with telephone, dictating machine, coffee maker, bar, even a small computer call-up screen, and he claimed to accomplish more in his couple of hours' commuting than at his desk at Braxton's.

In substance, his version of Braxton's predicament and his own personal bind largely corroborated what Kitty had said, but his rationale for it was new to my ears. According to Goldmark, Braxton's had been mediocre when he got there, slipping in the rankings each year and nowhere in profitability. But they'd been on a roll ever since, cutting deals they never would have even gotten a sniff at before him, cutting a few corners, too, and stepping on some people's toes, sure, but who the hell didn't? That's what they'd hired him for in the first place. Behind the genteel facades, the business was cutthroat, but the profits he'd made Braxton's were humongous. And why shouldn't they be? What the hell else were they in business for, if not to make money?

"Look, Tommy," Goldmark said, "all this shit about insider trading? It's been going on for *years*! The Street's *based* on it, couldn't survive five minutes without it. So what's the difference? I'll tell you what the difference is."

Another phone interruption, followed by: "Where was I? Oh yeah, the difference. You know what the difference is? It's the old-boy network. All those guys—Charlie Braxton, for instance—they never had to spell it out, no contracts, nothing. They did it with the wink of an eye, the pull of an ear, a buzzword here, a buzzword there. And nobody got caught. They ran their own show. But then they let us in, you know? Jews, wops, anybody with brains. But we didn't speak their fucking language, we didn't go to the same schools, we didn't give a shit about their Union League Club, which nobody ever heard of anyway.

"Look, why do you suppose they hired me in the first

place? Because Braxton's *wanted* a Jew? You gotta be kidding. The day I made Managing Director—and I was going to leave if I didn't—the entire Union League Club pissed in its pants. No. It was because they finally woke up and realized there were too many people around they couldn't even talk to, much less do business with.

"But"—turning abruptly toward me, with a suddenly boyish grin—"I don't have to tell you, Tommy. You know what I'm talking about. Hell, you're one of them. Is that why you don't like me?"

"It could be," I answered.

What it was about him that made me want to tell him the truth, I've no idea.

"That's okay," he said, brushing quickly past my reply. "Since when do you have to like somebody to do business with him?"

Still, he said, it was no accident that of all the people who had already gone to jail, who had actually gone to jail, not a one of them had gone to Andover or Groton or St. Mark's or any of "my" fancy prep schools. That was the old boys' revenge. And they'd do it to him, too. He was going to save Braxton's for them (single-handedly, it seemed), but if they found out he himself was in trouble on the side, they'd run like rats from the sinking ship.

"I had two goals when I got there, Tommy. The first was to make Managing Director by the time I was thirty, and I've done that. The second was to have a net worth of a hundred million, and I'm going to do that, too."

"It doesn't sound as if you're off to too good a start on that score," I said.

"Temporary," he said with a wave. "It's all temporary."

"But how could a guy as smart as you," I said, unable

to resist the dig, "get himself into such a fix? With his
hand in the till on top of it?"

"Impatience," he admitted freely. "I got carried
away, made some mistakes. Bad timing, bad luck, bad
judgment. But nothing I can't weather. It's only a liq-
uidity problem."

"If that's so," I said, "why does the number keep
changing?"

"What do you mean?"

"What you need," I said. "Kitty tells me she's already
lent you money, but now you need more. A hell of a lot
more, from what she tells me."

"Shit," he said, "you don't need me to tell you how
volatile the market's been. Up and down, up and down,
nobody knows where it's going. I'm subject to margin
calls just like everybody else."

That part was true enough. The major market indices,
which had been on a steady upswing for several years,
had lately started to yo-yo, with big swings day to day
and heavy trading. Still, Goldmark must have had some
margin calls. When I pointed this out, he admitted—
freely again—that instead of simply covering himself at
Braxton's with Kitty's money, he'd tried to recoup in a
hurry, which had only compounded his problems. But
now all he wanted to do was cover, and he described
how he intended to go about it, with my help, accom-
panying his words with succinct strokes of his hands.

"The way I've structured it, Tommy," he said,
"you've got to look on it purely as an investment, and
a pretty fair one too, I'd say. You'll make a regular loan
agreement with the account I name, and I'll countersign
it myself. I'm ready to pay prime plus three—plus four
if it goes past the first of the year, but it won't. Plus an
extra point to you personally if you twist my arm. Now

how many deals does Stark-Thompson have that are better than that?''

"And supposing you can't pay up?"

"What do you mean, supposing I can't pay up?"

"It happens," I said, thinking: *even to very smart people*.

"It won't happen to me," he answered.

"Well, that's fine. But what kind of security can you give me?"

"You mean to tell me my handshake isn't good enough?" he asked, grinning.

"No, I'm afraid not."

He shook his head.

"Kitty warned me you'd be a tough nut to crack," he said.

We had, by this time, already passed through upper Manhattan, where the traffic, joined by the commuters using the bridge, had slowed to a virtual standstill, and Goldmark, communicating with the driver by intercom, had instructed him to try the local streets. It occurred to me, not for the first time, that he and Kitty played a strange game, sometimes echoing each other, sometimes contradicting each other directly. They bad-mouthed each other freely, yet hadn't Kitty mortgaged her company to help him save his neck?

"What can I offer you, Tommy?" he asked with an apologetic smile. "My house? This car? Sorry, Braxton's leases both for me. If I had the collateral unencumbered, would I be talking to you in the first place? And paying a premium on top?"

"In that case," I answered, "I don't see how I can help you."

To his credit, he didn't flinch or bluster or, as I expected he would, bring the blackmail element into play. Not yet, that is. Instead he fell silent—for the first and only time that morning—until on a green light we'd inched a few blocks farther south, through a kind of no man's land which made me glance to be sure the car doors were locked. Then, smiling as though at some inner thought, he said:

"There's one thing I could put up, of very definite value. Only I'd have to swear you to secrecy, Tommy. Someone we both know would cut my throat from ear to ear if she ever found out."

"What's that?" I said.

"My share in Enterprises," he answered. "Katherine Goldmark Enterprises."

He watched me with the same conspiratorial smile, enjoying, I suppose, my dumbfounded reaction.

"You mean she never told you about it?" he asked.

"No."

"Well, it's true," he said, laughing. "I own fifty percent of it. Drives her absolutely bananas—not that it should. Who do you think financed it? Raised the capital for it? She's always tried to buy me out, but I've never let her. It's too good an investment. Hell, why do you think she lent me money, Tommy? Out of the goodness of her heart? She thinks maybe I'll default, and if I default, there goes my fifty percent of Enterprises!"

And if that were true, I thought, why would she have pushed me to bail you out? But I'd been doing another mental calculation, as always with Goldmark: How old could he have been at the time, if he'd actually financed Kitty?

"I always understood it was her husband who'd floated her company," I said.

"Who? Sprague? You gotta be kidding. Oh, maybe in the beginning, when she was working out of her kitchen. But when she really got it going? With an office? Employees? Hell, he turned her down flat! That's when I

stepped in, with every cent I could scrape together. I
knew it was going to fly. But that was the dumbest thing
Sprague ever did, and she never forgave him. She de-
stroyed the fucker.''

''What do you mean by that?'' I said, feeling myself
tense.

''Just what I said,''. he answered noncommittally.
''She's a real ballbuster, my sister. Though why she ever
married him to begin with I'll never understand.''

''People do a lot of funny things when they're on the
rebound.''

''What rebound?'' His eyebrows raised in a question.
I hesitated.

''I'd gathered she lived with someone for a long time,''
I said. ''Before Sprague.''

''Oh, that? The piano player? The one she likes to say
walked out on her?''

''That's right.''

''And you believe that bullshit, Tommy?''

''I didn't know it was bullshit.''

''No? Well, who do you think threw who out? The
guy moved in with her, they lived together three months,
six months max. Then one day, everything of his out on
the street, including the piano. She even changed the
locks on the doors. I know because—''

He stopped midsentence, as though he'd said more
than he'd wanted to. He reached idly for the phone, which
hadn't rung, then gazed out the window a moment, thinking, then back to me, grinning that boyish grin again.

''Well, I helped her. She asked me to. He wasn't such
a bad guy, either. Better than Sprague. Said she didn't
want to pay his bills anymore. Well, hell, that's my sister
for you. Don't say I never told you, Tommy: she eats
guys alive.''

Laughing again.

The first time he'd said it, it had been me. Then, I think, me and himself. Now it was men in general whom Kitty ate alive—me, Goldmark, Sprague, the piano player. That was a hell of a way, I thought, to talk about someone who had been trying to save him, even if she had something to gain by it.

I felt a sudden claustrophobia in the limousine, an urge to get out and walk. But our business was unfinished, and, trying to look at it as objectively as I could then, maybe I'd rather have had the Funds own half of Kitty's company, if it came to that, than somebody else Goldmark might peddle it to.

"There's something you've left out," I said.

"What's that?"

"From what Kitty said, it sounded like blackmail."

"Kitty could make anything sound like blackmail. What do you mean?"

"What will happen if I say no to you? What will happen if you don't raise the money?"

"Oh, that," he said offhandedly. "Let's leave that out of it."

"Let's not leave anything out," I said sharply.

"Oh, come on, Tommy, maybe you want to call it blackmail, or she does. Call it what you want. All I said was that under pressure—I mean under oath, under interrogation . . . Hell, you're an attorney, you know what I'm talking about . . ."

"You mean, if you had a chance to plea-bargain?"

"That's not what I said." Then, smoothly: "Look, Tommy, let's be honest about it. I'm not saying it'd even come up, ever. Maybe it'll never have to. But I happen to know a lot about you and Kitty, your activities. And I'm not just talking about Safari, either."

"Then what are you talking about?"

"Thorne, for one."

I had to at least give him credit for his chutzpah, if nothing else.

The last part of the conversation had taken place in the street in front of my building, where the driver had double-parked, Goldmark's side toward the curb. We stared at each other. There was no menace in his expression, no desperation, just the steady gaze from under thick dark eyebrows.

"What about Thorne?" I said.

"Shit, Tommy," he said scornfully, "who do you think ordered her to kill him?"

He opened the door then, holding it for me as he stepped into the street. I got out after him. We stood face to face for a moment while horns honked. I'd forgotten I was a good five or six inches taller.

"Either way," he said, holding out his hand, "I'm very, very grateful. But do we have a deal?"

I thought about it for a second even though I'd made up my mind in the car. I didn't take his hand.

"I want to see the papers first," I said.

"Great. I'll have them on your desk this afternoon."

I turned away, but he called after me.

"With or without Enterprises?" he said. "But you'll promise to keep it secret?"

"With," I answered.

23

The papers arrived that afternoon, brought by Henry Angeletti. I returned them the next morning, signed, by messenger. I saw Kitty very briefly, late that evening, told her only that I'd worked out a deal with Goldmark that I thought I could live with.

No questions asked; no answers given.

For all I knew, she'd already gotten the details from her brother.

His version.

In point of fact, I no longer had any idea whose version to believe. Like the Marxists, they took turns rewriting history until your head spun like a fortune wheel, and if I remembered, a long time before, Kitty exploding at me for believing her brother over herself (the question of the hundred-dollar bet), there were things he'd said in the limousine that I couldn't walk away from. Half truths maybe, exaggerations certainly, but had he invented them out of whole cloth?

I didn't believe for a minute that he'd ''ordered'' her to kill Thorne. Who could *order* her to do anything? But they might well have talked about it—which was bad enough—since Thorne, whom Kitty said she'd recruited and who had then been taken over by Goldmark, knew enough to bring them both down. (If anything, I'd have guessed Goldmark had argued against murdering him. Thorne owed him money. With Thorne dead, his chances of ever collecting were nil.) What counted, though, was that Goldmark clearly knew about it! Maybe the investigations into Thorne's finances had led the police nowhere (or so the Suffolk County detective had indicated), but what would happen if Goldmark were ever put to the wall and the Thorne link discovered? How far might he go to save his own skin?

I already knew Kitty's answer—very far, indeed—and I was inclined to agree with her. Stark-Thompson's loan to the Braxton account, however risky, looked to me like the only insurance I could buy.

Then there was the question of Katherine Goldmark Enterprises. That he owned fifty percent of my wife's business—and it would have been the same had it been twenty percent, or one percent—may have stuck in my craw, but it went a long way to explaining why Kitty, despite her son-of-a-bitch-what-else-is-new line, was locked into him in her business dealings. Whatever they thought of each other personally, they'd used each other constantly, and, I saw clearly, the common denominator was always money. Over and over again: money. I could even explain to myself why Kitty had never told me about it. In this respect, I bought entirely what Goldmark had said: it must have driven her absolutely bananas.

But what I couldn't swallow, or explain away, or in any sense come to grips with, was the way he'd demolished her story about the pianist. *And you believe that bullshit, Tommy*? Vividly I remembered the night after Wanda Russell's party when Kitty had disappeared. I'd hit the roof, and then, while I sat on the Récamier couch in the bedroom, she'd told me the story. I remembered every detail of it, down to how, visibly exhausted, she'd sent me home afterward. And ever since, whenever I'd encountered that imperviousness, that impenetrability, that hard granitic shell which formed such an important part of her personality, I'd thought, well, at least I know where it comes from.

So much for Kitty's baring of her soul.

So much for my amateur psychologizing.

And you believe that bullshit, Tommy?

Yes, I believed that bullshit. Or: I had.

Unless Goldmark himself were lying?

But why would he? Just to belittle his sister?

And you will say: Any reasonable husband, upon hearing his wife so accused, would have gone home and asked her about it.

I didn't.

Which, you will say, only goes to show how estranged I had already become from her.

To which I can only reply: Yes, and no.

I know we spent that weekend together, at home, but I've no recollection whatsoever of what we did or said, or didn't do or say. A total blank. Maybe we had guests. Maybe the Buddy Spodes drove over from Scarsdale. Maybe we reviewed the contracts for the licensing of Kitty Goldmark products—I remember her asking my opinion at some point. Maybe we played tennis, listened to Mozart. Possibly we even made love. Undoubtedly I continued my postmortems on this strange creature whose roof I shared, and bed, and table, and whose hand I had indeed taken in holy matrimony on our lawn, even realizing—as I surely must have by that weekend—that I no longer had any idea who she was.

No idea whatsoever.

But it doesn't matter. Not at all.

The postmortems, anything.

For that Monday—you will remember the date of October nineteenth—the stock market definitively fell apart, collapsed, and we were all in the water, every one of us.

PART
FOUR

24

Sometime that Monday afternoon, I simply got up from my desk and walked out of the office. I couldn't deal with it another minute. My phones hadn't stopped ringing. On the one hand, my blue-haired ladies, Wanda Russell in the vanguard—three, four, five times, hysterical, what were we doing, what did I mean we couldn't sell, we were going to be wiped out if we didn't sell, she *ordered* me to sell, raging, weeping, keening—like a bunch of Irish biddies at the wake of some great martyr of the Republican army, and Wanda, I remember, my great bosomy friend, Wanda, already threatening me with a lawsuit for "willful mismanagement." And on the other, the Thatchers I dealt with, abject, helpless—there *was* no market, no buying at any price, the ticker itself was all fucked up, nothing to do except wait for the bottom, ride it out, you have no idea what it's like, Tommy old man, it's a stampede, an avalanche, a tidal wave . . .

I even heard, just before I walked out, from my Chairman, Arthur Hallandale Thompson. Had I heard the

news? Yes. What were we doing? We were riding out
the storm. Good, he said, that sounds like a good idea
to me.

Little did he know.

Little did Wanda Russell know.

Little did any of them know.

The truth was: while all of them had been hurt, I had
been wiped out. As far as my blue-haired ladies were
concerned, I was way overdrawn and the amount grew
every fifteen minutes. For some time by then, I had been
pulling my prospective share of the estates' profits out,
pending their resolution and final accounting. Only now
these profits, if there were any at all, had been vastly
diminished. In every case, therefore, I owed them money,
in some cases a hell of a lot of money.

Nor could I look to Stark-Thompson for help, even
though it dwarfed them all. The value of our assets on
the day I took over as Trustee, that is, the day of Corky
Stark's funeral, had become the benchmark for my first
year's operations. By the time the market closed that
Monday, in a great rage, a cliff-jumping riot, of selling,
in which the Dow dropped over twenty percent, it was
clear that I could never hope to bring us back to a point
at which the Trustee's percentages would come into play.
And while, when the time came, I was sure I could
browbeat my fellow Council members into awarding me
an honorable stipend for my year's services, say a spare
million or so, for I'd barely had time to survey all our
existing assets before the crash, I already needed a great
deal more than I could ever expect—honorably, that is—
from my major source.

Through it all, there was one call I didn't get. I'm
referring to my brother-in-law, the eminent Senior Managing Director of Braxton's, Mr. Theodore Goldmark.
I'd had occasion to talk to Braxton's, to my resident

"Thatcher" who managed one of my accounts, but all he could tell me was that the place was a zoo, people running every which way, and that it was a good thing the windows in the building didn't open. By any logic, Goldmark would have been the first one out if they did, and for my sake it was too bad they didn't. He could, I judged, never survive this, and the implications for me, for Kitty, were so vast and varied I couldn't begin to think about them. Except for one implication: for some reason, out of some odd reflex of gallows humor, I kept thinking that now Stark-Thompson was going to end up equal partners in Katherine Goldmark Enterprises.

In the space of a few short hours that Monday, therefore, I was wiped out. Cleaned. Like the poker player who had nothing to sign but IOUs, and zero in the bank to back them up. My pockets pulled free, and inside out, and empty.

And therefore, in the midst of the biggest financial catastrophe in over fifty years, I walked out.

I remember our receptionist saying to me:

"Are you leaving, Mr. Thompson?"

"I guess that's what it looks like, Millie."

"But what should I tell everybody? When will you be back?"

"Tell them never," I said. "Unless it's my wife. If she calls, say I'll catch up with her later."

From this day of dire and, for most of us, unprecedented events, I retain this other weirdness: never before, at least as an adult, had I felt so lightheaded as when I reached the streets that afternoon. I don't know what I'd expected to encounter: people running, cars crashing, towers toppling, the sky on fire? None of the above. The midtown scene seemed pretty much as usual: crowded, noisy, exhaust-filled. Peddlers, panhandlers, taxis, trucks, tourists, shoppers, people on important missions.

Black, brown, yellow, white. Two legs, two wheels, four. The pencil peddler on Fifth Avenue with no legs at all. But where were all my fellow victims of the crash? Already defunct? Or still upstairs in their shirt sleeves, sweating out their final hours? Why weren't they tripping their own light fantastic as I was?

For the first time in my life, I went into stores and browsed and bought and charged up a storm. Gifts for me, gifts for Kitty, for Starkie and Mary Laura, from Saks, from Doubleday and Mark Cross, from Tiffany's, all sent on their way by UPS. Eventually I drifted over to the club, usually empty in that trough between the lunch crowd and the five o'clock crowd except for stray jocks, but now there was one group hovering by a computer screen and another, larger and noisier, in the bar. I wondered if the Senator had ever paid his bill—no stray thought, for my resemblance to him, at least for that one afternoon, seemed both clear and hilarious. Broke, in debt to his eyeballs, bankrupt or near, with four ex-wives and how many mistresses strewn behind him, he still tap-danced his way through life gaily, stepping on toes now and then but always with that marvelous, and exasperating, insouciance. The Most Illustrious Member of Our Family. Perhaps tomorrow, certainly within a month, I would have become the Most Notorious Member of Our Family, but that was tomorrow or next month, and meanwhile—here was his secret!—I, too, could dodge the piper, let him catch me if he could. So I set up the bar I don't know how many times, toasting them all in pure Scotch malt, my peers and friends, and let them send me the bill!

The Senator's son indeed. By and by, I began to feel that other feeling, that tickle, that itch, that yen to preen my feathers before a damsel of my choosing, that throaty urge for the sweet words of love, and the gestures, and the touches. But there, in the club bar, the connection broke. Good-bye, Senator! For I wanted not just a damsel, any damsel. No pallid imitation for me. Even then, I confess it freely, that late in the day, in our day, with our world already standing on its head and the bells tolling, I wanted still her wondrous bosom, her devouring lips and her eyes half closed and rapturous and her thighs crushing down on me, her sweet heat, her musk, my Kitten.

There was one logistical problem, though.

I couldn't find her.

Not at her office; they thought she'd gone to her trainer's. Not at her trainer's; she'd been there and left. No message at Stark Thompson, P.C. The answering machine at the apartment. Not at the house, and no message. No, still not at her office; she'd called in, had said she wouldn't be back.

Typical Kitty: on the worst day of my life and, by extension, hers, to have abandoned me. Deflated, I finally made my way down to Grand Central and found a train home. It was crowded and (it, too) more clamorous than usual. I caught snatches of conversation—how So-and-So had taken the pipe, and So-and-So was hanging by his thumbs. It was always someone else who'd been ruined that day, never the speaker. Bravely resigned, the speakers themselves were riding it out. Sitting on the sidelines. Waiting for the bottom. Great opportunities acoming. Meanwhile the stir and hubbub of having experienced a great moment in history firsthand, the battlefield, at least Yale 29 Harvard 29, and the world would never be the same again, a brand-new ball game out there, chins jutting, heads raised in class defiance, and the communal garb of serge, flannel, tweed, and Burberry.

By the time I got home to our columned Colonial manse, I was dangerously close to sober. Sober meant

thinking about tomorrow and what I was going to do.
Sober meant thinking about Kitty and where she was.
Our Irish couple asked me if I wanted dinner served alone.
The phone had been ringing nonstop, they said, but no
word from Mrs. Thompson. I told them to forget about
dinner, that I would eat something cold later, and reached
for the Laphroaig.

I woke up diagonally. I was sprawled on our bed, face
down, clothes on. Shoes on. I thought it was the middle
of the night. (Had I just dreamt the dream again?) It
wasn't. Five-something. Dark outside, the lights on in
the room. I got up on my hands, elbows, to a monstrous,
blinding headache. No Kitty. How could there be if I
was diagonal on the bed? A taste of total inky rancidity
that only a bottle or more of pure malt can instill so
indelibly. A flood panic: that it was over. That what was
over? Everything.

I had to deal with everything. But one step at a time.

By the time I got downstairs, the headache was better
and the lights in our kitchen no longer hurt my eyes.
Kitty's car was still in the garage. On a hunch, I called
her driver. I think I woke him up. He said he'd had a
message from Mrs. Goldmark's office the afternoon before, telling him she wouldn't be needing him. Wouldn't
be needing him when, last night? Last night and this
morning too, he supposed.

The city, then. She must have stayed in the city.

I dreaded going, but I went. I drove all the way, beating
enough of the traffic to get to my office before it opened
for the day. I stood alone by our receptionist's desk,
listening to the tape she'd put on the evening before, at
closing. There'd been a number of calls then—two from
Wanda Russell—but none from Kitty. And no calls this
morning.

I left, ducking through the downstairs lobby lest any

of my employees spot me, and walked over through the morning throngs to Kitty's office. It occurred to me that I'd done this once before, a long time ago, when I'd been searching for her. Katherine Goldmark Enterprises on the twin glass doors. I went in. Some people were already at work. I think I frightened them. I barged through the premises—her own empty office with the secretary outside and the burgeoning ficus spreading sideways at her ceiling. People at their desks, startled. No, they hadn't seen Kitty, no, they hadn't seen Ms. Goldmark, no, they had no idea where she was, when she'd be in. How could they have no idea? How could the great and trusted Bettina herself not know? Who kept her calendar? Where was her schedule?

Finally (Bettina admitted), yes, she'd already called in, before anybody got there, to cancel all her appointments for the day.

I made them play the tape for me. Kitty's morning voice, cheerful enough: "Hi, this is for Johanna (her secretary), please cancel everything I've got on today. I won't be available. Talk to you later."

I think they—Bettina probably—even called Building Security, for on my way out— Was I that storming? That furious?—I passed somebody who looked the type. But by the time they'd have explained to him, I was long gone, back on the street.

I had saved the most logical place for last. No accident there. Even as I rounded the corner, I felt the dread suffuse through me. I must have been having trouble breathing. I remember stopping in sight of the park, the canopy, my sides heaving though I hadn't been running, and taking deep breaths, in, out. I was sweating, though I've no sense what the weather was like: hot, cold, wet, dry.

I know it rained sometime that day.

I hadn't been there in months. Even the nights we were out late in the city, she'd preferred to go home. On the rare occasions when I'd had to spend the night in New York myself, I'd used the club.

Kitty, of course, still used the apartment.

Ah, yes.

The doorman, however, recognized me readily enough. In fact he barred my way, as courteously as he could.

"I'm afraid I can't let you in, Mr. Thompson."

"What are you talking about, can't let me in? It's my wife's apartment, isn't it? Is she upstairs?"

"Yes," he said with obvious embarrassment. "But I have my instructions."

"You mean she told you not to let me in? What is this? Has she got somebody up there with her?"

He didn't answer, which was my answer.

"Please, Mr. Thompson. Please at least let me call upstairs first. It's my job."

"I'll tell you this much, Donald"—his name coming back to me—"if you so much as lift the phone, I'll have you out on the street by this afternoon. And that's a promise!"

With that I shoved past him, through the inner doors and on to the elevators.

When I got to our floor, my neck was clammy with sweat, the back of my shirt soaked, and my heart pounding as though I'd run up twenty-odd flights of stairs. Well, what did you expect? What did you expect? What did you expect? I kept saying it to myself over and over.

I'll tell you what I expected, though, fumbling for my key ring in that hallway, I couldn't have formulated it then. I expected to find Kitty with a man I'd never seen before, the new Tommy, so to speak. I might have imagined them in flagrante, yes, but just as easily in more civilized postures, eating breakfast, perhaps, in front of the familiar park view, their heads close together, making plans. How long they'd have been together, who could say? But it wouldn't have been just since yesterday. That wasn't Kitty's way. The Kitty I knew would have been grooming my replacement, as I had once been groomed, et cetera.

Et cetera. Et cetera.

How much of a cluck can one man be?

At least she hadn't changed the locks on me.

I let myself in, closing the door silently behind me. The lights were on in the living room, the disarray considerable. Remnants of food, drink, I think. Clothes strewn on the Chinese rug, a shirt. Empty of people. Something different in the way the furniture was arranged, or maybe it was new?

I thought I heard sounds. I crossed the living room to the small back hall. The door to Kitty's bedroom was open.

The lights on. My lungs struggling for air.

They were naked on the bed backward, heads toward me, feet at the pillow end.

Goldmark was on his back, head far back, chin raised, eyes closed, arms crossed above and behind his head and off the edge of the bed. His chest hair was dark and curly, too. His chest was heaving like a bellows, in, out, the air coming out of his open mouth in rhythmic snorts.

Kitty was on her hands and knees over him, body pulled back so that her arms were fully, stiffly extended. Rocking back and forth, head down and ass high up the glistening ramp of her back. Her face was hidden in his crotch, hair splayed darkly to either side but not concealing the rocking movement of her head.

The air had a haze of sex to it, and the sweet-and-sour redolence of Kitty in heat.

I don't think he saw me. I know she did. Whether or not she heard me, she pulled her head back abruptly. Her neck arched back. Her mouth still momentarily clamped his erection, or what was left of it. Her face was wet, smeared, and I saw her eyes go wide from tiny glittering pupils into a gasping expression.

It seems to me she must have gasped, must have shrieked. With her body if not her mouth. Maybe she did. But I was too confused as I turned, stumbling, to know where the noise was coming from, and it was only when I somehow got down into the street again, blinded by light again, and still heard the raucous, taunting clamor, that I realized the clamor was inside my head.

25

I must go fast now.

We never had a chance, not a one of us. Not Thorne, not Sprague, not all the other men she'd ever inveigled into her web of greed and deceit.

Not, finally, myself.

At least the pianist, as far as I knew, had escaped with his life.

To say that I realized this that morning, on Central Park South, would be an absurdity. I realized nothing. What I had beheld sickened me—yes, sickened even me. Next to it my poor recurrent dream, that nightmare of Starkie in danger which had haunted my adult life, seemed such meager fare. And this was no dream, no hallucinogenic horror show. This was the real McCoy. I had just seen the unseeable.

Nor will I try to describe the crazed life I led those next days, when I snuck like some renegade in and out of the wreckage of my former existence. I passed my nights in unfamiliar hotels, motels. I jumped at shadows, mostly my own. I did what I had to do, and I drove rented cars, and if I thought once that I had to go to her, in spite of everything, I thought it a thousand times. I couldn't grasp life without her. Yet each of those thousand times I saw her face as I'd last seen it, smeared, hideous, and each of those thousand times I understood what had been going on all along, and I choked on my understanding. The unexplained absences, the performances, the fights (always over the secrets she kept from me), the stonewalling, the lying. All to hide the true partner of her life, her darling, her curly-haired prince of finance, her brother, her lover.

His very name, the mere thought of it . . .

My God.

I made no attempt to contact her that week. Nor she me. I knew what she was plotting, though. It had to be. It was my turn to be strapped into the driver's seat, and hers to reach across me, left hand depressing the brake pedal, right hand groping for the shift, breasts brushing my lifeless knees, skirt tight across . . .

Why finally had she gotten rid of Sprague after all those years? Because, I was willing to bet, he'd found out the truth about them.

And why Thorne? Because Thorne had known, if not her incestuous secret, still enough to bring them down.

Whereas now I held both parts. How long would she endure the risk of exposure, the menace of my revenge?

I let it gnaw at her longer than I dared, almost a week. By then, though, sweet revenge had yielded to a grimmer instinct and I'd bought the gun, courtesy of American Express.

On Saturday I went to visit my children. I'd spent the night before in a Stamford hotel. (Could it have been the same one she'd stayed in that time? And had she really been alone that night? In a pig's eye!) Only in the morning, though, did I call the house—a reflection of my paranoia and clearly a mistake. When I told Susan I'd be there in fifteen minutes to pick up the children, she hit the roof. How could I do this to them, just show up like that? I'd never done it before, what was so important now?

What was really bothering her, it turned out, was that she had another man there, and once I'd wormed that out of her, I couldn't keep from bursting out laughing. And then apologized, congratulated her instead and told her not to worry, that if he and I ran into each other, I'd be my most civilized self.

I never saw him, not Susan either for that matter. Mary Laura and Starkie met me at the door. I hadn't seen them since the wedding. Either they'd since taken their teenage vows of silence vis-à-vis adults, or they were pissed, or both.

"What's up, Dad?" Starkie said, still in the doorway.

"Nothing's up," I answered. "I had an impulse to see you, that's all, and I've acted on it. Look," I said, glancing from one uncomprehending face to the other, "I know you may have other things to do, but in that case I have to ask you to cancel. Bear with me, please. Just go make your phone calls and let's get going."

Instead they trailed me out to the car. Starkie asked where my new Mercedes was. I told him that I hadn't come from home, therefore I'd rented a car. (The Mercedes? Was it still in the New York garage where I'd left it?) We drove off, Mary Laura with her arms crossed in the back seat, Starkie repeating:

"But what's up, Dad? Is this some kind of surprise thing?"

"No," I answered. "Maybe the way to think about it is that every once in a while adults get crazy ideas. Just like you."

"But you've ruined our day," Mary Laura said from

the rear. "And you've never done this before, just show-
ing up."

"True," I said.

Silence. Then, from Mary Laura:

"Well, where are we going?"

In fact, I had no idea.

"It's still October," I said. "Maybe we could go over
to the beach, take a walk together."

"The beach!" she said, astonished. "We'd freeze to
death!"

And so it went, back and forth, my stabs at enthusiasm
blunted by their sullenness, and short of telling them the
truth, I don't suppose it could have been different. Still,
I stuck it out, and made them stick it out, through lunch.
We ate in one of those long-menued deli diners we'd
been to before. Mary Laura couldn't find anything she
wanted. Starkie, I think, had a hamburger and a shake.
They answered my questions in monosyllables—about
school, their work, their friends, sports, fads—as though
there was absolutely no way they were going to let me
break through their resentment.

When I took them home, I kissed Mary Laura good-
bye on the cheek, then made Starkie stand still for a hug.
This, too, was new—normally we shook hands, if that—
and I could feel his body wriggle in embarrassment. Too
bad, I thought. Maybe someday he'd remember it, maybe
not. In any case they were free of me, and I got back
into the car and drove off, realizing that neither of them
had once asked about Kitty.

Then I had nothing to do except wait for my call or,
rather, wait for news when I called in, which I did periodically. Two days before, I'd hired a detective agency,
the same one I'd previously used for Susan. Their assignment was simpler this time: I simply wanted to know
my wife's whereabouts round the clock. No, there was

no place they could reach me; I'd be on the road, but I would call in for their reports.

Early that morning, before I'd checked out of the hotel, she'd still been at the mansion up the Hudson, Goldmark's place, having driven there the day before. Now, when I turned the car in at its Stamford lot before walking across the street to rent another, yes, she was still there. Was there anything else I wanted them to do?

No, I said, just keep up the surveillance.

I drove west slowly, to another motel not far from the river, and there I stayed, all but completing this account. My life was reduced to one activity and one goal. I was going to see her again. For diversion, I dismantled the weapon, stripping it to its components and laying them out on a motel towel. My obedient fingers wiped them clean. I held a square of gauze to the far end of the barrel and sighted through, looking for dust. There was none. Then I put the pieces back together again.

Shortly before noon on Sunday, they both drove off, she and Goldmark, in separate cars. In accordance with my instructions, only she was followed. Was that correct? Yes, that was correct.

The rest of Sunday, I called in every hour. She had gone home, I learned. Her car was in the garage. She hadn't moved since. As near as could be determined, she was alone.

I waited. There was a chance that he, or someone, would show up for dinner. Seven o'clock, eight o'clock. No one did.

With my nine o'clock call, I canceled the surveillance.

I showered, shaved, dressed, and packed my belongings. Sometime before eleven, I got into the car and drove off. I drove a little slowly, in minor traffic. I could find none of her Mozart on the radio. Out of nowhere instead—some attempt at black humor?—came thoughts of mythical and literary figures: the homecoming sailor in the Tennyson poem; Odysseus back in Ithaca, looking for Penelope; even old Van Winkle, geographically closer, stirring from the dead. Except that I was only in my forty-third year, no beard, no white, and I had been awake, at least in theory, since the end of World War II.

Then nothing except the winding lane, the dark trees, mailboxes, fenceposts.

I parked at the edge of our property. I was wearing a heavy black turtleneck, wide-wale black corduroys, rubber-sole shoes. New purchases. I walked in through the trees toward the lights of the house, the night air cold in my face.

The garage, where my old Aries still stood. The tool bin. The smells of polish, wax, in the darkened dining room. The center hall, alight, where Kitty had tripped on the stairs while Goldmark drank Scotch in the living room.

I froze, startled, when the hall lights went out behind me.

Only the system at work. Random selection.

Silence.

Our door, our room, upstairs. Listening. Entering.

Kitty asleep. The dim light, lime green, from the Victorian lamp. Her dark hair against a sea of pillows. Her nightgown, dusky pink, silk, rising, falling.

I listened to her breathing, my own. Yes, my last silent good-bye, whispered, brief requiem.

And then she looked up at me.

"Go on, Tommy. Do it. Show me you have the guts."

When I didn't immediately respond, she threw back the covers and got up abruptly. She brushed past me as though I wasn't there and padded barefoot across the carpet toward her antique dressing table.

The pink silk of her nightgown trailing behind her body.

"The only thing I've been wondering," she said without turning, "is what took you so long. You look like shit. Did it really take you that long to screw up your courage?"

No mockery in her tone, however. I stood there, watching for what she would do next, conscious of the weight in my hand.

She sat down at the dressing table. Switching on the lights above its three-paneled mirror, she eyed herself in the sudden brightness, glanced up at my reflection, presumably the gun's as well, then back to herself. She picked up a hairbrush. Pulling her head down, first one side, then the other, she worked it firmly through the dark curls.

"How long has it been going on?" I asked. "Between you and your brother?"

"*It*," she repeated, the brush poised in midair. "You can't even bring yourself to say the word, can you." She put the brush down and, leaning forward into the mirror, smiled exaggeratedly at herself, frowned, then reached toward a squat porcelain cosmetic jar. "Well, *it*, for the record, has been going on for as long as I can remember."

"Then why me?" I asked. "Was all this—from the Christmas party on—just a trap waiting for the mouse?"

"Do you need me to answer that?"

"I do."

"Really?"

"Yes."

"Well, as far as Theodore R. Goldmark was con-

cerned, you were handpicked. He knew all about the
Stark-Thompson Funds long before you did."

"And what about you?"

She seemed to hesitate. Still leaning forward, still scru-
tinizing her face, she dipped her fingers into the porcelain
jar and began to massage the skin under her eyes.

"As for me," she said into the mirror, "I had my own
reasons."

"What reasons?"

"What difference does it make now? We both blew
it. Teddy panicked."

Somehow, although I don't remember moving, I'd
come within reaching distance of her. Only the lower
part of her face reflected in the mirror. Her lips, her chin.
I could smell the familiar rose-tinged odor of the cream
she used.

"And now he'll go to jail?" I said.

"Oh, I doubt that."

She'd stopped rubbing. She wiped her fingertips on a
linen hand towel and swiveled toward me in her seat.
Her cheekbones glistened from the cream, accentuating
the criss-crossed circles of white skin around her eyes.
Her pupils stared up at me, dark, small.

"Either you're going to use that, Tommy," she said
with a short nod at the gun, "or you're not."

"You don't believe I will, do you?"

"Whatever," she said with a stray gesture. "But if
you're not, I'd like you to leave now. I really need to
get some sleep."

No tremor, not the slightest apprehension. Just: *I need
to get some sleep.*

I started to laugh. At last, I thought. That was what I
had come for: that summing up of our relationship.

"You mean," I said, smiling bitterly down at her,

"you're not going to fuck me first, Kitten? One last time? Just for old times' sake?"

Only then did I see the anger flare, and then Kitty rose up at me in all her faded, furious glory.

EPILOGUE

MEMORANDUM TO FILE (THOMPSON)   CONFIDENTIAL
FROM: DMC

This memorandum is based upon, and reconstructed from, notes taken in the course of the events described.

I was informed of the apparent death of Stark Thompson III on October 28th, 1987. I was, and remain, his attorney of record. It was I who prepared his Will and was named coexecutor of his Estate along with his wife, Katherine Goldmark Thompson, a.k.a. Kitty Goldmark. My name is Dwight MacGregor Coombs. I am licensed to practice law in New York State.

Ms. Goldmark, and so I shall refer to her, informed me of the event by telephone. It was a generally unsatisfactory conversation, due, I thought, to her shock at the news. The event had taken place in the early morning hours the day before. A car, rented in her husband's name in Stamford, Connecticut, had plunged through a construction site on the Tappan Zee Bridge and into the Hudson River. The car had already been recovered by the authorities and contained certain possessions which Ms. Goldmark herself had identified as belonging to her husband. But no body had been found inside.

I had met Ms. Goldmark only once or twice prior. (I had in fact attended their wedding in June 1987.) She had struck me as very self-possessed, and I know she had obtained quite some success in the business world. The woman I spoke to on October 28th, however, hardly resembled her. She contradicted herself several times. On the one hand, she said she was certain, positive, that Stark Thompson wasn't dead, that it was all a mistake. On the other, she wanted me to press the police to find his body. She wanted to know how long it took for someone presumed dead to be declared legally dead. She questioned me about her husband's Will. How long would it take to be probated once he was declared legally dead? What about his life insurance? When would the beneficiaries collect? But then again she repeated that he wasn't dead. She even implied that I knew his whereabouts.

This was not true.

Ms. Goldmark then offered me money if I would represent her interests vis-à-vis the investigating authorities. I declined, at which she ended the conversation promptly by hanging up.

There were two reasons why I declined, although I gave neither.

The first was that I suspected I wouldn't be a suitable representative for Ms. Goldmark.

The second involved a potential conflict of interest, as follows:

The same day as Stark Thompson's death or disappearance, I had received the typescript to which this memorandum is appended. It arrived by Express Mail, postmarked White Plains, New York, and the package contained the following letter, which I cite in full:

My dear Mac,

It was good to see you again last week. You seemed in excellent form.

What you may have deduced about my current situation I can only guess, for you were your usual discreet self. The fact is that I am in some difficulty. I cannot begin to explain why, but at the risk of sounding melodramatic, I have reason to fear that I may be in personal danger.

In the event you learn that something of the sort has happened—*but only in that event*—I ask that you open the enclosed package and read its contents. You will find, at the end of it, a second letter addressed to you. I would prefer that you save the latter until you've finished reading, and this not because I'm being deliberately mysterious or obfuscatory, but because I doubt it would make much sense to you otherwise.

And if nothing happens? Well then, just keep it all in some safe place. One never knows!

We may or may not see each other again. The latter would, of course, be a source of very great regret to me.

With kindest personal regards,

Sincerely yours,

The letter was undated, typed, but signed in his own hand: *Tommy.*

I began reading his account that evening. I did not finish until the weekend following. Perhaps I should only say that my eyesight has deteriorated, but I feel compelled to add that certain revelations shocked me greatly. At times I was obliged to put the pages aside. That this young man, whom I had known since his infancy and had always liked, could have committed such crimes—

and for what? For her? Insane acts, I am tempted to call them, and yet he appears to have been in full possession of his faculties.

My God Almighty, I thought when I was done, how little I know my fellow man! Not at all, in fact. Not after all my years of living.

I must continue.

Pursuant to Stark Thompson's instructions, I then read the second letter, handwritten, which I now cite in full:

My dear Mac,

In haste.

Since you're reading this, the worst must already have happened.

To business:

In the matter of the Estate of Edgar Sprague. While I doubt sufficient basis exists for opening an investigation into Sprague's death, please look into your firm's own files. They contain ample documentation concerning her dealings in Manderling's stock.

In the matter of Safari, etc. The records of Stark Thompson, P.C., plus the report and testimony of Henry Angeletti, will provide an excellent point of departure in support of my contentions. I would guess that, properly handled, Mr. Angeletti could be persuaded to cooperate, particularly if the Senior Managing Director of Braxton's goes up for indictment?

In the matter of the death of Robert Thorne. Please inform the appropriate authorities of the following:

1) The Thorne murder weapon is in the tool bin in my garage, wrapped in a pillowcase. This is where I put it after we moved in. I believe it is a #2 iron. It belonged to Thorne. I would bet anything her fingerprints are still on it.

2) Tell them to look under the mattress in Thorne's bedroom, at the bottom side, for traces of blood. She scrubbed it that night, and then we reversed it. Alas, I did dispose of the sheets and towels.

Finally, in the matter of the demise of Stark Thompson III. I leave this to you, dear Mac, depending on the circumstances.

I do realize, Mac, that none of this is quite your bag. You would much prefer, I imagine, to avoid the ugly situation it is bound to create. Act if you can. If you feel you cannot, them I am appending a list of people, all attorneys known to me and probably to you, to any one of whom you could turn this over. But I have chosen you instead, relying on your skill and discretion to carry out the last wishes of one who remains

Your loyal friend,
(signed) Tommy

I have debated this second letter's contents at length, particularly the last paragraph. It is not that I have any intention, whatever I might personally wish, of shirking my duties toward a client. Rather I doubt my competence. I have little experience in criminal matters, none whatsoever in homicide. I am also concerned about possible libel charges should I in any way "publish" or "cause to be published" Stark Thompson's allegations, in his account as in the letter. I have decided finally to proceed, but prudently.

Stark Thompson's disappearance has aroused a considerable stir in the media, particularly given the police investigation's inability so far to determine precisely what happened. Despite repeated attempts to drag the bottom of the Hudson River in the area concerned, no body has yet been found. Furthermore, I have learned that there was something strange about the crash itself. Under normal circumstances, I am told, it is extremely unlikely that any vehicle short of a truck or bus would be able to breach or jump the bridge's retaining wall, even at high speed, so as to plunge into the river. It was only in the temporary area of the construction, where systems of barricades and warning lights and arrows led drivers away from the wall, that a car could in fact plunge through. This, I have learned, has made the investigators somewhat skeptical about accidental cause, though in their minds Thompson could still have been either the victim or even the perpetrator of the event.

According to the testimony of those who knew him (I am simply repeating now what the media have reported), including his wife and brother-in-law, Stark Thompson had been newly and happily married. Only three days before his disappearance, he had visited his two children, who lived with his ex-wife. He seemed normal to them. Ms. Goldmark has told interviewers that she last saw him that Sunday night. He had been away for the weekend, had arrived home late, they'd gone to bed shortly thereafter, and when she awoke in the morning, he had already left. An early meeting, she had assumed. She had no idea where he had been all day Monday, or Monday night. He hadn't been to his office. To date, she is the last person known to have seen him.

No mention has been made yet of the financial difficulties he describes in his account.

I myself have been approached by the media for background material on my client and information about his Will. Of course I am reticent about the former and have divulged nothing of the latter's contents.

I know only one thing which is not common knowledge: Either Stark Thompson lied in his account about the events of that Sunday night, or Ms. Goldmark is lying about them now.

MEMORANDUM TO FILE (THOMPSON)   CONFIDENTIAL
FROM: DMC
SUBJECT: THREE MEETINGS

This memorandun is based upon tape recordings, telephone conversations, notes and recollections.

After a series of skirmishes, I succeeded in convincing the Suffolk County Sheriff's Office, notably Detective Robert Hammerson and later his superiors, that I held important information concerning the death in their jurisdiction of one Robert Thorne. A client of mine, whose name and whereabouts I refused to divulge, had furnished me with a full description of how Thorne had been murdered, with suggestions for further investigation. I recommended to Hammerson that the mattress on Thorne's bed, which allegedly had been scrubbed and turned over during the crime, be re-examined. I also suggested that Thorne's golf clubs be checked, if they were still on the premises, to ascertain if they comprised a full set.

Apparently these suggestions bore fruit, for I soon found myself threatened with withholding evidence in a police investigation, concealing a material witness, and so forth!

To these tactics I replied that I would not divulge further information without a written guarantee of confidentiality for myself and my client. The Sheriff's Office refused to give me any such. Finally, to break the impasse and since further action on their part would require both a search warrant and the cooperation of authorities outside their jurisdiction, I agreed to meet one-on-one with a local magistrate to review the situation.

I then visited Judge Regis Fontaine in his chambers, at the county courthouse in Riverhead, Long Island, during which meeting I read aloud to him from the Thompson

account and the second Thompson letter, and showed
him selected relevant passages.

On the basis of this meeting, a warrant was issued and,
despite efforts by Ms. Goldmark's counsel to oppose it,
a search conducted of the Thompson residence by the
competent authorities. The alleged murder weapon was
discovered as indicated in my client's letter and im-
pounded by the police for forensic study.

On December 8th, 1987, a subpoena was served on Stark
Thompson, P.C., with copy to me, by the Federal District
Court in New York, requiring Stark Thompson, P.C., to
produce all records and documents pertaining to all transactions involving the securities of certain named U.S.
corporations made from the establishment of the firm to
the present.

By arrangement, I then received a visit from one Simon
Schwartzenberg of the U.S. Attorney's Office, who in-
formed me that Stark Thompson, P.C., had been named
in an ongoing investigation of the investment bank of
Braxton's, and specifically of the conduct and affairs of
Theodore R. Goldmark and his immediate staff.

Of course I was generally aware of the so-called Goldmark scandal, that Goldmark had been suspended from
his duties at Braxton's, and so forth, for it had been amply
covered in the media. But as I told Schwartzenberg, while
I had represented Stark Thompson in certain personal
matters including the preparation of his Will, I had no
involvement whatsoever with Stark Thompson, P.C. I
was therefore of little help to him, and our meeting was
brief, if reasonably cordial.

Of course were a similar subpoena served on me, de-
manding that I produce all such records and documents,
it is technically possible that I might have to furnish the
Thompson typescript. A neat legal question there. But

since Schwartzenberg made no reference to it, neither did I.

On the same day, by coincidence and upon very short notice, I received a visit from Ms. Goldmark herself, accompanied by her attorney, a certain Roy Lanceman of New York, whom I knew by reputation but had never met. I have no taped record of our meeting because Lanceman, upon entering my office, insisted that I refrain from making any, to which I agreed.

I had, I should say, continued to receive telephone calls from Ms. Goldmark. I regarded them as fishing expeditions. Under the pretext of questioning me about her husband's Estate and Will, she clearly tried to trick me into admitting that he was still alive. By the time of this meeting, however, her calls had all but ceased, possibly because she had herself ascertained that the liabilities in Stark Thompson's Estate would far exceed the assets.

Roy Lanceman, who is reputed inside the profession to be something of a street fighter, opened our conversation in a pointed, even aggressive manner. I will try to reconstruct to the best of my ability.

"My client and I have learned," he began, "that you have in your possession certain documents authored by Kitty's husband and which may be extremely derogatory in nature toward her. Is this true, Counselor?"

I have ever been suspicious, I admit, of fellow attorneys who address me as "Counselor." I told Lanceman I felt under no obligation to answer his question, citing the confidentiality of the attorney and client relationship.

"Is that so?" he said. "Come, come, Counselor. I wouldn't like to have to force your hand. We'd much prefer to deal with this amicably."

"I'm afraid my answer is the same," I replied.

This seemed to nettle him to no end. Standing, he began to pace and, thumbs in the slit pockets of his vest, proceeded to threaten me substantially as follows:

"Let me spell it out for you, Mr. Coombs. If the documents, as we have reason to believe, contain material which, by revealing her private life, would greatly embarrass my client or are, in addition, of a slanderous nature, accusing her falsely of crimes of which she has no knowledge, then we are dealing with a very serious matter. Your refusal even to acknowledge their existence makes a mockery of good faith among attorneys. We know they exist. And I'm putting you on notice, Counselor, that any attempt to publish them, or cause them to be published in the legal sense, by you or anyone else, will leave us no choice but to pursue to the fullest the remedies of which I'm sure you're well aware."

I suspected Lanceman, wrongly perhaps, of grandstanding for his client's benefit. I said:

"What exactly is it that you want, Mr. Lanceman?"

Up to this point, Ms. Goldmark had left the talking to him. Suddenly, however, she could no longer contain herself. She burst from her chair, brushed aside her attorney's efforts to intervene, and attacked me in no uncertain, and indeed slanderous, almost physical, terms. Among the appellations, I recall "crook," "liar," and, however vulgarly and inappropriately, "cocksucking old fool." We all knew what was going on, she maintained. I'd joined forces with her husband against her, and I'd done it with my eyes closed to how crazy and malicious he was. Because things had gone wrong in his business life—thanks entirely to his own mistakes, his own stupidity and greed—he was now determined to ruin her. He'd blown it; therefore she was supposed to blow it. And I was helping him! We had even sicced the police onto her, did I think she didn't know that? Did we really think she was going to spend the rest of her life defending herself against our trumped-up charges?

Above all, she insisted he was still alive. And that I knew it and was helping him cover it up.

"I'm going to get the son of a bitch," she hurled at me, "if it's the last thing I do. You tell him that for me. I'm going to make him wish he never fucked Kitty Goldmark. And that goes for you too, Mac Bastard. I'm going to put you out of business. As of now, you are *ruined*. You're going to get disbarred, and by the time I'm done suing you, I'm going to take you for every last penny."

I endured her venom in troubled silence. There was little else to do, and though the Thompson account describes such moments with greater skill and detail than I am capable of, suffice it that I too was subjected to the rageful passion of the woman, her wide-mouthed grimace, the shrill reverberations of her voice, her accusing, clawlike hands.

Eventually, whether through his efforts or because she had exhausted herself, Lanceman induced her to leave. She was tearful by then, her face buried in a handkerchief, which sight, however, failed to move me to much sympathy. If the purpose of her visit had been to intimidate me, she had failed. She was, among other things, too late for that.

Roy Lanceman subsequently called to apologize. I commented to him that I failed to understand what he had expected the meeting to accomplish. He said words to the effect that his client had insisted on it.

I cannot also help speculate as to why he agreed to represent her in the first place and why, apparently, he continues to do so. The only answer that comes to mind is that we lawyers have to take our business where we find it.

I dictate these notes in random form for inclusion in a file which, if it must remain open, yet has little more for me to add to it.

As of this writing, the final disposition or whereabouts of Stark Thompson III remains unresolved. I will return to this point.

His account and ancillary documents were finally wrested from my control by subpoena in the matter of *The People vs. Katherine Goldmark Thompson*. At one point, much to my discomfort, it appeared that I would be called to testify concerning their authenticity, but I was saved from that ordeal, ironically enough, by Roy Lanceman himself. After a prolonged, pre-trial battle over the question of their admissibility as evidence, Lanceman won, the documents were kept out of the trial and returned to me, for inclusion in this file.

I followed the courtroom proceedings with considerable interest. Indeed it would have been difficult not to, given the intensive media coverage. I thought Lanceman's line of defense probably the only one realistically open to him: that Stark Thompson, not the defendant, had killed Thorne because Thorne had threatened to expose his financial dealings, and that if the defendant had helped him, however unwillingly, it was because she'd loved him and wanted to marry him. Despite his eloquence, however, Lanceman had trouble dealing with some of the evidence, and the prosecuting attorney succeeded, over Lanceman's constant objections, in demonstrating how important a role the defendant had played not only in her husband's financial affairs but in Thorne's as well.

In this connection, obviously, the testimony against

her of her brother, Theodore R. Goldmark, was devastating.

(Clearly Goldmark's testimony grew out of his own plea bargaining, for the sentence he received for his own crimes—two years, I believe—was surprisingly light.)

I must confess to a certain, however grudging, admiration for the way Ms. Goldmark conducted herself throughout. Gone was the shrewish creature who'd ranted and raved in my office, as well as in the pages of Stark Thompson's account. In her place was this handsome and poised woman whom I saw many times on television, entering and leaving the courthouse, ever calm, even gracious, before the jackals of the media. Apparently she gave the same impression inside the court, never flustering under close questioning and maintaining her composure—no mean feat, one would assume—even when her brother took the stand.

I admit, rather to my surprise, that I found her pretty.

Some of this impression, I imagine, must have been shared by the jury. There was no other basis, in my opinion, for them to have brought in a verdict, disregarding the judge's charges, of manslaughter in the first degree. Of course, as any lawyer knows, the quickest way to lose money is to bet on what any jury will decide.

She is now serving her time. I know this because I hear from her occasionally by mail. She continues to threaten me. She is still going to sue, to have me disbarred. She is absolutely convinced I know where he is, and she demands that I now tell her.

I have never answered.

I must conclude, however irrelevantly, with some conjecture as to what happened to my client on that night of October 26th–27th, 1987. I do so not without pain, for

I was fond of the young man, having known him virtually since his birth and having been, despite our occasional differences, a good and longtime friend of his late father.

Even though an old man and an attorney, neither of whom should be shocked by much that happens in this world, I continue to be dismayed by Tommy's account, parts of which I have referred to again from time to time. Most of it I am inclined to believe. Somehow, through some moral failure of his own, aggravated by the actions and failures to act of those around him, and swept, I am sure, by the trends and tendencies of this period of our history, as well as—most of all!—by his total infatuation with this formidable woman, he participated in the worst of crimes. More even than his own role in the murder of Robert Thorne, I was overwhelmed by the slaughter of Corcoran Stark, whom I myself knew slightly, and still more, though I am neither psychologist nor literary critic, by the almost casual and remorseless way he described it. Certainly he deserved the highest penalty for his crimes as much as his wife did.

Returning to the night of October 26th–27th, I am compelled to say, however reluctantly and late in the day, that I am now inclined toward Ms. Goldmark's belief. This is not at all, I add, because she has so steadfastly maintained it. Certain unanswered questions to the contrary, I indeed thought—or wanted to think—that Tommy, after he had been unable to bring himself to kill her that Sunday night, had experienced such terrible despair and hopelessness that he in fact took his own life, either deliberately or accidentally. In the continued absence of any physical evidence (such as his body, which, I had been assured, must one day float to the surface if it did go into the river that night), I thought this solution best fit the warped psychology of a man who still craved vengeance even though, by his own account, he had failed miserably to achieve it.

I now believe I was wrong. I also believe that Tommy used me.

Not long ago, I was visited, by appointment, by a man mentioned several times in the Thompson account, one Crandall Fly Jr., who identified himself as the Trustee of the Stark-Thompson Family Funds. Mr. Fly, a most personable man and a prominent architect, asked my discreet help in sorting out a highly confidential matter. In substance, it appeared to him, and had just been confirmed by independent audit, that there was a cash shortfall in the Funds accounts amounting to just over five million dollars, which dated back to Stark Thompson's brief tenure as Trustee. Although they had managed to track other transactions of his during the period in question, this one remained an enigma. Could I shed any light on the subject for him?

In fact I could not. There was no such item in the list of assets I had drawn up, and, I regretfully informed Mr. Fly, in the best of circumstances, and even assuming the obligation could be proven, Stark Thompson's Estate would never be able to make good on it.

Mr. Fly did not seem overly concerned by this news. We chatted a few moments, inevitably about the mystery surrounding Tommy's disappearance, and then he left. I have not heard again from him. I doubt that I will.

Five million dollars, however.

A reasonable stake for a man on the run.

But whom am I to tell it to?

The police? But they have already closed their books on the Thompson case.

The Stark-Thompson Family Council? To judge from Fly's attitude, as well as the Thompson account, they will scarcely miss the money.

Mary Laura, Starkie, and their mother (who, recently remarried, has at last ceased pestering me for child-support payments)? But what good would it do them?

And, lastly, Kitty Goldmark? But what good, finally, would it do her?

My God, though, Tommy . . .

In truth—a sad realization—I have no one to tell it to. Yet it weighs heavy. Therefore I confide it to this file.

MEMORANDUM TO FILE (THOMPSON)   CONFIDENTIAL
FROM: AE, SECRETARY TO DMC
SUBJECT: ATTACHED LETTER

I have asked Mr. Rogers what to do with the attached latter, addressed to Mr. Coombs and received from Kath-erine Goldmark shortly after Mr. Coombs passed away. Upon Mr. Rogers' instructions I am adding it to the confidential Thompson file, pending the disposal of Mr. Coombs' personal papers

Dear Macaroon,

Here's the irony of it. I have the proof. The proof of what I've been saying all along, and you've been so busy denying—at least you used to be—is sitting beside me as I write. It is a picture postcard, Mac. On the one side is a photo of a curving beach, with palm trees, on the island of Tobago. On the other is his message, It says: "Hi Kitten." That's all. Just "Hi Kitten." His hand-writing, his sense of comedy, but true to himself he didn't have the guts to sign it.

Now I wonder who it was, if not you, who gave him my address?

So, you'll ask if you ever ask, where's the irony in it?

The irony is this. I have no one now to do anything about it. My high and mighty lawyer, the shyster Lanceman, has fired me. And you, if I had to guess, toss my correspondence into the circular file, unopened. (Unless you forward it on to him?) So who should I show it to? The warden?

Besides, what's to do?

The days are cold and long here, Mac Bastard. The nights colder and longer. Not cold inside my room. Cold inside me. Days, weeks, months, a long, cold blur. But I promise you this much. I'll never forget any of you.

Not you.

Not Tommy.

Not even my darling brother.